Walk Tall in the Wind

Dennis Swan

Pen and ink illustrations by Christa Scheck
Gray Dove illustration by ArtHolistic at www.fiverr.com/artholistic

ISBN-13: 978-0997738018

ISBN-10: 0997738014

Island City Publishing, LLC, Eaton Rapids, Michigan

DEDICATION

I dedicate this book to my wife Kathi, who stood by my side, helped do research in the libraries, and let me stay home and write whenever I wanted. And to the memory of my step-son, Michael, and my brother Charles, who both left us way too young, and to my parents.

I also want to thank the Eaton Rapids Writers Group, who taught me the art of writing. I was pretty green in the beginning. And to Dee Cassidy for not only editing my novel but for encouraging me on my journey.

A big thank you to my old friend, Rebecca Payne. You gave my novel the 'that certain polish' it needed.

And to Island City Publishing LLC and Celeste Bennett for having faith in me as a writer.

MAY YOU BE STRENGTHENED BY YESTERDAY'S RAIN,

WALK STRAIGHT IN TOMORROW'S WIND AND

CHERISH EACH MOMENT OF THE SUN TODAY.

Native American prayer

WALK TALL IN THE WIND

INTRODUCTION
MICHIGAN TERRITORY – 1835

This novel is about the early days of a small town in the central part of the lower peninsula of Michigan. Some of the characters are real. Some are distant relatives whose tombstones the author visits. Many are figments of imagination. The story line follows true history; the characters follow author's imagination.

The virgin forests of Michigan were fortunate to have a great diversity of trees and shrubs. Conifers (softwood) prevailed in the northern regions and deciduous (hardwood) trees in the south. One could faithfully describe the peninsulas of early Michigan as a single forest full of soaring trees. There were oaks, maples, sycamores, beech, walnut, hickory, chestnuts, and so much more, along with many species of pines.

Trees were the giant and majestic sentinels of the land. Many were ancient when the early French explorers paddled up the river the native Pottawatomie called "O Washtenong," which meant "far off" or "extending far inland," or as the French called it in the 1600s "la Riviere Grand."

In the area described in this book, a brook merged with the river, forming a small point of land the Natives called the "Forks." For the previous two millennia, Native American men, woman, and children flourished in this area and called it their home.

It was on this small peninsula of land, where the present Spring Brook flows into the Grand River, the settlement of Eaton Rapids would eventually come to be. Back then, the river was still wild as it tumbled over rocks and ledges in an eighteen-foot drop in the four miles before Spring Brook flows into it.

The original formation of the county of Eaton occurred in 1829, Section 3 of an act passed by the Legislative Council of the Territory of Michigan in Detroit, on the 29th of October in that year. In 1842 the Township of Eaton Rapids would be split off from Eaton Township, to join Bellevue and Vermontville Townships. This is the first written record of "Eaton Rapids."

A German immigrant, John Jacob Astor, became the owner of The American Fur Co. on Mackinac Island after the War of 1812 and controlled the fur trade in the Michigan Territory. Astor annually imported over 5,000 gallons of whiskey to trade to the Native Americans for their furs. Although selling alcohol to the Native American population was against Federal Law, Astor bribed Territorial Governor Cass for special privileges. Encouraging the Native Americans to become addicted to alcohol was disastrous for them. Astor wanted to control them and to be able to buy their furs cheaply. Others sold them liquor in order to steal their land, and in later years, their minerals. Astor made a million dollars on the fur trade but destroyed thousands of lives doing it. Alcoholism kept the Native American population in turmoil and broke up their traditional family unit.

The winds of change continued blowing in the 1830s. Americans from the east coast and Canadians, as well as European immigrants, hungry for rich farmland, timber, and minerals, would no longer live in peace with the Native Americans. The French voyageurs (fur traders) and missionaries had lived in harmony with the Native Americans for generations, but the new Americans no longer needed them to hunt and trap for furs. Nor did they need their political allegiance against the British and French governments. The Native Americans became an unwanted obstacle to the settlement of the territories, of no use to the politicians in Washington or Detroit.

PART I- 1835

CHAPTER 1
LATE AUTUMN

Olive

Olive hadn't expected the baby to arrive until after the traditional "Breakin' Up Christmas" on the sixth of January. When her labor pains started, she hoped the cramps were from something she had eaten, as her stomach had been restless all day. Then her water broke, and she was sure of another miscarriage. Her husband Simon was away, and there were no other settlers that lived close by.

She remembered the three friendly Pottawatomie women who regularly came to their trading post, Flying Cloud Woman, River Woman, and Early Dawn. Two were Native Indians, the other a Black Indian. She'd gathered that Cloud Woman was their band's healer and a midwife. Their Winter Camp was to the south of the settlement, down closer by the river. The women and their menfolk had either been too old or too sick to travel with the rest of their band to Fort Mackinac.

Olive called to her two youngest boys, James and Joseph, who were playing up in their sleeping loft, to come down.

"Now listen real careful. The baby is coming. The both of you run down to the Indian Camp. Find Cloud and River. Tell them the baby is early and your father is still away. Ask them to come back with you. Now go as fast as you can run."

The boys ran. They knew all about the Native Indians, where their wigwams were and in which one the old women lived. Those boys knew everything that went on in their neck of the woods, no matter how busy their mother kept them. They knew how to sign and had picked up a smattering of French and Ojibwa playing with the Native children during the summer when the tribe was there.

Olive cleared off the rough-cut, slab-top table. It served as her work table as well as their dinner table. She spread several old quilts over the top. She clambered up on the table as labor pains wracked her body.

The boys found the three old women seated around the fire in the center of their dome-shaped wigwam, sewing and telling stories. The boys burst in, both talking at once in Ojibwa.

"Grandmother! The baby is coming! Mother needs you to come to help as she is all alone. She said that the baby is coming too early. Please, will you come and help?"

"Yes, we will come," said Cloud. "River, my medicine bag is beside you. Dawn, you come, too. I may need your help. Come boys, help an old grandmother up."

Cloud slowly stood with the boy's help, and she stretched her cramped legs. She was tall and thin, her steel-gray hair in a long plait down her back. "Boys, fetch those baskets hanging on the wall. They are full of dried herbs, medicine that I may need."

The boys brought the Indian women to the cabin. They examined Olive and confirmed her fear, that she was indeed in early labor. The baby was already on its way.

"The baby is small, and you are big. The baby should have no problem. I will make tea for you to drink, to make the baby want to come faster."

With tears in her eyes, Olive said, "Will the baby be large enough to live on its own? I thought it would be another month before it came. I'm not that big."

"That is in the hands of the Great Spirit." Cloud felt Olive's stomach. "I can feel the baby move; it is still alive. That is a good sign. It will be the way it is supposed to be. I cannot change that."

They made strong herbal teas for Olive to drink. She didn't remember much until the next morning. When she woke, Rain brought over the tiny bundle. Tears again came to Olive's eyes as she thought, "Another lost baby."

Rain gently laid the baby in Olive’s arms, "A baby girl you had, tiny little thing, but she healthy, and she hungry! She has nursed several times throughout the night when you were still under the medicine spell. You do not remember. She is small and only nurses a little at a time."

It was then the tiny bundle let out a loud cry that could be heard for miles, at least it sounded like it in the small cabin. Rain gently helped

Olive so the baby could nurse. Olive's tears were now joyful.

The three old women took turns staying at the cabin, looking after Olive and the baby. They had the boys dig a hole beside one of the old oaks out back. They buried the afterbirth with a ceremony, telling Olive the baby would be protected by the tree spirits. Then they blessed and cleansed her, the baby, and the cabin with a smudge of sage and sweet-grass, and said a prayer with a rosary.

The women boiled herbal teas to make her milk flow and tonics to help her to heal. They had the boys heat water from the artesian spring north of their cabin, in the huge copper kettle on the fire pit. They brought pails of the hot spring water in. Olive and the baby soaked and bathed in the waters in a wooden wash tub.

Cloud told Olive, "Native women always come to the springs around the Forks to bathe after they give birth. It prevents fevers and sickness. The waters here are good medicine."

Olive usually bathed and washed her hair in water collected in the rain barrel or from the brook. The artesian mineral spring water smelled faintly of rotten eggs.

When the old women were sure that the baby and mother were safe from any fevers and on the road to good health, they gave strict instructions to the two boys on how to take care of their mother and baby sister. One or more of the three came every day to check on them, to see if she needed help. Afterward, they sat in front of the fireplace, sewing, talking, and drinking their herbal tea. Olive had come to love the old Indian women and felt they cared for her, too.

Olive knew that many settlers thought the Native Americans were no more than dirty savages. Some called them heathens and said they were no better than animals. These Indian women came to her as sisters when she needed them most, and helped ease the birth of her child. They had been gentle and kind when she was at her most vulnerable. Olive was sure that the reason she and the baby were alive was due to the midwifery skills of the Native American Indian women.

Simon and their middle son Glyn had left to gather winter supplies for their trading post. They traveled south, out of the primitive wilderness of central Michigan, to the more populated southern regions of the territory. Olive reminisced about her husband, the man she loved and missed with all her heart.

CHAPTER 2
THE COURTSHIP

Olive married Simon shortly after he was home from fighting in the War of 1812. She knew he would never settle down to till the soil in the mountains of Massachusetts like their forefathers before them. They attended the same Quaker school when they were young, by the small village of Deerfield. She left after the eighth grade to attended Mrs. Rowson's Female Academy in Boston for her higher education. When Simon left, he went to Yale and was accepted at the renowned Litchfield Law School. When attending Litchfield, Simon signed up for the militia to fight in the Northwest Territories. Olive had not seen him after she left for Boston, until a chance meeting.

When they met again, it was summer, and she was visiting her parents in Deerfield. She had been invited to an Abolition Society meeting with some Quaker friends one Sunday afternoon at the VanCort Mansion, after their weekly meeting.

Simon was there. He had matured into a tall, confident young man, almost six feet tall, slim and broad-shouldered, with wavy ginger hair. She had never really noticed him much before, except as one of the many annoying neighborhood boys that teased and pulled at her braids.

He came over to where she was seated with their hostess, on a brocaded Federal sofa in front of a white marble fireplace. Mahogany bookcases, filled with old, well read, leather-bound volumes extended along the walls on either side. A few comfortable wing-back chairs circled the sofa and were occupied by older gentlemen. Olive had been playing the Chopin etude “Tristesse” on the pianoforte that stood along one wall. She had stopped to let another young lady play.

“Mrs. VanCort, Miss Olive, Gentlemen,” Simon gave a stiff, military bow to his hostess and her guests. He looked quite handsome in his pale, fawn-colored trousers, white linen shirt with a simple knotted cravat, and dark waistcoat. He was clean shaved, with his hair combed back from his high forehead.

"Not sure if you remember me, Miss Olive," said Simon in his rich baritone voice. "I'm Simon Chatfield, one of those annoying Chatfield boys that lived down the road a ways from your father's farm. You play marvelously. I enjoyed it very much. I play the fiddle but have never tried to play such an elaborate sonnet. Since it is warm this afternoon, may I fetch you a cup of punch?"

Olive gracefully stood. She was tall and slim and was suddenly glad she had worn her best summer gown, the one with a high Empire waistline in a light gray cotton percale print and matching 'straights', or heelless slippers. Her glossy dark hair was done up in a knot under a tulle cap tied with a bow. She had a long curl that hung down on each side, framing her face.

"Yes, I was just going to get one. It is quite warm; I'll accompany you." Olive turned to her hostess; her voice was clear, strong and precise. As a teacher, she needed to be able to project it to the back of a classroom where even her naughtiest pupils would hear and obey.

"Mrs. VanCort, please excuse us. Is there anything I can bring back for you all, drinks or refreshment?"

"No, no, we're fine. Friend Mathews and I, along with these other gentlemen, are discussing the Slavery Issue. You two young people go on and enjoy yourselves," said Mrs. VanCort with a twinkle in her eye and a smile as she waved the young couple on, always the benevolent matchmaker.

Olive, too, smiled as she turned and walked out of the double drawing room with Simon. "And yes, I remember you well, Mr. Simon. You took my best bonnet when we were in fifth grade, and you would not give it back till I told on you. Miss Sacket made you sit at the front of the class the rest of the day."

"Why yes, Miss Olive, that was me; you have a good memory. You were always studying and reading books. I wanted you to pay more attention to me. But getting put in front of the class was not what I had anticipated. I wanted your attention, not the ridicule of the whole class!"

"Well," said Olive, coyly smiling, "I'm sure you were not responsible for putting the frog in my desk in sixth grade either. You know, I took Mr. Frog home and made a pet of him. He stayed on the back stoop in a crock of water, with a rock to sit on, for a week before he jumped out and left. My older sister said that is what all men do."

Simon grinned for the first time in a long while.

They crossed the spacious hall with its graceful cantilevered staircase and entered an immense dining room. The many guests were standing about talking and visiting with one another. A Brussels carpet with pale blue and rose-hued flowers covered the center of the parquet floor, under a dining room table that could seat twenty. On it was a vast array of silver and china dishes, filled with sweet and savory tidbits. Antique walnut paneling covered the rooms walls. The ceiling had ornamental plaster work that set off the Waterford chandelier. Floor-length windows opened to the veranda. A slight breeze blew the gauzy, lace curtains just enough so the heat was not oppressive.

They walked over to a marble-topped Chippendale serving table. Simon ladled out two cups of switchel, a popular and refreshing vinegar and molasses fruit punch, for them to enjoy. Several guests were admiring the samovar and punchbowl. They were of the new style, a blue and white porcelain that the English called Flow Blue for the way the dark cobalt blue flowed out of the pattern and blurred slightly when it was fired. The ladies loved it, a change from the monotonous white ironstone china which was mass produced at the time.

Olive and Simon made small talk with the guest they knew as they enjoyed their punch, and slowly made their way out through the open windows and onto the shaded veranda. "So Mr. Simon, tell me what you have been doing with yourself? Last I heard, you went off to university, then to read law."

They came to the end of the veranda, walked down the steps and out into the garden. The damp, cool smell of fresh cut grass and the heady aroma of flowers soothed one's senses. The drone of bees could be heard as they lazily pollinated flowers in the humid heat. The couple talked as they strolled the curved, oyster-shell paths while admiring the graceful marble garden urns which were entwined by dark red and white blooming roses.

"I did go to Yale, then law school for a while. Then I got anxious to do something with my life. I joined the militia and fought with General Harrison on the Great Lakes frontier. My regiment was the one that chased down and killed Chief Tecumseh.

"I came back home this spring to read law. But someday, I'm going to go back to that part of the country. It's still a wilderness, but a man could make a decent living there. Around Detroit, the country is not that different from here, with small villages and farms, and the people are mighty friendly, too."

"Let me ask you, Mr. Simon, are you no longer a Quaker? Friends seldom take up arms. I was quite shocked when you told me that you had. We have always been pacifists; what happened?"

Blood drained from Simon's face. He became as pale as the oyster-shell paths they walked, and his body became as tense as the strings of a fiddle. Olive noticed a scar that stood out below one eye. It ran down over his high, chiseled cheekbone. She had to stifle an impulse to reach up, to sooth the tension from his haunted face.

Simon began to talk in that low, rich baritone of his, concentrating on each word. "I don't really know. I was a strong believer in the Quaker philosophy that I, that we, grew up with. But in college, studying history, it dawned on me that someone had to stand up to the tyrants of the world. It made me so angry, the way the landed aristocrats taxed their people in the old countries of Europe, to pay for their endless wars.

"The common, everyday citizens of Europe are being reduced to paupers and peasants, the very people that the aristocrats depended on to grow their food and bake their bread. The ordinary man is nothing more than chattel to the ruling class, who do not care a whit if they starve. If a people cannot pay their taxes, they are thrown in debtor's prison, their property seized, and family put in work-houses.

"Most of my family on my mother's side came from the Alsace-Lorraine region in France, or Germany, depending on which principality controlled it at the time. Boundaries are always changing because of the wars. My family was fed up with it all: the land-owning aristocrats, coming in and conscripting all the young men in the village for military duty. At times they even made the peasants walk in front of the army. Old men, women and children. They used them as nothing more than cannon fodder.

"If the young men who were conscripted did, by chance, make it back from war, many were scarred for life. Missing arms or legs, or not right in the head, because of what they had seen, or were made to do. Their governments gave them nothing for their service or for their care. If they came home crippled or deranged, they became a burden on their family or were forced to beg for a living. Many froze to death on cold winter nights where they slept, covered in heaps of wet leaves outside some church or convent.

"Well, that's why my family came to this country, for the freedom to live the way you want, and not be afraid of your rulers. To mean something more to your government, other than just a vassal to be used and discarded. Governments should be for the people, not the tyrants of the people."

Olive strolled quietly by Simon's side while he continued on.

"Then the war started. I had friends and classmates that enlisted. I thought fighting the English is what I should do, because of my philosophy. I'm still a Quaker at heart, but I no longer attend the Friends Meetings because of my military service. It might make some uncomfortable, and I would probably be asked to leave. Maybe it was a mistake, my enlisting. I don't know. But I did it, for it's what I believe in. George Fox said, 'carry your sword as long as you can' to William Penn, and I will not change my thinking. My only regret is that you may think less of me for it."

Olive was moved by his sincerity. Being in the army had changed him. Besides the obvious, the growing up and maturing, there was something just a little mysterious about Simon Chatfield that intrigued her. It was a little shocking to her that he no longer attended Friends Meetings and had been in military service. But she could understand being lost at that young age, questioning one's life path and faith. She had also wondered about one's spirituality. She thought any intelligent person would. She decided to keep an open mind. After all, he had been sweet on her since the fifth grade.

"I'll let you in on a little secret in our family," said Olive while they walked and she told him this story. "During the Revolutionary War, my mother's mother, Grandmother Lydia Darragh, lived in Philadelphia, stayed there during the British occupation...

CHAPTER 3

Philadelphia, Pennsylvania-1777

Lydia Darragh

Sept-26-1777- "General Howe, I implore you to let my family stay in our home. It is only myself and my two young children as my husband is in England on business. If you put us out into the street, we will become destitute, and my two babies will die of starvation as we have no place to go. Because we are Friends and do not believe in taking part in conflicts, we are neither Patriots nor Loyalists. We are outcasts to our neighbors. No one would take us in out of the cold."

Lydia, a lace hankie in her dainty hand, dried tearful eyes. She had come to Gen. Howe's headquarters to plead her case. She had been told by a captain of the British occupying army that morning that she and her family would be evicted from her house by the British, who now occupied Philadelphia.

"Oh, all right. You can stay in your house since your husband is out of the country. If I find out he or you are engaged in espionage of any sort with the rebels, I will hang your husband and throw you and your children in the brig of a ship, and throw you all overboard between here and England. Is that clear?

"My captain tells me, after he inventoried your house, that you have a large front room. We will need it in a moment's notice to hold meetings. That is all for now, good-day Mrs. Darragh."

"Oh, thank you, good sir." Lydia turned, still drying her eyes.

She walked out of the big parlor of the mansion house that British

General Howe had confiscated for himself. It was a house that belonged to John Cadwalader. Her house was directly across the road. Mr. Cadwalader and her husband were both serving with the Philadelphia Light Horse Brigade. Her two eldest boys were in the rebel army; the oldest, Charles, with General Washington's Second Pennsylvania Regulars. Lydia had been spying on the British for Gen. Washington since they came up the river. Gen. Howe, in taking the house across the road from hers, was her good fortune indeed. She had to put on a sad story to be able to stay so close to the enemy.

She was slightly older than middle age, short, a bit plump, with graying hair. And she was able to weep on cue. She looked to be anyone's grandmother (young grandmother, she thought). Her two youngest children were twelve and fourteen. The fourteen-year-old made regular trips to meet up with rebel agents, to pass on information that she wrote down in code. She sewed the report into the sleeve of his old coat, which he then exchanged with the rebel agent for an identical coat to wear home again.

Dec-2-1777- "Yes, yes, no need to pound the door down, I'm coming. Yes?" Lydia asked as she unlocked and opened her front door, to find a young British captain before her.

"Gen. Howe wishes to inform you that your front room will be needed tonight at six o'clock. You and your family are to vacate the first floor while we are here. You are directed to furnish candles and light refreshments. We will notify you when we leave, Madame." The captain nodded, turned and left.

At six o'clock, she unlocked the front door and let the Captain in. He escorted her upstairs to her room. The children and all the servants were in their bed-chambers, with strict orders to stay put. But Lydia wasn't going to let this meeting go forth without her.

Earlier in the day, she made sure all the door hinges were well greased with tallow. She quietly left her room and silently made her way down the servant stairs and down a back hallway. She slipped into a closet that backed up to her big parlor where General Howe was meeting in. Lydia had removed everything in the closet earlier, except for a chair. All that was between her and Howe was a thin panel of wood. It was like she was sitting right next to him.

She sat quietly and listened, mentally gathering information about the British. They were fine-tuning a major offensive against the American rebels, who were moving to their winter camp in White Marsh on the fourth. The British planned on surrounding them with 5,000 men,

13 pieces of cannon, and 11 boats on wheels (the Conestoga Wagon that were used for ammunition and supplies), plans which were thoroughly discussed. As the meeting broke up so they could enjoy Lydia's refreshments, she quietly made her way back to her room and slipped into bed.

The Captain had to pound loudly at her chamber door three times before a yawning, sleepy-eyed Lydia answered. She acknowledged that the meeting was over, and the Brits were leaving her home. She even asked the Captain to lock up on his way out.

Lydia was in a dilemma; she had vital information to be given to Gen. Washington before the end of the next day. Her son had taken a correspondence the day before. It would be several more days before he could again go without raising suspicion from the British.

The next morning she rummaged through her rag-bag for old clothes, rubbed a little soot on her face and hands, and dressed in the ragged clothes she had found. They were dirty, wrinkled, and threadbare; clothes she wouldn't dress her servants in. She took an empty flour sack and went to British headquarters. She asked to speak to a Corporal Barrington.

"Yes, Madame, how can I help you?" asked the young Irish corporal to the poor old beggar woman standing before him in his office.

"Are you not Matilda Barrington's grandson?" asked Lydia, a bit loudly, as though she was partly deaf, and with a slight Irish brogue. "She and I are cousins. She wrote and said you were with General Howe's Regiment. How are you? I am Mrs. Darragh. We would be second cousins, once removed. I am so glad to meet you. My, you look just like your father."

Lydia had never met his father, but her distant cousin Matilda had written and told her he would be in General Howe's regiment and that she worried for him because he was a bit daft, like his father.

"You must come by the house on your day off and have a meal with us. Well, not a meal, maybe soup and a bit of bread? You see, it is only me and my two youngest children and with this war, food is getting scarce. Which is why I am here. We have been out of flour for a week. My children have had not a morsel of bread. A man that owed my husband a little money came by and paid me a portion of what was owed this morning. What I am seeking is a pass out of the city so I can go to a gristmill for a sack of flour. Would you know who to ask for such a pass?"

"Oh, I can sign a pass for you. I have one here on my desk. You take it. It was for another person, but I can write a different one out for him." Corporal Barrington signed the pass and gave it to Lydia.

"It was nice meeting a cousin from back home. If I ever get time enough off, I will come and see you and your children. But I haven't had a day off in a fortnight, and I don't know when I will.

"If you have any trouble, come and see me, again. Good day, Cousin Darragh." The corporal spoke briskly as he shut the door, for he was not looking forward to breaking bread with this poor old woman and her dirty, American brats.

Lydia smiled, took the pass and left. She walked through the snow. It was several miles out of the city before she came to the gristmill she favored. She left her sack to be filled and walked a few more miles to the Rising Sun Tavern. There she found Thomas Craig, a member of the Pennsylvanian Militia, and passed him a worn needle case while they shared a tankard of ale. She told him to get it to General Washington before nightfall. Then the old beggar woman in her threadbare clothes made her way back to the mill and retrieved her sack of flour. Carrying it over bent shoulders, she trudged her way back to the city through the deep snow.

Upon receiving the needle case, the General found within its various pockets old needles, folded scraps of paper and in one, the neatly rolled up plans for the British invasion against the Americans on the fourth of December, which would have been a smashing defeat for Washington. Instead, when they came and saw that the Americans were ready and waiting for Gen. Howe's army, the British forces turned and marched back to the city for the winter. General George Washington knew it was thanks to his secret Philadelphia spy, Mrs. Darragh, who saved the Continental Army from certain destruction."

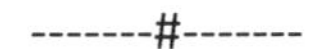

Simon smiled at the end of the story and chuckled. A woman who could tell a good yarn would always keep a man amused.

"Enough about me, Miss Olive, what have you been up to? Still on the farm with your parents? Or, have you moved on?"

"I left our country school the same year that you did, to attend Mrs. Rowson's Academy in Boston. I graduated and stayed there for a few years to teach. I came home this spring when Father had a bad spell, and Mother needed time to care for him. You remember that my parents ran a school for poor immigrants, as well as Indian and Negro children? They could not afford to hire a teacher, and were sad that they would have to close it.

"The truth is, they both are getting quite elderly. I came back to help. But now, thanks to a generous donation from Mrs. VanCort, and to several Friends who have volunteered to help, I am not needed anymore. So I have been thinking of going back to teach at the Rowson Academy in Boston."

"I am sorry to hear that," said Simon. "I was hoping that you could accompany me next week to a lecture on missionary work in the Indian Territories. Afterward, we could go to a pleasure park for supper."

"Well sir, that sounds most enjoyable. I think I may stay a little longer before going back to Boston. The new term doesn't start for a month yet."

They had frequent outings together. Olive even persuaded Simon to go back and attend Quaker Meetings with her. It wasn't long until they fell in love. They courted and married in less than a year. Olive never made it back to Boston to teach, and Simon decided to leave the law. They said their vows in front of family and Friends at the Quaker Meeting Hall they both had attended as children. Then they hitched up a covered wagon loaded with all their possessions and left Deerfield and the Massachusetts Mountains for good. As Horace Greeley said, "Go west, young man." They made it as far as the western part of New York State, to the Erie Canal. Her parents were not happy with her.

"Olive," her mother had said, "are you positive you want to marry this Simon Chatfield and move away from your friends and family? You always wanted to teach. You put a lot of time and effort to your education. You could find a good position at any Academy you wanted. Young Mr. Chatfield has no money to speak of, and your grandmother's inheritance will not get you far in this world. Wanting to be a wife and mother is a noble and good thing, yes. But do you want to be a drudge to housework and raising babies all your life?

"Living on the frontier is dangerous. You have no idea of the hardships you will have to endure. It is hard enough to raise children here where it's civilized. On the frontier, you will not have adequate help in case of an illness. Diseases strike out of the blue, accidents happen. You will not have close neighbors to watch out for your welfare. How will you be able to give birth to your children with no one to help?

"Of course, if you are sure this is what you want, I support and bless you for it. I do not think I could endure such hardships, so please think hard on this, for this is your life."

"Yes, but Mother, think of all the opportunities there will be on the frontier. I will be able to teach all the children from surrounding farms, and the Indian children. I can teach them how to be good Christians and put their heathen ways in the past," said Olive, a bit naive about the reality of frontier life.

"Between being a mother and a wife, I doubt you will have much time to teach all the heathens in the neighborhood, whatever their race. Remember one thing. You have to respect them and their way of life, or you will never gain their respect. And you will never be able to teach them if they do not respect you as a woman."

Simon opened a blacksmith and harness shop in Albany. Simon's father had been a hard-working blacksmith and harness maker, as well as having a farm. He had had twelve children to support with his first wife, and eight more with his second wife. Simon worked and trained to be a blacksmith with his father while growing up. He was good at it, but never much enjoyed it. Now they needed to make money before they moved to the frontier. The Erie Canal was under construction, and business was brisk. Crews of men and teams of horses were required, harnesses, tools, and machinery wore out and needed constant repairs.

There were giant stump-pullers that took six men to operate and a team of horses to pull. They had eighteen-foot tall wheels with a screw and cable that could wrench out the largest stumps in no time. One team could pull 30-40 stumps a day. This was one of the time and labor saving-machines invented while building the canal. Before the stump-pullers, it would take a team of men all day to dig out one stump, and the canal was being dug through thick forests.

Blacksmiths were kept busy repairing and making improvements to the equipment. Another time-saver invented at this time was a plow with a sharp blade that could cut through tree roots. The 3,000 Irish immigrants that came to work on the project could then dig roots out much faster than before. And a one-wheeled, hand-held wagon that dirt and roots could be tossed into, wheeled out and dumped, which got the name "wheelbarrow," was also a labor-saving invention.

The Erie Canal was a huge project that the Government took on. The Federal Government first tried to tackle the project, but the Senate deemed it too costly and vetoed down the spending bill. Then the Governor of New York, Governor Clinton, took on the project for the state. It was nick-named "Clinton's Ditch."

They hired engineers and contractors, who in turn hired subcontractors, who hired anyone with a team of horses to work on digging the canal. Great Britain already had a large canal system that criss-crossed their land. American engineers went over to observe the canals and saw how well the Irish maintained them. Thousands of Irish were hired by the canal-builders and emigrated to the US.

Simon and Olive sold the blacksmith and harness business when construction on the Canal was completed. He and Olive then opened a tavern/stage-coach stop, between Buffalo and Rexford Flats, where people could stop for food or a bed. Olive worked hard to ensure the business was one of the most reputable around. The food was good home-cooking fare, served on ironstone or pewter tableware. They would use none of those wooden trenchers that some taverns used, that were nailed to the wooden tables so no one would the steal them.

Olive made sure all the rooms were aired out each day, and the bedding kept free of fleas and bedbugs. There was no hanky-panky, gambling, or card-playing in her establishment. The men could go elsewhere for their entertainments. All this while raising five rambunctious boys.

Simon also worked hard, either in their livery stable or the blacksmith shop while fetching supplies, and doing upkeep on the large, old buildings of their establishment. But Olive knew Simon was getting antsy again. She had thought that by this time, Simon would have given up on his dream of homesteading in the territories, but the itch was still there. Every day, more people were leaving for the Northwest Territory, stopping at their wagon-tavern, telling stories of cheap land and talking of the endless opportunities.

Two years before, Simon had ventured to the Black Swamp in northern Ohio to stake a claim, but the best land had already been taken up by land speculators. Prices rose to a dollar and twenty-five cents an acre, from the twelve cents paid by the first settlers. Then the land had to be drained before you could raise a crop. Mosquitoes were so thick that when a person wiped the sweat off the back of their neck, their hand would be bloody. Bears, wildcats, and wolves, especially the wolves, were a great menace, as well as rattlesnakes, as long as a man and as thick around as his arm. Simon was not impressed.

It was said that good land could still be bought in the Michigan Territory at a fair price. All one had to do was to clear the trees and brush to raise a crop. But Olive and Simon were now getting too old to clear a homestead and farm. They were now in their mid-forties.

CHAPTER 4

NEW FRONTIER

They left Buffalo by the lake steamer "New York" and traveled to Detroit, that ancient French village that had grown to be Michigan's largest city of five thousand and the capital of the Michigan Territory. They missed the cholera epidemic that had swept over the city the previous year. They traveled overland by ox-wagon from Detroit to Dexter, gathering enough supplies along the way to open a trading post. Dexter being the last town of any size before they entered the wilderness. Then traveled on through the forest and swamps to the little cabin by where the two rivers met, a place the Native Americans traditional called the "Forks."

There were already plans for a sawmill three miles upstream on Spring Brook, where the "Old Clinton Trail" crossed. But Simon thought that the Forks, by the old Indian camp, would be a better location for a flourishing town. He picked out a parcel he liked, staked his claim, and with the help of his two oldest boys, built the two-room cabin of rough-cut logs from the primeval forest. Here they would live and sell groceries and supplies to the pioneers and the Indians that passed through.

Business had been very good that summer; they sold out of most the stock they had brought. Many folks were passing through on their way to Grand Rapids and other small settlements, like Ionia and Grand Haven. The next trading post wasn't till Ada, the one that old Joseph La Framboise and his Ottawa wife started in 1796.

Simon and their middle son Glyn set off the first of November to ride down to the larger towns of the more populated regions of southern Michigan. They needed enough supplies to hold them over till spring. Their idea was to ride their horse, then sell or trade it. They could then buy two teams of oxen and load two wagons with the much-needed supplies, and be back by the end of November. The oxen could be butchered for fresh meat during the winter, or sold with the wagons.

But it was now the middle of December and still no sign of them. Olive knew in good weather a team of oxen and a wagon should take about seven days to reach their cabin from Dexter. But early winter storms came through shortly after they left, blanketing the land with deep snow. It had been cold and windy since.

She was now worried. She knew of a hundred things that might be keeping them. The roads were nothing more than trails that the Indians had followed for centuries, and they could turn into a quagmire in bad weather. Wagons could become mired in the muck of the swamps, the oxen could go lame, or the men themselves could have met with an accident or sickened and died.

She wasn't too worried about the Indians. Not with the war and disease that the white man had brought upon them like proverbial plagues that decimated their population. She was more worried about unscrupulous white men that would slit a person's throat for a pint of whiskey.

Even though they carried no whiskey to sell, there was still a chance of some young Indian brave or French voyageur making a nuisance of themselves. Olive told Simon not to buy any more whiskey to sell. The Quakers were trying to do away with the practice of cheating the Indians out of their land and furs with alcohol, not to mention all the other problems alcohol brought to the frontier.

The two younger boys kept firewood in good supply. They hunted and fished to keep fresh food on the table, and to trade with settlers passing through. Olive was glad that the whiskey had sold out so quickly. Everyone needed a jug for snakebites and a little something when company called. The Indians knew that it was against the white man's law to sell whiskey to them, but there was always someone who would.

She had several loaded flintlock rifles in the cabin, intended more for protection from wolves and bears, but she and the boys were prepared to use them against other types of intruders, too.

Olive was still tall and lean, with the dark hair all her people had, but with a muscular physique a pioneer woman needed. After raising a brood of five boys and running a tavern on the Canal, she was not a woman anyone wanted to mess with.

Olive lay on her rope bed and listened to the wild, lonely sounds as she watched her newborn baby sleep. The river was high from the early snows and freezing rains. Olive could hear the turbulent rapids, breaking wild and chaotic as they surged over time-worn boulders and rushed through the rocky outcroppings in the O Washtenong. The night was pitch black, cloudy and cold. The savage wind ravaged the last leaves that clung to the majestic oaks as they swayed in a synchronized dance performed since time immemorial. Wolves howled in the not too far distance.

The fire crackled and popped in the wide fireplace as a log fell and sparks flew. She did not keep a roaring hot fire, as she did not want the clay and stick chimney to ignite. Instead, she had several small fires in the stone fireplace. That way, a person could have several pots or pans cooking at once.

The gale force storm shrieked and shook her little cabin. Olive was fearful that the oak shakes on the roof, only held on by weighted, pinned poles, would fly off in the wind. But the giant sentinels that guarded the little cabin seemed to come together, to surround her sacred home and hearth from harm.

She watched the tiny baby as she slept in Olive's old cradle, snuggled down under soft, hand-knitted blankets. The two youngest boys were asleep on robes made from the tanned hides of black bears and warmly wrapped in patchwork feather quilts. Their two 'stray' dogs that followed them home one day from the Indian Camp slept curled next to them. They were all crowded together in front of the fire. Most cabins in these parts had only dirt floors. The floor of their cabin was made from split ash puncheon, and only lightly smoothed by an adze. The cold wind snaked its icy fingers though the chinking of the notched logs of the cabin walls. It was impossible to keep the chill out. In the morning, she would find more animal dung and mix it with mud, to fill in the cracks caused by the constant shrinking of the curing green logs.

She stood up from the bed where she had been reminiscing when her hungry baby began to cry. Olive picked the baby up, cradling her in her arms. She walked around the small room as she nursed the newborn. When the baby fell back asleep, Olive gently laid her in the old cradle. She checked to see that the latch strings were pulled in, and she banked the fire. Nights without Simon were long and cold. She should lie down and try to sleep.

She knew that this would be her last child. A baby girl. She had always wanted a girl. The others never lived longer than a year or two, if that, although the five boys were healthy. The three youngest boys still lived at home, while the two oldest had families of their own. They took over the running the tavern back east in New York. And they promised to follow Olive and Simon after they were settled in their new home.

Earlier she had made bread dough, and it was rising in large wooden bowls by the fireplace. She kept hot coals in the bake oven, so that it would be thoroughly heated by morning. Her bread and rolls were popular. Men from around the settlement came to the trading post for them. Even the Indians loved her baked goods. They would stop in to trade nuts, dried fruits, and/or their beadwork for it and other supplies. That was how she had become acquainted with her three friends. It was about the only food of the settlers they preferred over their own.

Native American Indians ate flat, unleavened fry bread made from the wild grains and nuts that they gathered and pounded into flour in a poodahgon, or stump pounder. This was a primitive mortar and pestle made from a birch tree. They would add a little water to make a sticky dough, and bake it on hot, flat stones near their cooking fire. They used this bread to scoop up the stews that were always cooking in the iron kettles at their campfires. Because of their primitive table utensils, Indians prepared their meat and vegetables by chopping into bite size pieces before cooking. The greeting when entering a Native Americans' wigwam was not "How are you?" but "Have you eaten yet?"

Olive knew that Simon and Glyn never traveled at night. Not with cougars, bears, and packs of hungry wolves preying on lone travelers. It was difficult enough to traverse the wilderness in daylight. She remembered an old story about a young man, who was traveling alone, with provisions for his family. He was caught out in the woods at night, unable to reach a shelter before dark. All they found of him was his wagon, an empty gun, and his hat. A pack of wolves and other scavengers had eaten and scattered everything else.

She heard the scream of a lynx in the distance. The wind had died down. She felt the temperature drop as the cold seeped into the cabin, stealing the warmth. Olive checked on the sleeping baby in the cradle which was next to her bed and close by the fireplace. She pulled the homespun wool wrapper closer around her shoulders and straightened her muslin night cap.

She was happy with her life. Yes, it had been hard, but Simon was always at her side and worked just as hard as she. He was her friend and confidant; and she loved him, even his flaws.

The losses of her babies were the most tragic events in her life.

Simon felt the loss just as much as she. They shared their grief together. The boys were their biggest joy. It was her hope that the two eldest, Elmer and Joshua, would come with their families in a year or so. She missed them and her grand babies.

Her mother had been right; the frontier could be a lonely place. Simon and Glyn were in all probability at somebody's cabin, maybe as close as Amos Spicer's a few miles up the brook. She wished they were home, but wherever they were, she prayed for them to be safe, and God willing, she would see them soon.

CHAPTER 5

Simon

The oxen were strong and sure and slow. Horses or mules could never have traversed the trails people jokingly called roads. The only sign that they were still on a trail was the ax blaze on some of the trees, and the deep, frozen ruts.

And it was cold. That type of damp cold that sinks into your bones with an ache. Icy drops of condensation dripped down the back of Simon's hat brim, slid under his collar and down his neck. Simon thought his leather gloves were frozen to the reins that led down to the oxen. He mused on his life so far as he rocked slowly back and forth as they drove over the rough trail, froze to the wagon seat.

He had a loving wife, five fine boys, with a baby on the way. He remembered when their first child was born; he was so proud. He took all the workers at his shop to the local tavern, and bought a round of 'shrub', a popular vinegar, fruit juice, and alcohol drink, for everyone there.

Six months later the whole village turned out for her funeral. She was fine that morning, laughing and smiling. She became ill in the afternoon and was dead by midnight. The doctor said it was "dropsy of the brain"*(meningitis)*. He hardly remembered those few days. A black fog settled over him that sucked all the joy and light out of his world. It seemed like his soul was down in a pit that he couldn't climb out of. And the pit was filled with all the corpses of the young men he had seen die in his army days, both white and Indian. He felt a great sorrow for the lives cut short, the futures that were never to be. Men who should have lived, to love and have children of their own. Cut down in the prime of their life. And for what?

If they had not gone to war, would anything really be any different? Politicians always negotiate peace treaties in the end. He tried to stay strong for Olive, but it was like he could sense a dark shadow that followed him every place as though it was he who was at fault for all the injustice that mankind thrust upon itself. He carried this weight on his shoulders like Atlas. He thought about morality. Was he a moral man? He had done things when he was in the army and had things happen to him. But was he damned? Did he not do what he had to, to survive?

Later, after the oldest boy, Elmer, was born, slowly, things got better. Business was brisk at his blacksmith shop; he had no time to sit around to ponder fate. He was proud when Olive delivered their second son. They started to make plans to enlarge their business. Then they lost two more girls in a row. The dark shadow came back, leaving him a haunted man. Whiskey helped, but Olive was a strict teetotaler and did not like him drinking in excess...

Glyn called out, waking Simon from his musing. He could see lights up ahead, through the rain and fog. They must be coming up to a small farm. Down a small incline, up another hill, and there was a good-sized log cabin, with a few outbuildings in a clearing. With the early darkness of the coming night, he had noticed a lone wolf following them. He could hear other wolves howling in the woods. "God, just in time," Simon thought. He wouldn't be surprised if they had to pry his frozen backside from the wooden seat!

As they approached the homestead, two figures came out with a lantern and their rifles, having been alerted by their barking dogs that something was afoot. After seeing it was two weary travelers, the men gestured them to the barn. All the people they had found in these parts were friendly and eager to help the strange traveler in need.

"Welcome, welcome! You need a place for the night? We have plenty of room. Draw your wagons up to the barn. We've got room inside for your oxen. The wolves won't bother the wagon, although the bears might! But the dogs should keep them at bay," one of the young men said while opening the barn door, "Bring the oxen right into the barn."

After they had unhitched the oxen, fed and bedded them down for the night, Simon and Glyn were invited into the cabin for supper. After wiping down and oiling the leather harnesses, they went to eat. The brothers both had good wives, and a grand supper was had. A ladle of steaming cornmeal mush covered with milk in a large wooden bowl, topped with maple syrup, warmed up a man in no time. This was followed with a large venison steak with roasted wild leeks and turnips, and with all the spongy wheat bread, topped with cranberry sauce that they could eat.

After supper, Simon and Glyn regaled the brothers and their wives with news they had gathered on their journey. After all, that was what the homesteader wanted most. Living so far from any neighbor, they craved to know what was going on in the world. They had very little outside contact and seldom traveled to pick up supplies or mail. They rarely had visitors, except for an occasional Indian passing through.

"We came out here about three years ago," Hiram Pickens was saying. "Came out with Joe and my two youngest brothers from the Mohawk River Valley. Took the steamer "Henry Clay" to Detroit. We were going to stay there, but some of the troops aboard ship came down sick. It was a company under the command of General Winfield Scott, came to fight in the "Black Hawk War." Soon as we heard that people in town were dying of the same illness, Asiatic Cholera we were later told, we high-tailed it out of there just before they posted guards to keep people from leaving.

"We took the Clinton Road up here. A good thing. We were told that along the Territorial Road, guards were posted at Ypsilanti to try to keep a stagecoach from Detroit out. During the confrontation, someone accidentally shot and killed one of the horses. That was a dumb thing to do since they were kind of stuck there after that."

Joseph picked up the story, "We traveled around some and decided we wanted to find some land as far away from that city as we could. Someone told us about this area. We came and liked what we saw. Our brothers, Guy and Saul, went to the land office at White Pigeon and staked our claim while we stayed and started to clear land and build the cabin.

"When the boys came back, they had both decided to go back east to stay for awhile, before coming out here to live. Saul heard that a school was to be set up at Kalamazoo, the Michigan and Huron Institute. He was always the one that had a good head for learning and decided that he would get a teaching certificate, then come out and teach. Guy noticed that women around here were scarce as hen's teeth. He's had his eye on a gal back home. She's going to take some persuading to come out here and homestead, but he's going to try.

"We all stayed here that first winter, and boy, that was a bad one. We almost starved to death. We had just about given up when a band of Indians came through. It was cold, bet it was twenty below. They wanted a place to stay warm, so they lived in the cabin with us for a week until the weather broke.

"They shared their pemmican and their dried corn. We pounded that up into meal and made it into hoe-cakes. They went hunting every day, always brought something back, even if it was just a possum or beaver. Possum fat with hoe-cake's not too bad when you're starving, and a beaver tail roasted on the fire is a real treat.

"When they left, they gave us enough corn and pemmican to last 'til spring. Said they would come back though here again, but we haven't seen them since. Some of them had been to the mission schools up north, spoke English and French real good, and were quite knowledgeable about politics. They weren't happy about some of the treaties being signed by people claiming to be their chiefs, and being cheated out of their land."

One of the wives came from the fireplace with a fresh pot of steaming chicory coffee and poured everyone a cup of the fragrant beverage, to go with their mincemeat pie. She was still quite young and pretty and was showing her pregnancy. Simon thanked the young lady and told her he sure did appreciate their hospitality. She blushed and said that having company was the real treat.

"I came up here last summer, with my two oldest boys," said Simon. "We staked out a place at the junction of the O Washtenong River and Spring Brook. Built a two room cabin and went back to New York. This spring, I brought my wife Olive and the three youngest boys back to Michigan. We bought two pair of oxen and two wagons in Detroit. Drove on to Dexter, buying all the supplies we thought we would need. Then we took the Old Clinton Trail up to our claim and set up a trading post. They're planning on putting up a saw mill next spring on Spring Brook, but I'm betting the real town will be at the rivers' junction.

"We've been there about six months now and sold most everything. Bet we had someone coming through there every day. By taking the flat-bottom boats downriver, it's a lot easier than walking or riding a horse, especially the way the trails are. Had one fellow come through, a ship builder from Detroit. Traded his horse off so he could take a boat the rest of the way to St Joseph, wanted to start his own business there for the Lake Michigan trade. And we always have Indians in their dugouts and canoes, stopping to trade their furs for powder and lead.

"We thought we'd better go back down to Dexter to buy more stock before winter sets in. Good thing too. All the homesteaders have been paying in paper money from the wild-cat banks. When we got to Dexter, no one wanted to take paper money. Rumor is that President Jackson is going to try to shut down banks that don't have Federal approval. First of the year, the "Specie Circular Act" goes into effect and land offices will only take hard currency for claims. People are afraid that the paper money issued by the wildcat banks will be worthless.

"We were lucky and found a bank that would still take paper money and gave us hard cash so we could buy the supplies we needed. Bought the yokes of oxen and wagons, and bought up what goods we could find. We traveled the Chicago-Detroit Road and then the Jackson-Monroe Road searching for goods. When we stopped at the Walker Tavern, a couple there told us to go to Parma before heading home, that a cooper had the barrels that we needed. That man told us someone at Oyers Corners had some kegs of black powder and a couple pecks of dried beans to sell."

After the coffee and pie were gone, the Picken boys pulled out their fiddles and ripped off a few tunes like "Money Musk," and "Zip Coon." Glyn taught them a new tune "The Devils Dream," with gusto. The women sang, and they all had a good time with newfound friends.

Simon thought they should have been able to find Oyers Corners before dark, but with the rain and fog, and fresh snow on the ground, they had lost their way. Thank the good Lord above, they had found the Pickens homestead. He hated to think what a night like tonight would have been like out in the open. Simon offered that he and Glyn could sleep in the barn with the oxen, but the Pickens women soon had a bed made up for them on the floor in front of the huge fireplace, where their wet clothes were hung up to dry.

In the morning, after a hefty breakfast of pork steak and brown gravy, with hot rolls and tea, they hitched up the oxen. They all shook hands and with a parting gift of a half keg of nails for the Pickens men and a roll of calico cloth for the wives, and directions to Oyers Corners, Simon and Glyn set off on the last leg of their journey. Simon figured they should be home in two days. It shouldn't take long to finish up their business. They had just got turned around in the hilly forest and swamps between Parma and Oyers Corners, but had made new friends. About four more miles to Oyers Corners, then on to the Forks. Another day or two, and they would be home. He missed his wife, and the boys, and prayed they were well.

CHAPTER 6

Glyn was having the time of his life. He was seventeen, tall and slender with black hair in a plait and the sky blue eyes he got from his mother's family. He wanted to settle down with a nice girl and raise a family back east, like his older brothers. Then his father decided to uproot the family to come out to this god-forsaken Michigan Territory. Everyone knew from reading the papers that Michigan was nothing more than mosquito infested swamps, swimming with rattlers and Indians. Everyone had heard the rhyme:

"Don't go to Michigan, that land of ills;
That means ague, fever, and chills."

Glyn was sure they would all be dead of ague or brain fever within the year but was proved wrong. Michigan was wild but filled with open prairies as well as swamps and primeval forest that never ended. He had never heard the kind of music the birds made that first spring. Every tree and bush were filled with songbirds, all singing, and somehow it was harmonious.

There were grand trees, so massive and loaded with intertwined limbs that a squirrel could run from one end of the territory to the next without touching the ground. And most tree limbs didn't start until they were 30-40 feet up on the trunk so that a man could drive a wagon team unhindered beneath them.

He had seen one tree with a hole in the base of its trunk large enough for a man to ride a horse in and turn around. But it was easy to get lost; all those trees looked the same. The Native Americans had established trails their people had followed for generations; some had been trod into the ground two feet or more. In other spots, Indians from long ago had bent and tied saplings to the ground, alongside the trails. Now those oddly bent trees showed the way through the forest, and settlers followed these trails, too.

His father bartered supplies with a man who traded Simon his horse, having decided to take a boat down the river instead. Horses were scarce around these parts. They were not much use with the lack of roads and the poor trails. His father thought that they could ride the horse to Dexter, trade or sell it, then buy a yoke of oxen and wagons to bring supplies back to the trading post.

Two days out on their journey, they found an abandoned lean-to to spend the night. Glyn liked horses, loved to ride and was a good horseman. He disdained the slow oxen and the ox-carts but knew they were necessary. He knew enough about horses, that if he hobbled the critter, it would graze nearby and alert them if any animal or people came around during the night. The next morning, the horse was gone.

Glyn rationalized that that meant the horse either knew the culprit or at least recognized their scent. And since his previous owner was far away by this time in St. Joe, the horse must have belonged to someone around here. They searched the ground until they found tracks and followed them.

Just as Glyn suspected, about dark they came to a large camp of Pottawatomie who were making their way to their winter village, stopping to shoot wild game for their winter provisions.

Glyn and his father hid under some brambles and waited. The natives were festive and had large fires burning in the center of camp. Somehow, the young braves had acquired a jug of whiskey, and they were indulging. As Simon and Glyn watched, a few wrestling matches broke out and quickly turned into fist fights. It was not a good time to walk into the camp and demand the horse back.

The women of the tribe got after the braves and broke the jug on the ground. The reprimanded young men retired for the night. A few older grandfathers sat around telling stories of their youth to the young children until they too drifted off and settled into their blankets.

The camp settled down. The fires were tended, and all was quiet. Glyn made his way to where the Indians hobbled their horses. He led them far from the camp and let them go. He found his horse and led it around to where Simon was keeping watch, waiting to sound an alarm in case the camp was aroused.

Glyn was almost back to where he was to meet his father. He was crossing a small stream when an Indian maiden stepped out of the tall cattails. The girl had been having a wash in the cold water. She had both arms up, over her head, wringing the water out of her glistening, long black hair. Moonlight gleamed off her wet, dark skin. He could see the muscles as they rippled under the taut skin of her thighs as she moved, graceful as a fawn. She stopped, startled.

The sudden appearance of the girl also startled Glen, who was more taken aback by her nakedness than anything else. He did the first thing that came to his addled mind. Glyn put his hand up in sign language for quiet. She stood motionless, her dark eyes never leaving his face.

He had picked up signing by the Native Americans that came to the trading post since most of the old ones claimed they could not speak English and only a word or two of French. He knew that if he showed how frightened he was, the girl would sound an alarm. Then, he and his father would be caught and probably would be slowly tortured to death. His Father often told the story of George Washington's land agent, William Crawford, who was abducted by Indians in the Ohio River Valley, scalped and roasted alive in 1783. He quickly signed that he would not harm her if she stayed still. He squared his shoulders and with his horse, walked straight and tall into the wind.

Glyn led the horse out of the water, jumped on its back and galloped back to his father. Glyn motioning for Simon to quickly jump on, and off they raced. He thought the Indian girl had roused the hunting party by now; he could almost hear their war cry. After they had ridden hard for several minutes, his heart started to calm down, and he began to tell his father what had happened.

"That was close. I thought sure that Indian girl would get us both killed. I found the horses and got them to follow me. Then I led them into the woods unhobbled them and let 'em all go, except ours, which I was bringing over to where you were. I was almost across the stream, and this girl stepped out from under some low-hanging tree branches and tall cattails, right in front of me. Startled me something good. Thought I was keeping a good watch of everything, and she just walked out from nowhere. She didn't have no weapon or nothing, think she was startled, too. So I signed to her. Told her to be quite, and she would be all right. She just stood there, so I kept on walking." Glyn found the episode both exhilarating and terrifying at the same time.

"Slow down," Simon chuckled. He thought they were in the clear and that Glyn had way too much imagination.

"It'll take a while for the braves to sober up and find their horses. I don't think the tribe will want to cause any trouble over a horse that they stole in the first place, but we'll watch our backs."

By the time they found the old lean-to and retrieved what gear they had left, dawn was upon them, the eastern sky slowly turning red and pink. The good weather that they had enjoyed looked as though it was coming to an end as clouds gathered in the west, with a cold, damp wind. They traveled throughout the day until they came to Manchester and found a tavern.

By then the snow was falling, and a fierce wind blew. After a hot meal, they secured a place to sleep and stayed the night. The next day they picked up what news could be had, and prepared to leave. The storm had stopped, and the world sparkled in the bright sun. They found a good trail that would take them on to Dexter. For what more could they ask?

CHAPTER 7

Gray Dove

Blood covered the ground. Gray Dove's face and buckskin dress were splattered in blood, and her hands were covered in red gore. She held a bloody knife. Bone shards, hair, and pieces of skin clung to it. She and the women of the tribe had just finished butchering the last of the wild game the men killed on this hunting trip, the most important of the year.

The small children gathered dry, dead wood, and placed large piles in the center of camp. Drying racks were propped around the fires that had burned for days where strips of venison and bear meat were hung to dry slowly to a tough, leather jerky that Gray Doves' people made into pemmican, and lived on during the coldest months. Skins were stretched out to cure, after having been scraped and rubbed with brains and urine. The white man prized the soft, buttery leather they called buckskin, and paid a good price for it.

She arched her back, stretching the sore muscles in her back and legs. She was taller than most girls of her tribe, and she was muscular, with good bone structure. Her grandmother, Cloud Woman, whom she loved dearly, told her that some of their ancestors had been Frenchmen from the north country. That seemed likely since the French had been trapping and trading with her people since the 1600's.

The older women quit the butchering chore and were feeding men fresh livers, quite the delicacy, leaving the last of the work to the younger girls. It was time to gather up all the tools and take them down to the stream to scour in sand and water. She could hear the young men in camp, laughing and shouting. They had had a good hunt, with enough meat to last through cicakkisws, the "Moon of the Crane," which was when food ran low, and game could be scarce. She thought they had enough skins to make into leggings and shirts, with enough left to trade with the Americans for guns and powder.

"Girls!" she shouted in Ojibwa. "Let's hurry and finish cleaning up. Maybe those boys will leave us some food, and not just bones and gristle."

The girls groaned, they had been up before the first light. They were hungry and wanted to join in on the merriment. "We need to hurry before dark, so we can see. Shaking Leaf, bring those baskets. We can fill them and take everything down to the stream at once and be back before your brave eats everything!"

They all laughed. Shaking Leaf, Gray Dove's best friend, liked a brave that was known to eat a lot even though he stayed small and slender. They quickly gathered everything and ran down to the stream. They worked fast as a team, the smell of roasting meat and squash making their mouths water.

Done at last, they brought all back to camp. Packing everything up would begin in the morning. They joined the feast. The roasted meat and vegetables tasted so good; they were starved. The older women had made sure to save some for them. A young brave Gray Dove liked came over and gave her a portion of his fresh liver. She thanked him as they sat around the campfire. Gray Dove loved to talk and eat with the other children she had grown up with, they all were quickly becoming young adults.

She knew some were already thinking of having families and were pairing off. Gray Dove had attended the mission school of Reverend William Ferry at the Presbyterian Mission at Mackinac Island, every winter since she was a small girl. She wanted to become a teacher or an interpreter, or to do mission work in the interior of the country. She was fluent in both English and French. She knew this might be her last summer with her band before she left. And she did enjoy spending as much time as she could with the tribe. As much as she loved the traditional life, she yearned for knowledge.

A few young men, older than she, but not yet paired off with a woman and a family, started fighting and drinking whiskey. The elder women soon regained control and sent the trouble-makers to bed. After a while, most everyone started drifting off; tomorrow would be another long day. As the young men quieted down, the old men told stories. Women gossiped among themselves, on which son or husband had brought home the most game. Gray Dove wanted to go down to the stream to wash off the blood and sweat. She had to hurry before the fires burned too low. The smell of blood was sure to draw wolves and bears, as well as wild cats.

She had just finished scrubbing her long black hair and skin with sand and was wading out to the center of the stream, when a white man, an American, stood in front of her with the horse that had been captured the night before. She was as still as a doe. What else could she do, standing in the cold water up to her knees, stark naked. She didn't know if this white man who stood in front of her, intended to kill or kidnap her. She was alone. Gray Dove knew that the young braves were drunk on whiskey while the old grandfathers would be snoring, fighting the battles of their youth in their sleep.

He signed to be quiet, and no harm would come to her. Then boldly walked past her, tall, and into the wind, with his horse. He did not hear her quietly say "adieu" to his back. She had thought the handsome young American brave to pull off such a coup. She didn't know if the warm tingling she felt was fear or admiration.

The brave who had stolen the horse had been very annoying. He had been bragging about stealing the horse back that he had sold earlier in the summer to another white man. She could not wait until morning to see her brother's face when he found the horse gone from under him. She now remembered the handsome young American was from the new trading post at the Forks. Her band stopped there early in the fall to sell some pelts, and her grandparents decided to stay the winter at the camp there. She thought it would be pleasant to see him in the spring when they returned.

CHAPTER 8

Simon and Glyn

They were more than two weeks behind getting back to Olive and the boys. Simon knew Olive's due date was close, and he wanted to be there for her and the baby. Giving birth was the most dangerous, and the most wonderful thing he could imagine. Olive being with child had not been in their long-term plans. It had been over ten years since the last boy was born; they both thought that that part of their life was behind them. Olive hadn't told him that she was with child until they were aboard the steamer, heading to Detroit. A brand new start for them and their new child, she had told him.

The early winter snow held them up for several days in Dexter; finding supplies had been cat and mouse. Those who could afford to, stocked up on supplies that would be needed for the coming winter and next spring. Prices were high, due to the shortness of cash. Salt pork was forty-four dollars a barrel, and flour, fourteen dollars.

It had been a tough going but eye-opening trip, seeing how fast the villages in the southern part of the state were growing. Marshall now had a first-class tavern, the "Marshall House," and a stagecoach made a regular stop as it was on their route between Detroit and Chicago. Jackson, what had been known as "Puddle Ford," then "Jacksonburg," now had four stores and a tavern. Brooklyn, Concord, and Grass Lake were all small but thriving settlements. John Baptiste Barboux at Henrietta, and old man Goodwin at Napoleon, both had thriving trading posts that started out with them buying furs from the Indians. A new mill was being built in Leoni, and the Ball Tavern was thriving in Parma.

Glyn and Simon stayed at a small trading post-tavern in Oyers

Corners, their oxen bedded down in the lean-to next to it. It wasn't much, more of a shanty with a loft. But it kept the weather out. They were starting early the next day for their final push, the eight to ten miles to their cabin. They had found a settler who claimed he knew a trail that would get them there in one day. He had a brother that had a small farm near the Forks. He had wanted to see him anyway so he decided that he would join them. Simon hoped the weather would clear.

"I just can't believe how this part of the country has changed in the last 25 years. When I came through here, there was nothing much past Detroit, just some Indian villages," Simon said as he finished up his supper of tough, gamy bear steak and onions. Not as good fare as at the Pickens, but they had eaten far worse on their travels. Simon was still tall, broad shouldered and slender, with light brown hair and a short beard that was turning gray. His eyes were the same ginger color as the steaming hot spiced shrub they were drinking.

"What are you talking about, Father, when were you ever through these parts? Thought you and Mother had always had the tavern. I just remember living in Albany above the harness shop. You always worked hard, you and the apprentices. Men were lined up at the door, morning till dark, waiting for you to mend their broken harnesses or fix their broken machinery. Even remember fist-fights at the door when someone would try to cut in, thinking they were more important."

"You remember all that, do you? Those men worked on building the Erie Canal. They lost money when their teams weren't working. Most of those men were just one day from losing their horses and their livelihood. If they couldn't work, the crew captains would just hire someone else, and their families would go hungry. They had to be there first thing in the morning. Digging that canal was hard work, and took a long while.

"No, I came through here in the war. I left school and signed up because the money was good. After the massacre at Frenchtown in '13, the federal government didn't have much of an army left in the Northwest Territory. Colonel Winchester surrendered to Major General Henry Proctor on the promise that the wounded and the prisoners would be safe until they could be transferred to Ft. Madden. Early that next morning, a couple of hundred liquor-crazed Indians under Tecumseh came into town and set it afire. Those that could escape the burning buildings were murdered and scalped, the rest burned alive. "Remember the River Raisin," everyone said. In all, only about 60 men out of 1000 survived the massacre and made it back alive to the fort at Maumee.

"The army had to pay good money before anyone would enlist, and they needed the new army fast. Still, it took them months to raise that many men and for them to train us. By then, the British, along with that damn Tecumseh, controlled all of Michigan, all the forts along the lakes, and were invading Ohio, killing Americans and burning any American settlements they found.

"First I was sent with the Detroit militia and was sent marching towards Fort Dearborn. When we were halfway there, we were ordered back to Detroit. Then I was under General William H. Harrison, Commander of the Army of the Northwest."

"My regiment was sent off in pursuit of the British and Indian forces that were under Proctor and Tecumseh. We caught up with them on October fifth, what's called the "Battle of the Thames." We killed Tecumseh and drove Proctor east, deep into Canada. Admiral Perry went on to recapture Detroit and drove the British and their Natives American allies north, to Fort Mackinac.

"Then we returned to Detroit. We lacked the provisions to go farther into Canada in pursuit of Proctor. The fighting was finally over on the Lake Erie front. We controlled Lake Erie and the St. Clair River, which cut off provisions to the British at Fort Mackinac. Then a cholera epidemic swept through Detroit, killing over 700 troops. The armies were short on adequate food and medical supplies. After that, the militiamen disbanded, and we went home."

"Was the war over then?"

"No, it was over as far as the North-East territories and Great Lakes were concerned. We sent the British fleet packing. There was still plenty of fighting going on along the Eastern coast and down in the South, as well as up and down the Mississippi. We hoped that the Canadians would also rise up against their British overlords. Nothing came of that, though, just rumors."

Glyn was silent, musing over the story he had heard for the first time. He always thought of his parents as just his hard-working mother and father, never as two real flesh and blood people, with stories and adventures of their own. No wonder his father knew so much about history; he was a part of it! Even though he and his brothers had always attended school in the community where they lived, both parents had taught their children at home as well. The simplest of tasks would be turned into a history or math quiz. At night, after the evening meal, the family would gather together to read or tell stories. Sometimes his father would bring out the old guitar and show the children how to pick a song. He knew his mother could play the piano, but since they could not afford one, she only played when at a friend's house.

He finished his supper and was sopping up the last of the flour gravy on his wooden trencher with a piece of hard corn dodger. Simple and cheap, a dodger was just cornmeal, water, and salt mixed into a ball and baked in an iron spider on the hot coals of the fireplace. Glyn couldn't wait to be home and taste his mother's cooking again. They had been able to find twenty bushels of wheat and had it milled at Clinton. He hoped the flour would last until spring.

They climbed the ladder to the sleeping loft the tavern kept for travelers. Indians and Negroes had to sleep in the lean-to with the livestock. The loft was one room, divided in half with a rope and blanket when women were present, of which there were none tonight. There were no beds. They simply rolled their blankets out and settled in for the night. They were starting out early the next morning, so that they could get to the Forks before dark.

There were two other men sharing the loft. One suffered the ague, which left him to shake and shiver. He would have the sweats before morning. Glyn thought the two hadn't bathed since last spring. He was used to that; men who were single or had wives back east or in Canada tended not to take care of themselves on the frontier. Bathtubs and barbers were few and far between, so were laundresses or, for that matter, single women.

He was thankful that his folks had taught him to take pride in his appearance, no matter where he was. There was no excuse to be unwashed or slovenly. It was no problem in warm weather; he and his brothers went to the river and took a swim. In cold weather, he broke the ice in a bucket and took a cold bath. He didn't need to shave but once a week, on Saturday night, so he would look presentable on the Sabbath. His father showed all the boys in the family, when they were old enough, how to keep a straight razor sharp and use it without cutting their own necks. Glyn thought as he fell asleep, that maybe he understood why his father was so strict about their appearance if he had been in the army. But strict as his father was, his mother was worse.

CHAPTER 9
SIMON'S WAR

Simon laid on the floor of the sleeping loft on his back, his arms folded behind his head, listening to Glyn breathe. He could hear the wind howling outside and felt icy drafts as they danced across the floor. This trip had made Glyn and him closer. He came to realize what an amazing individual his son had grown to be, and how much he loved him. He was so busy when the eldest two were growing up, that they were grown and married before he knew it. He made a mental note to himself to not let that happen with the two younger boys.

He hadn't told his son, or anyone, about the nightmare the war had become. Food had been scarce, and what rations they had quickly rotted or were worm-infested, making it inedible. They had to hunt and scavenge for provisions. His uniform was filthy and ragged, his boots full of holes, his feet always damp. Fleas and lice crawled over his body. They were in his hair and beard, in every crease and crevice. He was tempted to shave his whole body. They said the Indians did and Simon had read that Caesar had his hair plucked out when he was on campaign. But mosquitoes and black flies bit any exposed skin, so hair and beards helped there.

It seemed they chased Tecumseh and Proctor halfway through Canada, through thick swamps and endless wilderness. They were tired. Half the men were sick with ague. The Indians stayed to the rear, hid, then ambushed the troops, only to melt back into the trees. After weeks of chasing them, they thought they might have gained the upper hand—that they had worn the Natives down. There were only a couple dozen or so braves left, but Proctor kept pushing on. Simon's' sergeant thought the enemy intended to meet and regroup with more fighters, so their unit kept the chase up through the difficult terrain.

One rainy afternoon Simon's' unit finally surrounded them. It was by the Thames River, in a hilly location. The Indians were trapped, surrounded in a deep, bowl-shaped ravine. There were only a handful of Tecumseh's braves left. The battle was brief. Some said it was like shooting fish in a barrel. The sergeant said to wait until morning to investigate if any of the Indians were alive, hoping that any of those wounded would bleed out. Simon was put on guard duty with orders to shoot anything that moved. He was to keep watch on top of the highest hill, on the farther side of the ravine. The army would make camp on a hill on the other side.

About midnight the clouds broke, and a full moon came out. Simon stood, he could see a brave creeping through the long grass. Simon crept a little closer and could hear him chanting. He crept down the hill, keeping thorn trees and stunted red cedars between him and the brave. He quietly came out behind the man. By his dress and his height, Simon knew it was Chief Tecumseh himself. He stood in front of a tall stone obelisk, which was itself surrounded by four smaller obelisks in a circle of stones, each one large enough to sit on, which was at the center of the bowl-shaped ravine. The full moon was directly overhead. Simon did not know it, but this was the Algonquin's most sacred ritual site. It was where Tecumseh was headed all this time. Where he wanted to make his last stand. It was here he wanted to die.

Simon thought that maybe if he could capture the great Tecumseh alive, he might get some kind of promotion or recognition. He was quiet as he sneaked up behind the great warrior. Simon could see that he had been wounded, as he had a bloody rag tied around his head. Little did Simon know that Tecumseh had been waiting for him.

Tecumseh spoke, in perfect English. “Been waiting for one of you damned, stinking Americans to come. You are now in the People's most sacred circle. Why could you not just leave us alone? We would not have harmed you if you had left us alone. Why would you not honor your treaties? We lived with the French for so many years in peace. Your people will not be happy until we are all gone, and the land and lakes yours. Do you also want the air we breathe, as well as the sky? Do you even want to enslave The Great Spirit?”

Swiftly, he swung around and kicked the rifle out of Simon's hands. Simon was startled that Tecumseh had spoken so eloquently and moved so fast. Tecumseh tried to sucker punch Simon several times. Simon blocked the punches and sought to get him in a headlock. Tecumseh jumped back and then charged Simon, a dagger appeared in his hand as they went down on the ground. Tecumseh sliced Simon's cheek open as he tried to gouge his eye out. Simon rolled on top. His blood dripped down on Tecumseh's face, while Tecumseh was chanting a curse on Simon's soul.

Simon and Tecumseh both held the dagger in a death grip. Simon was able to turn the ceremonial blade away from his face. Their hands slick with blood, sliced open from the sharp obsidian blade, their blood intermingling. As Tecumseh rolled on top, Simon managed to plunge the blade into Tecumseh's heart. Tecumseh's eyes grew wide, then dimmed as his life's' blood pumped out. He said in English to Simon, "I die a great warrior, but may you be damned forever" and breathed his last breath of life in Simon's face.

Simon felt as though the knife had gone through him, too. The pain was searing, bright lights blinded him, then he fell into utter darkness, the breath knocked out of him as he lost consciousness...

Men from his regiment found them early the next morning. They thought Simon, still under Tecumseh, soaked in Tecumseh's blood, was dead as well. But he regained consciousness after one of the men poured cold water on his face. He woke, but was delirious. His gibberish made no sense; it was as though he was talking Indian. One of his buddies helped him, half dragged him, to the river where they washed the sticky blood off his body and his ragged uniform.

Simon slowly remembered the events of the night before. His hands, deeply sliced by the ceremonial dagger, the sharp pain still in his chest. As he washed the blood away, Simon thought he would find a stab wound in his chest, but neither he nor his friend found any injuires, except for his hands and the gash down his cheek.

At camp, after one man tried to sew Simon's wounds up, most of the regiment left to chase down General Proctor. Simon rested with a small group of the sickest men. They stayed to bury the dead warriors. The men dug a trench in front of the obelisk. They desecrated the braves and flung their bodies in on top of each other, with no kind of ceremony, Tecumseh last. One of the men pulled the blood-covered dagger from Tecumseh's lifeless body and tossed it to Simon. It landed at his feet; Simon looked down at it. Then they toppled the obelisk into the trench and covered the mass grave. The People's Sacred Circle was destroyed. It would always be a haunted place. The remaining regiment gave chase to Proctor and his remaining troops but soon ran out of provisions. In the dense Canadian countryside, they lost sight of them and came back empty handed.

-------#-------

They marched back to Detroit, only to find cholera had broken out in the fort and city again. They called Simon's regiment in for guard duty, the others having caught the contagion. It was not long before Simon started to feel ill. First watery diarrhea, then vomiting. He was sent to the crowded infirmary. No medical personnel were there to take care of the sick and dying. Dehydration quickly appeared with cholera, which caused a rapid heartbeat, low blood pressure, and body cramps. Simon could not endure the thirst. Men were dying all around him, wreathed in a thick miasma of death and sickness.

It wasn't until the next day that men came in and started carrying out the dead. Simon couldn't believe it—they actually picked up his body. He screamed at them that he was still alive, but it was like they couldn't hear. They threw his body on the wagon with the others, piling more corpses on him. He still screamed. He could see the ghosts of the other dead men, rising out of their bodies, following. But he wasn't dead! Why could no one see that? What kind of nightmare was this? The wagon started moving to the burial grounds. There, trenches were already dug, and they began tossing bodies in.

They picked Simon up. He took a huge gulp of air and screamed, "I am not dead!"

One of the men dropped his arms, "This one is still alive, heard him take a breath. Should we toss him in any way? Don't look as though he's going to make it, be a blessing to end it for him."

Simon was still screaming "Noooo, I'm still alive, can't you tell!"

"Well," the other man said, "We better take him back. Might get in trouble burying a live corpse. Throw him off to the side. We'll check on him later and decide."

They threw his body on the hard ground. What didn't hurt before did now. This was agony. All Simon wanted was a drink of water, just one drink. His mouth was so dry. His tongue was cracked and bleeding. He could not open his eyes because his lids were stuck to them. He was covered with flies. It was getting late and would soon be dark. The men quickly finished burying the corpses. They checked to see if he was still breathing. He was, so they threw him back on the wagon and left. At the infirmary, they carried him back into that hell hole. The stench was so strong it was like a living demon that swirled around him, waiting. They threw him down on a filthy pallet on the floor, stirring up a swarm of flies.

Simon had never felt so sick, or felt so alone. He wanted to die; he deserved to die. He willed himself to give up, just die and be done with it! He heard a voice, deep inside his head, no, inside his mind. But it wasn't his voice. It was Tecumseh's.

"Just die? You think you can just die, and not grieve over all those you have slain? No Simon, you will never die. I will stay and haunt you forever. Do you understand? Forever!"

A sharp pain pierced Simon's chest as he passed out.

It was pitch black when Simon woke. He could hear the cries and moans of dying men above the hum of flies. He felt stronger, strong enough to start crawling across the floor, which was thick with vomit, excrement, and maggots. A pail of water had been left by the door. He could smell it. It took him an hour of slowly crawling, stopping to rest, then crawling another inch or two, to reach it. By the grace of God, someone had filled it before they left. It took the last of his strength to raise up and take a drink, then another. He could feel strength flowing back into his tortured body as the cool, sweet water ran down his throat. He felt his innards soak in the moisture. He drank as much as he could without vomiting then poured the cool water over his head.

He lay there and rested for a while. Then, with all the strength he could muster he stood, and half dragged the empty bucket with his dirty, bandaged hands, out to the well. He lifted the full bucket out of the well and poured the cool water over his head, drinking in all he could. He felt a little more of his strength return.

Soon, he grew strong enough to carry a whole bucket of water. He carried it back to the infirmary and gave all the men drinks, not realizing that it was the very water from the shallow well that had sickened them all in the first place. A thick layer of clay below the sandy soil caused drainage from the burial ground and the latrines to flow back toward the fort, contaminating their water supply, and the village's. He went back and forth to the well. As the fort came to life in the first morning light, he was able to get several more men to help him care for the sick soldiers.

The doctor and the other medical men who ran the infirmary had died several days before from cholera, as had the Commanding Officer. With no one in charge, men were simply brought in to die, then hauled out to bury, with no one to care for them. If you were too sick, you died. Simon felt a burst of energy, as well as anger, and took over the infirmary. He knew nothing of medicine, but he could keep the men as clean and comfortable as he could until new people arrived to take over. Every man in his unit that had fought in Canada had died. He never forgot what it was like to be thrown as a corpse on to the dead wagon...

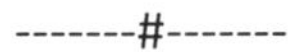

Simon and Glyn were up before dawn the next morning, the oxen hitched to the wagons, provisions packed, ready to set out. After a hearty breakfast, they paid the tavern-keep for their room and board. Glyn thought some should have been taken off their bill for all the lice and vermin they picked up in the sleeping loft, but his father said they were lucky that's all they got. Glyn wasn't sure what that meant.

Phineas Phelps came riding up on his mule. He was short and skinny, with a big floppy hat that hardly covered his big ears, and an infectious, tobacco-stained grin. He was ready to lead the way to the Forks. It had dawned sunny and cold. The storm that buffeted the tavern during the night had passed. Snow that had melted into slush in the rain was now frozen solid. At least there would be no mud to contend with.

There was talk of putting a plank road in from Jackson up to the O Washtenong in Biddle Town, but no one believed it would ever be done. That would be about like trying to build a railroad through this wilderness. But there was an Indian trail that only a few people knew about that was a good route between Oyers Corners and the Forks. If a decent road were ever put through, this would be most promising. Phineas thought if they pushed hard all day they would arrive before nightfall.

The little caravan left Oyers Corners just as the sun rose above the trees in the eastern sky. Phineas was on his mule, leading the way, followed by two wagons, each pulled by a team of oxen. They headed east, then curved around until they were headed towards the north. They were soon surrounded by thick forest, with hills and swamps. The Indians had long ago found a fairly level path to follow. It curved around to miss the steepest hills and kept away from the deepest swamps. It would be easy to get lost without the proper guide.

CHAPTER 10

Olive

The baby was asleep in the old cradle they had brought from New York. It was one of the few pieces of household furniture she had insisted on bringing with them. All of her children had been rocked in it, as had she and her siblings, and her mother as well. The baby awakened an hour before dawn and demanded to be nursed and changed, then fell back asleep.

Olive had her first batch of bread out of the stone beehive bake oven, the loaves cooling on the long slab-top table in the center of the room. The same table the baby had been born on. The cabin smelled of warm yeast and the toasted pine nuts she ground and mixed into the dough and pressed on top. Olive had a good feeling that today was going to be special. Her mother always said she had 'The Sight,' inherited from her Scottish grandmother. She didn't believe in such things, but she had a good feeling this little girl was going to grow up to be a strong woman and that she would see her husband today.

She heard the cowbell as the door in the trading post opened. Olive gathered up loaves of hot bread on a large wooden tray and went through the connecting door. The trading post was a twenty foot square room connected to the cabin where they lived with a fireplace in the middle of the center wall. One door went through the center wall into their own living space, and doors opened out on the stoops on each side. Both sides of the cabin were identical, but this room was packed with supplies that a homesteader might need.

There was a slab-top table in front of the door that went back into their room, where sales were figured up and purchases bundled. Behind the table, on the wall, were cubicles for the US mail to be sorted, although very little mail came in. Every wall had shelves for ax and hammer heads, rolls of cloth and tanned buckskin. The ceiling beams had hooks for every conceivable tool for the homesteader. Shovels and pitchforks, harnesses and bridles were hung in an organization only Simon knew. Kegs of nails, crocks of sauerkraut, vinegar, and pickles were on the far wall, and rows of barrels for salt pork, flour, and dried apples, although most were empty and sat waiting to be restocked. Natives came in often; some would arrive by canoe with furs to trade for game traps, iron pots, tobacco, or knives. And they always asked for whiskey.

PRICE LIST

Young Mare	*$40.00*	*Pair of Shoes*	*$1.50*
Beef cow	*$13.00*	*Spider/Frying Pan*	*$1.75*
Bushel of Wheat	*$ .75*	*Door Latch*	*1 shilling($.371/2)*
Bushel ear corn	*$ .33*	*2 1/2 pound Cotton*	*$ .78*
10 pounds of sugar	*$1.25*	*1 pound of lead*	*$ .25*
Pound of Tea	*$2.00*	*One yard of Calico*	*$ .75*
1 dozen Fish	*$ .50*	*One yard of Muslin*	*$ .31 1/2*
3 pounds of Butter	*1 shilling ($ .37 ½)*	*Six Needles*	*$.06 1/4*
1 Bushel Apples	*1 shilling ($ .37 ½)*	*Gunpowder 1 ½ pounds.*	*$1.50*

"Morning, Miss Olive, thought I smelled your bread soon as I walked close to your cabin. Wanted to check to see if I had any letters."

Reverend Jack lived in a lean-to shanty down by the Indian Camp, took on odd jobs, and was sweet on Olive. Said he was waiting on the mill that was to be built, that he was a master millwright, and could keep any machine running. Olive thought he must be good at being a wheelwright, as he was always was covered in grease. Jack lived by himself, and would disappear from time to time for a couple of weeks, and then he'd be back. He always wore the same frontier clothes: moccasins, breeches and a shirt made out of tanned buckskins. In cool weather he added a coat and a cap made from coonskin. Simon said that Jack was a preacher and made rounds to the different settlements that would listen to him. She remembered the first time she had heard him preach, early in the summer...

-------#-------

Two pioneer brothers had settled on a claim halfway between the Forks and the Big Prairie. They cleared enough land to build a cabin. The older one, Samuel, went back East and got his wife and children. That was a year before Simon and Olive came out west.

The wife, Ruth, had been sickly most of her adult life, consumption they said. She had her baby in the spring. The stress of childbirth and pioneer living made her poorly again. One day, the men folk were out in the field cutting wheat, the children were helping by bundling the cut wheat, so it could be loaded onto a stone-bolt and be drawn back to the barn, to be thrashed. They were out in the field most all day.

When the work was done, they drove the stone-boat with the wheat bundles back to the cabin. They found Ruth dead in bed, with the baby crying in her arms. Samuel lovingly held his wife, then with tears on his face, tied her feet together and folded her arms over her breast. He tied a rag under her chin and over her head to keep her mouth closed and placed a coin over each eye. He did this in respect to his wife. He knew she would go into rigormortis in a few hours. They put her in a wagon and brought her to the Forks.

Simon and Glyn made a crude coffin from the boards off the wagon. They tacked black cloth to the outside, and a quilt lined the inside. Olive would dress her in a nice dress of her own since Ruth had none left. With the help of the Indian women, they washed and dressed her.

Her husband Samuel had no decent clothes either. His corduroy trousers were in tatters, his 'wa'mus' was so thin and ragged, he wore it as a shirt, and only a fragment of his cap was left on his head. It was said that you could tell how long a man had been in these parts according to his clothes. By the second year, he wore his best clothes every day, by the third year, he had cut his coat tails off to mend his sleeves.

Between Simon and Glyn, and with the help of other men in the area, Olive put together a halfway decent suit of clothes for Samuel to wear to his wife's funeral. They discussed where they should bury her, and decided on a pleasant meadow beside Spring Brook, where wildflowers grew abundantly. Jack preached a good sermon that everyone in the area attended. A neighbor of the widower took the children to raise until he could go back east to find another wife.

-------#-------

"Sorry Jack, no mail for you this week, maybe next." Olive always said the same thing. She never knew of him ever receiving a letter.

"That's all right. Why don't you wrap up a loaf of that bread, and I need some salt, black powder, and lead."

Olive wrapped up a loaf of warm bread and put a generous pat of freshly turned butter in with his purchases. Jack paid his bill; they talked a while, and he left. She went over to the fireplace, stirred up the embers, and put some logs on so the room would warm up, then went back into their living quarters. No one stayed the night, so she didn't have anyone but the boys to fix breakfast for.

"James! Joseph! You two get up and take care of your bedclothes. Take them outside and hang 'em on the bushes. The sun is out, and they need airing. I need you all to fetch some water from the brook. I need to wash clothes today, now that the sun is shining."

Her two youngest boys always stayed curled up in their bed as long as possible. "But Mother, we're hungry. Can't we eat first? The baby kept us up all night, and we're tired."

"You two get up. You can have a fresh biscuit while you're getting the water, and then I'll have your breakfast ready. Stop at the cow shed, gather the eggs and let the yard birds out. See if any Indians passing through stayed the night there. If so, bring them in for something to eat. You can do the milking after your breakfast. And I need more wood split to heat water. Start a fire under the copper kettle out back. And you're not sleepy. I had to listen to both of you snore all night. I'll be glad when your big brother gets back, so you can sleep up in the loft again. Now get a move on. Your father may not be here, but I know where he keeps the switch!"

The two boys and their dogs came tumbling out from under their quilts. It had almost become a ritual, she threatening them with a beating if they didn't get up and get moving. She knew, and they knew, she never would. They were really good boys; she didn't know how she could manage without them. They had been such a great help when the baby came.

The old cowbell on the trading post door clanged again. She went through to find two young Indian boys, Mani-to-corb-way and Shing-wauk, who were about the same age as James and Joseph. They wore traditional clothes, that is, not a lot. Frontier woman quickly got used to seeing the naked chest and backsides of the Native American male. They would add buckskin breeches, a shirt, and moccasins when the snow was deep. Olive wondered that they didn't freeze, but the cold didn't seem to bother them.

"Good morning, Mrs. Chatfield. Grandfather sent us to pick up a loaf of bread, and he would like a pinch of salt. Are the boys around?"

Olive knew the two boys well. They were playmates and good friends with James and Joseph. She knew their mother had died a long while back, and their father, because of his addiction to alcohol, was seldom seen. They lived with their old grandfather in the Camp. Their grandfather lived alone; his wife died of cholera the year before. It was quite evident that an ancestor of the boys, maybe the mother, had been a Black Indian.

Olive wasn't sure if he took care of the boys, or the boys him. They had been to a missionary school in Canada at some time and learned to speak perfect King's English with an English accent. They had impeccable manners around adults. She had seen them play and knew they could be just as wild and loud as the others. She wished some of their good manners would rub off on her boys.

"Here you go, the bread is still warm. I put the salt in a twist of paper. Now you two get back to your grandfather before the bread gets cold. James and Joseph are doing their chores. Be back here at mid-day for your lessons."

"Thank you, Mrs. Chatfield," the boys both rang out as they left.

Olive had been encouraging the few Indian children in the Camp to come and study with her boys. She hoped by summer, if enough settlers with children moved into the area, to start a proper school for them.

CHAPTER 11
THE ROAD HOME

On leaving Oyers Corners, the farther they traveled, the shanties of the homesteaders became farther apart, then seemed to disappear. Close to the settlement, the few farms were laid out in neat patchworks. Soon the road gave out and became a trail barely discernible to the eye. The shanties and the fields grew smaller and not as well tended, but you could see where the forest was being cleared. A lot of energy was going into clearing the land. They were about half way to the Forks, and the forest had enveloped them. The trail was only a path, and not much used. They saw only a couple of lone Indians in the distance, and not a white man since leaving Oyers Corners.

"I see horses up ahead," said Phelps. "Coming up the trail from Onondaga." He rode ahead of them on his mule, to show them the way. Phineas was not the most talkative sort but was pleasant enough company. He explained that most folks took the other trail to the west, a better trail, but the Holibaugh hills were steep and would be slippery in this weather. A person would have to spend the night at someone's cabin around Charlesworth. This old Indian trail wasn't used much, but if you pushed, you could make it in one day. Providing you stayed out of mud holes or didn't get lost. When the horses were closer, they could see it was three voyageurs coming their way.

"How goes there?" Phelps shouted, raising his hand when they were within twenty rods of each other. The trapping party hailed back. They pulled up beside each other, warily eyeing each other. All three were mixed race, two were French-Indian, the other a Black-Indian, although they looked and smelled about the same. Glyn thought they must specialize in trapping pole-cats. Phelps spoke to them in a combination of French and sign. He wanted to know their business and where they were headed. When the trappers learned they had supplies and were headed to the Forks, they wanted to barter some of their furs. Glyn thought they should move on and not waste the time if they were to make it to their cabin before dark. But Simon thought if he traded a few items the trappers wanted, it would take little time, and furs brought good money.

They got down to negotiations and quickly settled with each other. Glyn noticed the sly looking one, with a scraggly black beard and pale, watery brown eyes, looking at the barrels of flour they had strapped to the sides of the wagons. He signed he wanted a drink of whiskey. Glyn signed "no whiskey." The scraggly Black-Beard started to get agitated, then took a swing at Glyn. Glyn ducked and dived for Black-Beard's legs, and they went down in a hail of fists. The other two voyageurs acted as though they would join in on the fight until Phineas pointed his rifle and told them to settle down. Glyn, about 25 years younger than his adversary, was soon on top. Having two older and two younger brothers had made Glyn an expert at boxing and wrestling. Glyn punched the man a few times until his eyes rolled back in his head. Simon went over to the barrel, opened the top and took a handful of flour out and dumped it in the face of the trapper.

"No whiskey," Simon said in his guttural French. He helped Glyn up with one hand, holding his rifle in the other. They quickly picked things up, tied down the canvas covering the wagon, and set off. The two trappers lifted their bloodied and white-faced friend off the ground. Phineas stayed at the rear of their little caravan, watching out over his shoulder with his rifle ever ready in case the trio tried to follow them. After an hour or so it all seemed clear. Glyn smelled like polecats the rest of the way home.

"Ya gotta watch out for those old voyageurs. When they all git liquored up with their friends, no telling what they might do," Phineas said. "I imagine most of 'em are good people. Trying to make a living like the rest of us. Some of them old French trappers live in sin right with them Inguns, and still have their own wives and families back in Quebec. They have half-breeds running all over the country. As bad as those slave-holders down South. I hear they all have half-bred children on their plantations. And they claim they have a Christian right to own slaves. Sinners, all of 'em."

Phineas was a strict Methodist.

Finally, with the sun dipping down over the trees, they came to their fork in the trail. Another mile or two to the north was the Forks and their cabin. Phineas's brother lived a couple of miles down the trail to the east. Simon thanked him and invited him and his brother to their cabin before he headed back to Oyers Corners. The oxen set off in a fast walk towards the settlement like they somehow knew they were headed to their new home and a warm barn. More likely they sensed the lone wolf that had been following them for the last few miles. Glyn had noticed him through the trees, staying far enough away not to cause concern, just waiting for the darkness of night.

CHAPTER 12
HOMECOMING

They came into the Forks by the back way, on the seldom-used south trail. Most of the foot traffic came in from the west, following the old Indian trail that ran along Spring Brook to Spicer's Mill, whom some called the Hogsback. Or, the more traveled trail along the O Washtenong River. As they came upon the Indian Camp, dogs barked, and children stopped playing to look.

Several Native Americans stood outside their wigwams, warming their hands over the iron pots that swung above cooking fires, supported on a tripod of wooden poles. Wood smoke wafted through the air. Simon and Glyn waved a greeting and traveled on. Soon they could hear the whooping and hollering as two young boys and their dogs came running toward them. James and Joseph hopped up onto the wagons, talking and shouting as they hugged their father and brother, the dogs barking at their wheels. They wanted to know where they had been and what had taken them so long. They teased their big brother, told him he looked like a rag-man. He was dirty, smelled of skunk, and his clothes were torn and ripped.

They pulled up in front of the cabin. Simon jumped off the wagon as the door opened and Olive walked out, drying her hands on her apron. Simon rushed to her and lifted her off the ground in a big bear hug. She clung to him. He put her down and looked at her, never had she been so beautiful to him. He looked into eyes that were so blue they put an Irish sky to shame. He took her face in his large calloused hands and gently kissed her, and hugged her tight. Her dark hair, only tinged with gray, was braided up in a knot at the back of her head beneath her scarf.

"God, it's so good to see you and finally be home. I was so worried for you and the boys. You had the baby! How is it? Girl or boy? Are you well?" Simon knew he was talking too fast, but he needed to know everything.

"Yes, yes, I'm well, and the baby seems good and healthy. Come in and see her, she's asleep in the cradle."

"She!" exclaimed Simon. "We have a little girl! And she's healthy."

Simon raced into the cabin to where the cradle sat by the fireplace. He picked up the little bundle with care.

By this time the boys were crowding into the room.

"Look, boys; you have a little sister. She looks just like your mother!"

"Yea, yea, we've seen her. She cries all the time, and she smells." The infatuation had definitely worn off for the two younger boys.

"What did you bring us!" The boys were jumping up and down, remembering the promise that if they were good and helpful to their mother, a prize might be had.

"You two settle down," said Simon. "There are two wagons that need tending to. And if you look hard, there might be a sack of hard candy hid in there."

Simon couldn't take his eyes off his daughter. "Glyn, come over here and say hello to your new sister. You will have to watch out for her. She is so tiny, no bigger than a possum."

Glyn hugged his mother and walked over to where his father was holding his new sister. He put his hand out to touch the baby's perfect porcelain face. She reached up and grabbed onto his finger in her little fist, and would not let go. His heart melted at that moment. Tears came to his eyes, and he knew he would be looking after her all his life. Never before had he felt such a protective bond with a sibling. He took her from his father and sat down in one of the rustic chairs sitting around the long table. So, Glyn thought, so this is what it feels like to have a family that one loves and takes care of.

Simon reached over and pulled Olive to him in a hug. He smiled and thought, if this baby could melt the heart of Glyn, his middle son, who thought only about the next meal or the next adventure, she should be able to wrap any man around her finger.

"So tell us, what did you name her?" Simon asked in a gentle voice.

"Haven't yet, wanted to wait till you all were home. Thought we could pick one out together." Olive didn't want to say that she was waiting to see if the girl was going to live or not, but she was thriving like a weed in a garden patch.

"You boys go out and take care of the oxen," Olive told the two youngsters. "Leave the wagons up next to the cabin by the trading post door; the dogs will keep watch if any bears or vermin come around. We'll unload them in the morning. I'll get supper on the table, you all must be hungry. We'll talk about naming the baby and you can tell us everything that happened to you two."

Olive reached over, took the baby out of Glyn's arms, and put her back in the cradle. "You two go out back and take those filthy clothes off. I'll have to boil them for a week. I hung some clothes out this morning; they're hanging on the back stoop. There's a kettle of water still warm on the fire pit. Scrub yourselves good with that lye soap. I bet you're both crawling with bugs from staying in those filthy taverns, and I'll have none of that in my cabin."

James and Joseph unhitched, fed and bedded the oxen down. Then they wiped the harnesses down and hung them up. Glyn and Simon washed the lice and dirt off and put clean clothes on. They all sat down to a supper of stewed venison and hot corn bread with freshly turned sweet butter. Glyn regaled his young brothers of their adventures. Olive was worried that the Frenchmen might come back. Simon was sure they would never show up since they had said that they were heading to Detroit, to take a boat to Quebec. They talked for hours. All were happy that the family was safe and together again. The boys cleared the table off and fed the scraps to the dogs. Simon wanted to know what was wrong with them.

"You boys never got up and helped your mother without being told to."

"Cloud said she would whip us good if we didn't help Mother. We've been real good while you were away," said Joesph.

"Well, that makes me proud of you two. I'll have to ask Cloud what her secret is!" Simon laughed and hugged his boys. Later, three sleepy boys made their way up the ladder to the loft.

During the night, after the baby had nursed and had been put in her cradle, Olive snuggled close against Simon in their bed. The cabin was no longer a cold and lonely place for her, but a warm and loving home. Her fingers slowly played across his familiar, well-muscled chest as he stroked her long dark hair and smelled her warm, musky scent. Simon was glad to be home. He wanted never to leave Olive's arms again for a long time. And Olive wanted Simon at home, too.

"You have no idea how I have missed you, Olive. My love for you only gets stronger the longer we're together. The taste of your lips, the smell of your skin. I want to have you next to me every night, your skin touching mine."

"Simon, I love you with all my heart. You know what they say, 'Absence makes the heart grow fonder.' I never truly knew what that meant till now. Hold me a little tighter tonight, since I can't believe you're home."

"Have you thought what you want to name the baby?" Olive decided the time had come for the child to have a name. "I was thinking of naming her after your mother."

"That's mighty sweet of you, but I was never partial to Elvira. Mother was named after the town her mother's family was from. I was thinking something simple, a name from the Bible maybe? Esther or Ruth? What do you like?"

"I think I like Sarah. Simple, but the name means goodness of character. And our daughter is going to be a good and strong character."

"Sarah, yes I like that. Sarah Marie, that's a nice name." Simon mumbled as he fell asleep, still holding Olive in his arms.

PART II – 1836

CHAPTER 13

Olive

The log cabin Simon and the boys built had two rooms. The whole cabin measured twenty foot by forty foot, with a stone fireplace in the center that separated the two, twenty-foot square rooms. The family lived in one room. The boys slept up in the attic loft. The loft covered three-quarters of the attic, and a ladder led up to it. The loft stayed quite warm in the winter with the heat from the fireplace rising up, but was stifling hot in the summer. The trading post took up the other room, with an attic sleeping loft above for travelers. Outside, a stoop went across both front and back, with a door going in and out of each room. There were no windows, except for a bottle glass window in the eave of each of the sleeping lofts and a shuttered vent that could be opened in hot weather.

A lean-to at the end of the trading-post had a small forge for making the tools and utensils they sold. Glyn grew up pumping the bellows while his father worked, heating the iron red hot so it could be turned into useful articles. Now the two younger boys worked the bellows while Glyn hammered out nails. He could make nine hundred nails a day. First, the nail rods were heated, then they were dented at the proper length, put in a nail-header and broken off. Lastly, the nail head was pounded out and then dipped in cold water. A good nail-maker could do it in four strokes.

In good weather, the back stoop was an extension of their living space. The family would eat on a rough slab-top table, with blocks of wood for seats. A fire pit was not far from the stoop with a large copper kettle hanging over it, with water from the artesian spring heating continuously for cooking and washing dishes.

Water for washing clothes came from the rain barrel or the brook because it was softer. The artesian water contained too many minerals and turned clothes a rust color. Olive had her spinning wheel, hand loom, churn and sewing work table set up out on the stoop so she could catch the light.

The stoop looked out over the marsh that Spring Brook widened into before it gently flowed into the O Washtenong. The marsh was filled with water birds of every sort, swans, geese, and ducks. Cormorants and kingfishers could be seen diving for fish. Wading birds could be seen walking through the trees and undergrowth. Blue herons, egrets, and sand-hill cranes, as tall as a man but shy as a mouse, pecking the ground, looking for insects and tender shoots of grass. The area was like an elegant park filled with grand old trees. Birds sang from every branch and bush. The ground was covered with flowers of every hue. The air was filled with the crescendo of music and fragrance.

Olive sat on the back stoop with her Indian friends. She was teaching them how to do fine sewing and tatting. In turn, they showed her how to do the intricate bead and quill work of their tribe. They also showed her which herbs to burn to keep the bugs away. Sarah slept in an old sap trough. The baby had caught a bad cold that spring, but with the help of Native American herbal remedies the old women brewed up, she was much better and was now thriving.

One day when Olive sat sewing with her friends, she said to River Woman, who always smiled but had little to say, “Tell me your story.” River was silent. She was working on some beaded moccasins for the baby. Finally, she started to talk...

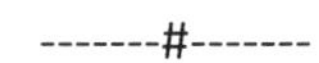

-------#-------

"RIVER WOMAN'S STORY"

“I was born in Georgia on a rice plantation. I fell in love and jumped the broom with a boy I grew up with, named Wild Cat. I was about fourteen, fifteen summers and he about sixteen. My, he had a fiery temper. We wanted to start a family as soon as we could. When slaves work in the rice fields, they tend not to live a long time. The rice swamps are full of disease and poisonous snakes. You have to stand in water and mud while digging and cleaning out drainage ditches, waist deep in mud and water, day after day. At night, you slept on the ground, wherever you happened to stop work for the night. You slept with the mud still clinging to you, for when it dried, it kept you warmer. Guards were posted to watch for cougars, but sometimes the guards fell asleep. On Sundays, they let you go back to the main camp.

"After I found that I was with child, we decided to run away, to Spanish Florida. We made it through the Florida swamps and met up with Billy Bowlegs, a half-black Seminole chief. We lived in his town, and we all called ourselves Maroons.

“You see, my mother and father tried to escape before I was birthed, my mother was too big and too slow, she was caught by the slavers. She was whipped and taken back. They cut her *(Achilles)* tendons so she couldn't run again. She heard my father made it into Spanish Florida and was adopted by the Seminoles. I looked but never found him.

“My man, Wild Cat, he kept going back to Georgia and bringing slaves to freedom. He was well known to the slave hunters, and a bounty was put on his head. One time he was cornered, and he fought his way out of the ambush. Several white men were killed.

“It was about January of 1818 when General Andrew Jackson came with a Navy fleet and with two mounted regiments and marched on Spanish Florida. They found the town we lived in, Billy Bowlegs' town. There was a big battle. Jackson was known for using savage dogs, ones that would tear your face off or bite a child right in two. The Black Seminoles by this time were quite powerful. We had a strong army and a good fort. But not strong enough for the US Army.

“We were defeated.

“The army captured many, including my man. Took him back to Georgia. Heard that he was put on trial, and whipped. They cut Wild Cat's head and hands off. They put his head on a pike in the center of the slave market. His hands they nailed to the gate. Last I heard they was still there, just a sun-bleached skull and a pair of mummified hands, to remind slaves of what will happen if they try to escape.

"A few of us did escape the slaughter. We went north and sought shelter with other tribes. We kept going north, kept passing on to the next tribe so we would be safe and could never be found by the slavers. I ended up being adopted by a tribe in the far North Country. Kept me and my daughter safe, until I became Wolf Jaw's wife.”

CHAPTER 14

Cloud Woman, the Healer

Olive had a rare shouting match with Simon one day over her Indian friends.

"I don't want them heathen, dirty Indians in my cabin or around our baby!" Simon had shouted, shortly after he had got back from his trip to fetch supplies. He had been out and trapped several rabbits for supper. While he was skinning and gutting them, his knife slipped, and he sliced opened his thumb. He came into the cabin, and Olive tore some clean cloth into strips to bandage the wound.

Cloud Woman was there. She took a pinch of dried plantain from her medicine pouch and chewed it. Then she reached over, spat the green glob onto his cut thumb and preceded to bind the wound tightly with the cloth strips.

All hell broke loose. Simon lost his temper and told the old woman to leave. Olive took Cloud Woman out the door, then turned on Simon and told him in no uncertain terms, that if it wasn't for those women, she would probably be dead, and their daughter, too.

His thumb healed quickly, without an infection. Olive said it was thanks to Cloud Woman's medical herbs. He thought it was a miracle he hadn't got blood poisoning. He had to admit that he was thankful for their help when he was away from home when Sarah was born. Olive didn't say, but she knew that if he had been home, he wouldn't have been much help. Birthing was a women's thing, better off when men were not around.

More than a week went by after his outburst at Cloud Woman and the women stayed away and had not come back. Olive was angry, and

Simon knew that if he wanted his loving wife back, he had to make peace with her native friends.

He took several loaves of bread, some fresh meat, and salt to the Camp and thanked the women profusely for all they had done for his family. He took baby Sarah with him and watched as the old people came out of their wigwams to fuss over her. The old men, as well as the women, all wanted to hold the little papoose. They told him how they missed their own families, who were now at their winter village up north. After that, the women started coming to the cabin again and told Olive that they knew how men were.

The truth was that Simon grew up hearing stories of how the Native American Indian had captured, tortured and killed the early colonists. They had come to America looking for a peaceful place to live and farm and were harassed by the Indians. The Native Americans took the side of French during the French and Indian Wars, and the English during the Revolutionary War. He had fought them as the enemy during the War of 1812 when Tecumseh had massacred the wounded troops at River Raisin. He had wanted to rejoin the militia to fight in the Black Hawk War in 1832, but Olive had persuaded him out of it.

Through long talks with Olive into the night, Simon came to see that his prejudices, although understandable, were not sensible. To hate an entire race of people because of the past misdeeds of a few was being very short-sighted. Their lack of tolerance to alcohol was no more their fault than their lack of immunity from European diseases. They were fighting for their own homeland; the Europeans were the aggressors. They had signed treaty after treaty with the white man, only to see those treaties broken time and time again. And the Indians could not understand the treaties they signed. French treaties had always given them gifts for the temporary use of their land. They thought it more of a temporary lease of the land. How could you sell something that belonged to the 'Great Spirit Father,' and had been given to them?

He hated to admit it, but Olive was right—again. Even though they were both raised as Quakers, she was brought up in a much more rigid Quaker household. Her father, a country lawyer, and her mother, a school teacher, opened a school at their farmhouse for poor children. They had even helped Indian and Negro students, as well as poor immigrants just coming into the country, and had been ostracized for it. Local townspeople threw manure on the walls of their house and even tried to set it afire once. But through perseverance, she had learned not to judge a person on the color of their skin, or their religion, or ethnicity, but as individual souls.

Olive reminded Simon how three from their Quaker faith had been hung by the Puritans in Boston in 1659. At the time, Pennsylvania Quakers were not allowed in the Puritan's Massachusetts Bay Colony under the penalty of death.

Simon had been taught to mistrust the German and French overlords of the old country, and the English and Native Americans in their new country. Those that were trying to take away the life he wanted for his family. He never told Olive much about his war, the strange happenings that took place, or the strange nightmares that haunted his sleep.

CHAPTER 15

Gray Dove

Gray Dove's band made it to Mackinac Island before the lake froze over. It had been their traditional winter campgrounds long before the French came in 1668 and opened a chapel and mission in Sault Ste. Marie. Gray Dove's people had been part of the uprising in 1763 that killed most of the British garrisoned at Fort Machilimackinac before the British moved the fort to the island in 1772.

But that spring, small-pox broke out among the white men, rapidly spreading to the Indian encampment. Gray Dove's brother was the first of her family to sicken, with a high temperature and body aches, then her mother. She went to the doctor at the fort's infirmary for help and was turned away. Her brother's skin turned black and charred looking. His eyes turned blood red, and he vomited constantly. He died on the fifth day, and her mother and father soon followed. By then people were leaving in droves, scared of the sickness they did not understand. People not yet sick rushed into the forest to hide. The incubation period is twelve days; most of those that fled to the woods died miserably and alone.

Gray Dove wanted to die. Almost everyone from her tribe on the island was dead. She stayed and nursed those that could not fend for themselves. Despite her care, most of them died. Only some of those who got the blisters died. Then she got sick; she was so tired, she simply crawled into her dome-shaped wigwam and waited to join her family. She thought about her grandmother, whom they had left with her husband and his first wife by the trading post beside the river. She hoped this white man's curse would spare them.

She fell into a deep sleep. When she woke, she had the rash on her body. She ached and had a fever. She woke up once and an old woman she did not know was bathing her face in cool water and forced her to drink a broth. She slept and woke again, alone. The rash was fading, and the fluid-filled blisters were starting to form on her palms and a few on her face, but she didn't feel as bad. That day went by, and then another. The old woman came back and brought more broth to drink and fresh water. The next day Gray Dove crawled out and sat in the sun. After a few days, she felt like she might live after all. The old woman came back when Gray Dove was stronger, gathered up a few items, and set the wigwam ablaze. Gray Dove watched as all she had left of her family turned to ashes. She noticed that all the wigwams had been destroyed.

"Thank you for helping me. I'm Gray Dove."

"No, it is I who should thank you. You nursed me when my husband and I were sick. You do not recognize me, for I was covered in blisters. My husband died, but I lived, thanks to you. The soldiers are burning all the Camps. I made them leave your wigwam, told them I would burn it when you were better. Come, I built a new wigwam with a few other survivors on the other side of the island. I'm Blackbird."

With Blackbird's help, Gray Dove made her way along the lake shore until they reached the other side. Out of the 3,000 inhabitants that had been on the island, only about 100 were left. Over 2,000 had died, and the rest had left the island. When the last ice leaves the lakes, the rest of the Indians will leave also. They were a ragged group, most still recovering from the sickness. Many were blind. They would go to the missions and seek help for those who could not live on their own.

Gray Dove shared Blackbird's hut with two other women. When she became stronger, she helped take care of those in need. When early summer finally came and the ice in the lakes melted, a few of their people who had heard about the epidemic came to see if anyone was left. They helped to take the last few poor souls either back to their families or to one of the missions where they could stay and be looked after. Blackbird and one of the other women wanted Gray Dove to stay with their tribe, which hunted in the upper Lake Superior country in the summer.

Gray Dove only wanted to find her grandmother, hoping that she was safe down in the O Washtenong River country and that she could find her. They found Gray Dove a small group that was heading south on Lake Michigan, to spend the summer at Fort Miami by the St. Joseph River. She planned to go as far as the mouth of the O Washtenong with them, and then go the rest of the way alone.

She said her farewells to her new-found friends and started paddling along the shore of the lake in a dugout canoe, going south. They were to camp and fish along the way. Unfortunately, it wasn't long before she learned that she was being treated as a slave, and not a passenger. She expected to do her share of the work, but when they came to Little Traverse Bay, she was sold to some voyageurs that were waiting for them. Little did the two Canadians know, that she knew this part of the lake well.

Gray Dove had to think fast. She suddenly found herself in a very dangerous situation. If she caused these two any trouble, she could end up at the bottom of Lake Michigan with her throat slit. No one would know what happened to her.

She signed to the two that they needed to stop at Wagonokezee, on the shore of La Petite Traverse to pick up supplies to last the trip and then start early the next day for Canada. Little did the unsuspecting men know that this was the Ottawa's capital village.

CHAPTER 16
THE FRONT STOOP

The talk today was about politics. Everyone was waiting to hear how the great Toledo War between Michigan and Ohio was faring. Simon sat on the front stoop of their cabin, talking to some of the local men, Amos Spicer, Benjamin Knight and C.C. Darling. The Forks was starting to grow, and the trading post had become the informal "Town Hall and Meeting Place." Simon built a flat-bottom boat to ferry people and goods across the O Washtenong River and back. And because he had had some schooling to be a lawyer, people came to him if a constable was needed to settle a dispute or have a proper legal contract drawn up.

Streets were beginning to be laid out and lots sold. A second blacksmith shop was in operation, and the sawmill at Spicer's Mill ran day and night. Plans for a grist mill and a carding mill were talked about. Now that proper lumber could be had, Simon wanted to build a tavern to cater to the increasing volume of people coming to the area. And a livery stable was needed. There was talk about petitioning for a permit to put a dam across the O Washtenong and digging a mill-race to Spring Brook to increase its flow. Immigrants were flocking into the new land from the hungry, war-torn, old countries of Europe. Michigan was attracting the young and ambitious, ready to turn a primitive land into a modern and successful nation.

"What have you heard from Glyn? Have they kicked those Buckeye asses back to Ohio?" Knight asked Simon as they drank the cool cider vinegar and ginger beer called "switchel" on the shaded front stoop of the trading post.

"Last we heard was a month ago. They almost caught a Ohioan Judge and his guards in a one-room schoolhouse with the windows blocked off in the middle of the night. Could have had them if they hadn't run so fast and kicked up so much dust!" Simon laughed.

When Glyn came in one night and told his folks he was joining the militia, they didn't want him to go. Simon thought this disagreement would blow over quickly, that it was really kind of silly, mostly politics. Olive was dead set against it. She had not uprooted her family and moved out here so her sons would have to fight, but so they could live and raise families in peace. She worried that her three youngest boys were drifting away from their Quaker beliefs. Out here on the frontier, they mixed with all kinds of people with different beliefs and religions. Their Quaker ways were slowly falling away.

But Simon remembered his military career, and thought maybe, if the boy didn't get his fool head blown off, the experience might help him grow up. Glyn had never been on his own before, always dependent on his family, but he was a hard worker.

"Have you heard any more about the Constitutional Convention in Detroit? Those fools have no idea how us people out here are trying to make a living. We need some sort of schools and funds for them. How do they expect us to pay for teachers? And when are some decent roads going to be coming through these parts? With all the new settlers coming in, we need roads that a person can use without getting stuck in a bog around every hill. And we need a bridge across the Grand." Knight wanted to build a store and make the settlement into a real town.

"I heard from a brother down by Detroit that they're going to set aside the proceeds of section 16 of every township for schools." said Darling.

"That don't make a lick of sense. What if in one township, section 16 is a swamp, and in another, it's the middle of a town. Some are going to have lots of money, others none." Knight was being argumentative.

"What I heard was that they're going to pool all the money together, and divide the interest up according to how many children are in the district. That way, all are treated equal."

Simon hoped that the Territory would soon be accepted into the Union. A bill had been passed by Congress in 1835 to grant statehood to Michigan. It only needed to have President Jackson's signature. As soon as the boundaries could be established, Michigan would achieve statehood. So many things were up in the air. Olive was schooling the children from around the settlement every day, in the afternoons and between chores. If more families moved into the area, a school building would be needed. A bridge would be nice too since the only way to get across the Grand was by boat or fording.

"We need to hold our own convention and send delegates down there, so they know what's needed up here. We need to elect some county commissioners, set up a court with local judges and sheriffs. We don't know yet where the county seat will be; I heard it'll be in the Big Prairie in the center of the county, but all that's there now is a tree with an ax mark on it, surrounded by old Indian corn fields."

"Fellow through here last week said he heard that Bellevue is where court's being held. There's a trail from the Indian Village in Walton, along the Battle Creek to Bellevue. And Territorial Road runs from Jackson to Marshall to Battle Creek, where there's a trail going to Bellevue. But there is no straight path to that side of the county; the Big Swamp divides us. Just no way through. That side should be another county by itself."

John Montgomery rode up on his mule and greeted all the men. He took a seat after he drew a cup of switchel from the crock that sat on a wooden stump on the stoop.

"As you all know," Montgomery said, "I've always been a strong anti-slavery man. Simon, can I count on you, what with your Quaker wife and all, to support me in forming an anti-slavery party. They let Tennessee in as a slave state. We don't need them bringing slaves into this state. Detroit and Mackinac both have slaves, but not many. We need to outlaw this sin of oppression before it takes root."

"What about the Indian problem? Settlers aren't going to want to live where Inguns come into your cabin to demand food and whiskey."

Simon spoke up. "There is no Indian problem. We've done broke their spirit around here. If the fur traders would stop giving them whiskey in order to steal their furs, they would settle down and farm, just the same as the immigrants coming in. We make the problem by not encouraging them to adopt our ways. The missionaries got the right idea, sending them to school to teach them a trade. And I heard that up north, the missions are buying up farms for the Indians so they can settle down permanently.

"Rix Robbinson is up on Mackinac Island right now with Henry Schoolcraft, finalizing a treaty with the Ottawas for all their land in Michigan, except for some small reservations they can hunt on and each will receive 40 acres to farm. The only way for them to become citizens is to own land, and it's against the law for Indians to buy land!"

And so the afternoon on the porch went on, the men talking politics but solving nothing.

CHAPTER 17

Glyn

Several months after Glyn joined the Michigan Militia, the 'Great Battle of Toledo,' or the 'Maumee Melee,' was over. Territorial Governor Mason went back to Detroit and put General Joseph W. Brown in as its commander, who promptly disbanded the troops and left the decision of the State borders up to Congress.

Glyn liked the militia and the camaraderie of the men. He had been in the saddle for weeks and thoroughly enjoyed it. Chasing the Ohioan judges across the country had allowed Glyn to see the farmers' fields. He decided that the military life wasn't what he wanted to do his whole life. It was fun for now, but farming was looking pretty good.

"Just look at these level fields," marveled Glyn. "The corn must be close to eight foot high. The wheat fields go on forever. If I could clear enough land back home to farm, I could build myself a cabin and raise a family."

He and a fellow soldier, Jean-Luc Marcotte, had become good friends and were riding back to Detroit from Monroe. After the troops had been disbanded, they worked on the steamboats that plied the Maumee, shipping grain out to the Great Lakes from the interior of Indiana and Ohio, and on out to the East Coast. After they had saved up enough money, they left the hard and dangerous work as boaters and headed back to their homes. Jean-Luc Marcottes' family had lived in Detroit since the early 1700's, an old French family that had a ribbon farm along the river.

"You need to come home with me. I wrote to Mother. They are expecting us. I am tired to the bone; you must be, too. We will stay there for a couple of weeks; then I'll come with you and see this great land of yours." Jean-Luc had lived in Detroit all his life. His family had come there with Antoine de Laumet Cadillac in 1701 when Fort Pontchartrain was first founded in the name of his Majesty, Roy Louis XIV of France. Jean had never ventured north of the city, although he had made several trips to France and even went to school there for a year. Jean-Luc was tall for a Frenchmen. Painfully thin, with dark blue eyes, prominent cheekbones, a nose a little too long to be called handsome. His jet black hair curled around his head when it escaped from his hat. He spoke perfect English, with a slight accent, since French was his first language.

"Are you sure it's all right for me to stay at your house? I can always find a tavern and stay there." Glyn knew Jean-Luc was the oldest of ten children. The oldest sister was married, and the next oldest brother was finishing his schooling in France. Glyn was afraid with eight children and a set of grandparents living under the same roof, it must be crowded. He hated to think of that many living in his family's two-room cabin.

"Do not worry, we have plenty of room," Jean-Luc said. "Mother would be hurt if you do not stay with us. And my sisters would be mad at me, too. We like lots of company, an excuse to have a party. We live on a farm, but we party like we live in Paris. You shall see.

"Ah, we are almost there now. We have to go through town and take a boat up the Detroit River. There are no roads to the farm; the river is our road."

Detroit at this time had a population of 5,000 people. On the outskirts of town were apple orchards and wind-powered cider mills. He could see saw-mills and grist-mills along the river. Many houses were of brick. They came to the First Protestant Society Church at Woodward and Larned Streets. Jean told him that was the largest and oldest Negro Church in the Territory. They stopped in front of the Territorial Capital Building that sat on Grand Circus Park. He had never seen such a beautiful building. It was 60 by 90 foot with a 40-foot cupola, and six, two storied pillars across the front. The business section of town had over 50 brick store buildings, and some were four stories high!

They came to the wharf and Jean found a flat-bottom boat to hire to take them home. Colorfully painted Natives, free Negroes, as well as Frenchmen and soldiers, were lined up on the banks and wharves of the Detroit River fishing. The farm was up river near Pig Island. On the ride, Glyn was able to look at the town, and Jean-Luc told him some history.

"First, remember that Europe was at war for 126 years, and the New World was just a pawn in that war. Peace did not come to Europe or to us until Napoleon was defeated in 1814.

“My family came here with Cadillac in 1702, to locate Fort Pontchartrain for France. It would be important. It would control 'Le Detroit' and the river traffic between Lake Huron and Lake Erie. It would keep the English out of the Great Lakes. That didn't work out so well for Cadillac. The King transferred him to New Orleans after nine years to be the governor of Louisiana. The English came and took the Fort in 1760, but by then, we Frenchman called this home. We had farms and businesses established; so we stayed. A few followed Cadillac to New Orleans; a few went to Quebec. And then the Americans came in 1796. Fortunes were made in the fur trade, but the land is rich here along the river. It’s a good place to live. This is home, but France is where we look to when we want culture and education.”

“This is incredible. I've never seen houses like these along the river. They look like those in old picture books, with thatched roofs and walls all crooked and covered with vines and moss. But you can tell looking closer they are well looked after."

“Yes, the Americans say our farms are run down and want to buy them. They want to build new houses. They say that the town is growing, and they need the land for expansion. The old families are holding out, but the younger ones, I'm afraid, will sell out, and that will force everyone to move. They want to knock down our old wharves. They need newer and bigger ones for the steamboats. Ah, here we are, this is our place.”

The boat pulled up to the wharf. Jean paid the old man and talked to him like an intimate friend, in rapid French. Glyn didn't catch everything said but picked up that he was getting old, and the traffic on the river was getting crowded, what with the steamships bringing immigrants in waves.

They led their horses off from the boat and started up the long drive. The house was long and low, with dormer windows on the second floor. The roof came down over the proper stoop that ran all across the front. Large trees grew behind the house and vines grew up the porch columns and onto the roof. A green lawn came sweeping down the steep hill to the river.

Ornamental bushes lined the drive and flowers grew in profusion along the house. Glyn could smell roses and lilies on the hot breeze. He could see the drive as it wound around the back of the house, past the trees where the farm building's old rail fences stood. A cow mooed softly in the distance, the sights and sounds of the city behind them.

CHAPTER 18

Gray Dove

If she could just keep their hands off her until they reached Wagonokezee, Gray Dove thought; she might have a chance. She couldn't believe she had been so stupid to fall for a trick like that: being separating her from her people and then sold to the trappers for a jug of whiskey. The sickness had caused her to let her guard down, and she forgot that not everyone had her best interest at heart. She tried to remember who had suggested that that group take her along. They had been unknown strangers from the eastern lakes and stopped at the island for provisions. They had quickly volunteered to take her to the mouth of the O Washtenong River.

The two voyageurs looked at her like she was a choice piece of meat. They reminded her of mangy, hungry bears in the spring, waiting for her to make a false move so they could devour her. She had no family left. No father or brother to protect her anymore. She had been the daughter of a very well-known warrior, who had songs of bravery sung about his deeds in battles. Now she had no one, except her dear old grandmother. Grandfather had been killed in one of the many wars years before she was even born. That was why her grandmother had married her husband's brother, Wolf Jaw, as was the Peoples' custom. Wolf Jaw had been sick the winter before with lung fever, never fully recovered, and was too feeble last fall to travel with the band.

They broke camp quickly as the men wanted to be gone back to Canada before anyone came looking for their new prized possession. She signed that she knew no French and was not from around here and that she did not understand the dialect they spoke. Then she signed that a trading post was up ahead and that they should stop for provisions. They would need more now that she was with them; it wasn't too far. She quickly gathered up all their camping gear and stowed it in the canoe; then they pushed off. The lake was calm, no large waves along the shore.

She nicknamed her captors Snake Eyes and Black Bear. After listening to them talk between themselves, she picked up that this was foreign territory to them. They were from northern Canada, far beyond Lake Superior, and only came down here to receive a better price on their pelts. Now they were headed back to their home area.

"Where you think she's taking us," Snake Eyes was talking to his partner, as he passed a flask of whiskey to him. "You trust her? God knows what she might be planning."

"She's fine. Signed that we needed more supplies to make it back up to our country. Think she really likes me. See the way she smiled at me. Might share her with ya if you quit your belly-aching all the time. Told you this was a good idea, to come down and trade with Astor. We made a lot of money and got an Injun squaw to keep us company back in the woods."

"Did you see the look she gave to that Injun that sold her, thought she was going to claw his eyes out. I don't know what she said to him, but he sure looked like he was glad to see the last of her."

"She was sweet on him and wanted to stay with him. After a couple nights with me, she'll never want to leave my bedroll, you just wait and see."

"With you? Funny that all your other women left. Thought we was gonna share. We both paid for her, and I think she likes me more. Caught her looking at me a lot. She looks at you like she smells something spoiled. That reminds me, hope they got some bear grease at that trading post, the black flies are coming out, and they bite like hell."

"We don't even know if she can cook yet. Some of those squaws can only cook stew. Even then, it tastes like they used the head and guts, and their fry bread's hard as a rock."

"Aw, if she can't cook, we'll trade her off at some outpost. Now quit your bellyaching, I said we would share. Can't wait till we get back in our own neck of the woods. Too many people around here."

They paddled their canoe around a large hill and entered the bay. The trees stopped, and there was Wagonokezee, the largest Native town in the Michigan Territory. It had a chapel in the center, with log cabins that surrounded it, and hundreds of Native families that lived in long houses down by the shore. Many Ottawas came here during the summer. Natives enjoyed their summer holidays and annual festivals, with singing and dancing. Hunting parties from as far away as the Rocky Mountains returned here each summer with captive slaves to trade for potential mates.

Gray Dove paddled hard to come as close to the town as possible before the trappers became suspicious. Snake Eyes shouted to Black Bear to hold up as he stared hard at the large Native town. Snake Eyes sat at the back, Black Bear at the front. Gray Dove stood up, and in one motion, stripped off her buckskin dress. Snake Eyes jumped up to grab her. She screamed her Indian family's war cry, "AAAAHHHHEEEEE." Her father had taught her to use this when in distress. At the same time, she used her paddle as a Lacrosse stick to smack Snake Eyes on the side of the head. Black Bear, being a little slower than Snake Eyes, turned around just as Gray Dove bashed his nose in, and she dived into the lake.

The water was cold from the winter ice, but Gray Dove swam fast toward shore. The men were paddling hard behind her, they weren't going to let their slave get away so easily, she had just cost them a jug of whiskey! Just as they pulled up beside her and reached down into the water, a shot rang out. The bullet flew over Black Bear's head. He fell backward onto Snake Eyes as his raccoon cap fell into the water, a hole through the top.

Gray Dove reached the sandy shore, just as several hands reached in to help her stand. Three young braves dashed past her and grabbed Black Bear as he raised his paddle. If he couldn't have her, no one would. They fell into the water. Snake Eyes saw his partner in trouble and dived in to help. More braves jumped into the water to help subdue the two intruders.

Gray Dove was assisted to shore, and someone covered her in a trade blanket. The two voyageurs were still fighting as they were dragged on shore. A large crowd gathered to watch, as one brave punched them, then another took his turn. The Canadians were soon fighting for their lives, but the braves were just having a good time, while all their past hostility poured out. Soon the two lay on the beach, alive but not moving.

By now, Gray Dove was surrounded by her People, and she told her story. The priest and the chief, who had been summoned by the commotion, made their way down to the crowd. They listened as Gray Dove told her story. The chief held his hand up for quiet.

"I knew this young girl's father. It saddens me that he is gone and that his daughter has been treated with such disrespect. I will leave it up to her as to what should happen to her captors."

"The White Man's holy book says an eye for an eye, these two should be sold into slavery and Gray Dove given the money so she can go home," said one old, wise woman, who had been a captive from the west herself many years before.

"And who would buy two such as these? They don't look like much. I say scalp them, kill them," said another old woman. A roar of approval went up from the crowd.

By this time Snake Eyes and Black Bear were beginning to stir, tried to sit up, only to be knocked down again. Both had bloody faces. Blood dripped down their split lips and broken noses, and their eyes were swollen mostly shut.

"Neither had a chance to harm me," Gray Dove said. "I do not want their deaths on my conscience all my life. I have seen too much death this winter. Please, just send them away. Put a curse on them if they should ever come back to our land, but send them away."

The chief and the priest conferred. "We will send them away. First, we will brand them as cowards, so any People that come in contact with them will know to be wary."

The chief motioned for the young men to take them away. Gray Dove knew that they would be lucky to escape alive, but that was not her problem now. Her only focus was getting back to the Forks to find her grandmother.

CHAPTER 19

Glyn enjoyed his stay at Jean-Luc's family farm and wanted never to leave. They danced every night, with all the young women from the old French families from Detroit. Jean's family had shown Glyn a lifestyle he had never seen before, the culture of an old society that knew how to have a good time. Jean-Luc had his sister, Magdelaine, teach Glyn how to dance, something he picked up quite fast.

The girls he grew up with in New York had all been Quakers. They had been very serious and bookish, not at all like the fun-loving girls of Detroit. They danced till the morning light, slept till noon, had lunch with Jean-Luc's sisters and friends at someone's house, then rode out with Jean-Luc's old friends until it was time for the next soirée.

Glyn shared a room in the old farmhouse with Jean-Luc and two of his brothers, Adriane and Louis. The large upstairs room at the end of the hall had a sloping ceiling and dormer windows that looked out on the river on one side, and the long fields of the farm on the other. Four single beds, several dressers and large wardrobes, were crowded in with bookcases and desks. Glyn slept in the bed that belonged to the brother who was in France.

At the other end of the hall was a large room much like this, where the sisters slept. In the center were four smaller rooms. One for Jean-Luc's parents with a nursery beside which was now used as a sitting room, and across the hall, two spare rooms that guests could occupy. A winding staircase led down to the hall on the main floor, which stretched from the front door to the back, a large space, 24 by 50 feet, that served as a ballroom when the Marcottes entertained. A double parlor was on one side of the hall, a library and dining room on the other. At each end of the house there was a small suite of rooms. One was for the grandparents, and the other was used as an office where Jean-Luc's father ran the farm and family business. The kitchens, pantry, and laundry were all in the basement. The old house had been added on to for a hundred years.

After a month, Jean-Luc came into their room early one morning and asked Glyn, "Do you still want to leave for your cabin in the wilderness in the morning? You must want to see your family?"

"I want never to leave here. I'm in love with your family, with Detroit, and with your sister Magdelaine. Never imagined that people lived like this on the frontier." Glyn had always lived life to its fullest, but never the way that Jean-Luc lived.

"No," said Glyn. "Don't open the drapes, my head is killing me."

"Well, you did drink a lot of wine last night. I don't know what Louis had in that flask. Some sort of corn liqueur concoction I suspect; it did pack a punch." Jean-Luc drew the drapes halfway and looked out.

"Nice day, the river is calm. Let's find a rowboat. See if we can round up some girls to take a ride with us, row out to the lake, or the island. Angelique whispered to me last night that she would be free today."

"We have to get Maggie to come, too." Glyn had begun to call Magdelaine by her childhood nickname.

"I tell you, Jean-Luc, I'm in love with your sister with the auburn hair, with skin so pale, so translucent. She is a flower, so sweet and innocent. Do you think she will come?"

"Innocent I don't know about. But if she thinks Angelique is coming, she will be there. Those two are great friends. Get out of bed, and get dressed. We'll go down to the cafe for some strong coffee and beignets. I'll tell Alice to pack us a lunch. We'll gather the girls and go rowing. Then we have to make plans when to leave for your settlement in the wilderness."

"Oh, you will love it there, Jean-Luc. Wild country, lots of game to shoot. The people are nice. A more friendly lot you will never find," mused Glyn, getting into the spirit of returning home.

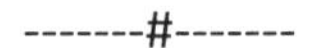
-------#-------

The sun was still shinning, although starting to set in the westward sky in a brilliant display of color. Not too hot for the end of summer. The water on the river was calm, with a cool breeze from the north. Magdelaine and Angelique were talking and giggling in French, seated in the center of the birch-bark canoe. Glyn and Jean-Luc were at either end, rowing home. They had been out all afternoon; enjoyed the picnic lunch which they ate on Pig Island, on a sandy stretch of beach. A lake steamer was paddling its way upriver. A couple of the old five-masted sailing ships were gliding along the water. Flat-bottom boats, full of supplies, were headed in both directions on the river. Natives in their dug-out canoes, faces painted in bright colors, paddled in unison, headed for their villages in the north country.

They glided up to a wharf. The two young men jumped out and secured the canoe with hemp ropes. The girls handed out the picnic basket, and the boys helped them out onto the wooden wharf.

"We have had the best day," said Angelique. "It was a perfect day for a boat ride and picnic. Hope we can do it again soon."

"Afraid not, tomorrow we set off for Glyn's cabin in the forest."

"So soon? I knew you were going to leave, but I thought we could have a few more weeks of your company. You boys just got back from fighting those awful Ohioans. Can't you stay for a little while longer?" said Angelique coyly, knowing full well that tonight's dinner would be in honor of the two men leaving.

"Glyn wanted to stay longer, but we do need to leave in the morning. We can't stay here and row you girls around all summer. Besides, it wouldn't be fair to the other young men courting you."

"Oh Jean-Luc, you know full well that all the other young men in this town don't hold a candle to you two dashing soldiers. When you leave, there will be no more excitement in town. Mother will have us weeding the garden every day."

They reached the top of the river bank. Natives, as well as immigrants, were fishing the river to get their supper. Smoke from cooking fires could be smelled from the Native village outside the fort walls, as well as manure from the mules and horses hauling wagons in the streets, the cows and pigs grazing on the green, and the raw sewage that was dumped into the river.

Every day, boatloads of settlers arrived in Detroit, eager to start a new life on the frontier. But could the old way of life, with the colorful Natives paddling up and down the rivers, French fur traders bartering for pelts, and the missionaries, out to save the savage soul. Could this old way co-exist with the new, thought Glyn, as they took in the tranquil scene.

Jean-Luc carried Angelique's picnic basket and left to walk her home, so she could change for tonight's dinner. Glyn walked with Magdelaine along the shore. They told each other about their dreams. Glyn wondered out loud about the future of their country, of all the changes that were occurring.

"Magdelaine, I truly think that this country is going to be one of greatest in the world, all the top minds are coming here, all the men that have great ambition and dreams, there is no telling what can become of us, don't you agree?"

"I don't know; France still has the greatest universities and art museums. You've never been to Europe, have you? I recently returned from spending a year there. The culture on the Continent is unbelievable. You should travel some day."

"Maybe I will someday, if you come with me. I know we haven't known each other long, but I fell madly in love with you the first time I laid eyes on you. What do you say, Magdelaine, will you marry me?" Glyn had no idea that she would say yes. He thought she felt towards him as a brother. They had talked and joked freely with one another from the beginning.

Magdelaine thought for a moment; emotions openly played across her face. She looked up into Glyn's eyes. "Yes Glyn, I'll marry you. I have feelings for you, too. Oh yes, let's tell everyone tonight at supper. Keep it our little secret until then."

"No, I need to talk to your father, receive his permission first. That's the only right thing to do." Glyn was suddenly dizzy with emotion. He never thought she would say yes. At most he thought she might string him along for several years. He was happy, he was ecstatic. He wanted to take her up in his arms and dance though the streets.

Magdelaine stepped up to Glyn and gave him a peck on the cheek and a chaste hug, just as Jean-Luc returned from leaving Angelique at her house.

"Well, what's all this? Can't leave you two alone in public without a scandal. Mother will have my head if she hears the way the two of are acting. Come on, let's find the canoe and paddle on home."

Supper that night was festive and gay. A dozen friends, as well as family, showed up for the send-off. The dining room was large, with a fireplace in the center of one wall. Huge old beams, black with the smoke of a hundred years worth of fires, criss-crossed the ceiling. The table was laid with the best French porcelain and silver, on a white lace tablecloth. Two large silver and onyx candelabras with beeswax candles were on the table, and sconces were lit on the walls, between the windows that looked out onto the wide porch and the Detroit River.

The women were dressed in the latest French fashions, tightly corseted, with wide V-neckline bodices with "gigot" *(gigantic)* leg-of-mutton sleeves. The tiny waistlines were decorated with fancy belts. The skirts were ankle length, full and domed shaped with many petticoats, finished with flat square-toed shoes.

With the rich meal over, the French wine flowed freely, and ices were served. The dancing would start in a few minutes. They could hear the servants clearing the hall and the musicians setting up. Magdelaine looked over at Glyn and took his hand. They both stood up. Glyn cleared his voice and rapped on the crystal wine goblet with his fork.

"May I have your attention for a moment. I would like to thank all of you here for showing me such a grand time while I have been visiting, and to thank Mr. and Mrs. Marcotte for their hospitality. I have never had such a good time in my life.

"And now, Magdelaine and I would like to announce our engagement."

A great roar of applause rang out, everyone talking at once, congratulating the new couple. After many slaps on the back and several toasts, the music started, and everyone moved to the hall for the dancing. A festive night became even more so. Wine flowed, and the dancing lasted until the sun came up in the east.

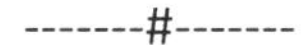

Sometime during the dancing, Jean-Luc left the party, silently slipping out an open door. Anyone who saw would have thought he was leaving to use the necessary house in the back. That wasn't his intention. He had, during the dance, asked his favorite serving girl to meet him at half-past three. They had been meeting like this for over a year, when they both could get away and his mother not notice. They usually met in the woods or their favorite spot, the haymow of a horse barn, way out back where no one could see.

They lay together after making love, enjoying being in each other's arms, breathing in the heady aroma of the fresh hay, the horses below them, and their own musky perfume. Jean-Luc nuzzled her chin, began to kiss his way down her throat to her breast.

"Jean-Luc, I heard in the kitchen that Glyn and Magdelaine are going to marry. I like Glyn; he's a nice man and always treats us servants like real people. I thought he was your friend too, so why are you letting him marry your sister?"

"I only heard about it at supper. It's not like I encouraged them. What difference does it make if they want to marry?" Jean-Luc was softly counting her ribs with velvet fingers while running his tongue across her breast.

"You would want your friend to marry a woman who is carrying another man's child? Does Glyn even know that Magdelaine is with child?"

Jean-Luc, startled by this pronouncement, stopped what he was doing, "I didn't know she was with child! What story is this? How do you speak of such a thing?"

Annoyed, the mood broken, he rolled over and stood up. "How could you say such a thing about Magdelaine? Why do you hate her so much? What has she done to you!"

"I don't hate your sister. I just like your friend and don't want to see him hurt. He is a sweet man. He could make someone a good husband."

"Someone like you? Is this what this is all about? You dragging my sister's name through the mud? You want to marry him?"

"Jean-Luc, that is a terrible thing to say! No, I do not want to marry him. You are a fool. I work in the kitchen and in the laundry. We know everything that goes on in the house. We know that Magdelaine has not had her time of month since she came home from France. Three months, what does that say? At first, we thought the trip must have tired her, but it's been three months! That must tell you something."

"Damn! If this is true, I can't let Glyn marry her, unless he already knows and is trying to do the gallant thing. It would be just like Maggie to do something like this. Good God, I wonder if Mother knows? Is this a conspiracy between the two? Women! I have to get back and talk to Glyn. Damn it, what a mess this has turned out to be!"

"No, don't go yet, I've hardly seen you since you got back, and you're leaving in the morning! Stay a little while longer. Everyone at the house is still dancing, and we have time. And I miss you when you're gone."

"No, I need to get back and straighten this mess up." Jean-Luc gathered his clothes.

"And as you can see, I'm not up to it now." He chuckled as he reached down to kiss her on top of her head.

"Oh, but I can fix that."

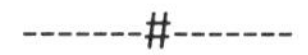

Jean-Luc reached the house as the sun peeked over the horizon. Most everyone had left the party; a few stragglers were still saying their goodbyes. Men were trading a final drink from their flasks, wishing everyone a safe trip. Jean saw Magdelaine climbing the stairs and caught up to her on the landing.

"Maggie, I need to speak to you. Now."

"Can it not wait till morning Jean-Luc? I'm dead on my feet."

"Yes, it must be tiring to dance all night in your condition."

Magdelaine looked up sharply at Jean. "What do you mean by that!"

They reached the top of the stairs. Jean took hold of her elbow and swiftly jerked her into one of the spare bedrooms. He looked around to be sure no one had seen them, then ducked in himself, closing the door.

"I was surprised to hear that you and Glyn are to marry. You have only known each other for a few short weeks. Tell me, what did father and mother have to say about it? They both seemed quite happy. Never thought either of them would have approved of such a rash announcement. Is that not what you were in Paris last winter for, to find a suitable husband? And now you're going to marry a Yankee settler, who has nothing but a cabin in the woods? Might as well marry one of the heathen Indians. Now tell me, what is going on?"

"Nothing is going on. We met, we fell in love. I thought you were the romantic one, telling father you would only marry for love."

"Nice try, but a little bird told me you were in a family way when you came home from France. Glyn could not be the father, so why are you marrying him? You do not love him. You always said you would not marry anyone who was not French, rich, and titled. Did you talk him into marrying you, or is this a trick? You think he is some backwards hick that won't notice. Glyn is a really good man; he does not deserve this."

Magdelaine slapped Jean-Luc across the face, then burst into tears, and threw herself on the bed.

"It's not like that, really it's not," gasped Magdelaine through her tears. "He said he loved me. Xavier-Francois Pontchartrain, his father is

Count Pontchartrain. He said he loved me, that he would follow me back to Detroit and marry me. He is a younger son of the Count. He said his Father would give him enough money to start a business here.

"We had plans. It happened the night before I left. He said he loved me and no other. I didn't know I was with child until I was back. I told mother and I also told her that as soon as Xavier came to America, we would be married. She and Father were so happy. The Pontchartrain family is well known and respected here in Detroit.

"Then I received a letter from him, saying he was sorry, but his father was marrying him off to a rich, noble family in Spain. That it is all settled, and the engagement announced. I wrote right back and told him I was carrying his child, that he had to come and marry me. Father said he would send a lawyer to Paris and sue him for breach of contract.

"I received a letter from him yesterday, said he was sorry, that there was no way he could get out of marrying his Spanish Countess. He would deny the child was his. Said that by the time I received his letter, he would be married and fighting in Spain to put Don Carlos back on the throne. He said if I loved him, I should throw myself in the river and drown."

Jean went over to the bed and gathered his sister up and held her until she cried herself out.

"Now I understand. You were very stupid. A woman never gives a man what he wants until she gets what she wants first. You can never trust a man, especially a Frenchman. But how did you get Glyn to go along with this? Did father give him money?"

"You are a pig, Jean-Luc! How could you think that no one would have me unless someone paid them. That's not what happened. Glyn does not know that I am with child. He asked me to marry him after we got back from the picnic. He is in love with me. He never has to know this child is not his. I will marry him as soon as I can and he will never know. I am truly fond of him. You are right, he is a good man. Jean-Luc, please don't ruin this for me, please. I told Mother. She said this is a prayer sent from heaven. She and Father are fond of him too."

"Have you made any plans or set a date? Are you going to marry before we leave? The sooner, the better."

"Jean-Luc, thank you so much for going along with us. I was so afraid you would be against it." Magdelaine hugged her brother, tears streaming down her face. "Please help me convince Glyn to stay and marry me, then stay in Detroit. He can work for father."

"I'll talk to him, only because I know that you will make Glyn a good wife. But he may want to take you to his home, to meet his family first. And his family may not approve. They are Quakers. If this is to work, we must get you two married as soon as possible. I'll talk with Father. He might have some influence with Father de Casson. The Church does need a new roof. We can tell them that Glyn needs to go to his family without delay, maybe a family member is on their sickbed."

CHAPTER 20

Gray Dove

The old chief took Gray Dove into his family's longhouse and said he would see to it that she was nursed back to health and would protect her. But she was anxious to find her grandmother and any remaining members of her clan. The old chief let it be known that he was looking for a hunting party to escort a member of his family back down to the O Washtenong River country. A party of five men, four women and a child were leaving the next day. They would be joining more clansmen at Rix Robinson's trading post on the Kalamazoo River. She would travel that far with the band, and make the rest of the journey on her own. She was afraid that if she waited too long, her family would leave the camp at the Forks, and finding them would be much more difficult.

The trip down the coast of Lake Michigan was uneventful. They camped at night at some sandy inlet and feasted on the fish they caught. The women were friendly, but Gray Dove kept a distance between them. She was still wary from her former captivity. She knew she was lucky even to be alive. She had lived through the small-pox epidemic and the French voyageurs. Gray Dove did not want to stretch her moment of good fortune. She was happy to be on her way to find her grandmother.

One night as the party was looking for dry wood to build a campfire on a sandy stretch of shoreline, Gray Dove told the young woman named Ash Leaf that this would be her last night with the party.

"In the morning, I will be off on my own. The O Washtenong River is where I start to go inland to find my family. The river's mouth will be along the shore, not more than half a day from here. I will go then, and find my way. It will be much faster than traveling overland from the Kalamazoo."

The next morning dawned bright and clear. The party quickly picked up camp and started packing their canoes. Ash Leaf packed their belongings in the canoe as Gray Dove came up.

She said to Gray Dove, "My husband and I will continue with you until we get you home with your grandmother. We talked it over last night, and Fox will not sleep well until you have joined your family. He promised the old chief that he would see you back with them. Storm can lead the others. He needs to find his dead wife's family so they can take care of Red Feather, their little boy. They will continue on. We will meet up with them later. Our People have had a bad winter, bad medicine for us all. We will go with you, stay until the time is right for us to part. That time is not now."

Gray Dove was touched by the gesture, and she set off with Ash Leaf and Fox. They paddled down the Lake Michigan shoreline until they found the mouth of the O Washtenong. Several bands of Ottawa and Chippewa were seen plying the river, fishing and hunting for food. Their temporary campsites were dotted along the river. A small settlement called Grand Haven was at the mouth of the O Washtenong, on the opposite shore.

They stopped at these Native fishing camps at night, finding old friends and making new ones. All had heard about the epidemic on Mackinac Island, and there had been outbreaks of fever at several other towns over the winter, both Indian and American. People were anxious about family and friends.

At night, around the campfires, some of the Indians talked about moving farther north to Canada, beyond Lake Superior, where there were fewer white men and their sicknesses. Others talked of driving the Americans out of their land, but everyone knew that would never be. The white man was here like a plague that would never leave and could never be stopped.

They paddled on up the river, meeting fellow natives and voyageurs. But the large majority of river traffic was immigrants on their way down river to homestead or to start businesses in the many new towns that were springing up. It was a steady flow of boats and canoes. Small villages that were just an isolated trading post in Gray Dove's childhood were growing larger every day. And there were fewer Native villages and fewer Natives on the river.

Eight days after leaving the hunting party on Lake Michigan, Gray Dove began to notice familiar landmarks. They were coming closer to the Forks, with its ancient trees and large marsh at the mouth of the brook. It would be filled with birds this time of year. They heard the chopping of wood, and the sawing and hammering a mile or so before they came upon the settlement. She could see the half-built log cabins and shacks of the growing settlement. Some were no more than a lean-to with a roof. She was surprised that so many buildings were being built.

They paddled on until she could see the smoke of cooking fires from the Indian Camp. Before the canoe had a chance to come to rest on the rocky shore, Gray Dove was out and running. She saw the wigwam that her father had built the summer before, with a cook fire in front with an iron pot hanging over it. She rushed up and ducked inside. And there, sitting on a bearskin robe, was her grandmother, Cloud Woman. Gray Dove had never been so glad to see a person before.

"Grandmother, you're safe and alive! I was so worried that I would never see you again. The sickness took all the family. Mother, Father, and Brother are all dead; the whole tribe is gone. Everyone who went north with us is dead. I was so sick that I wanted to die, but I thought of you and wanted to see you again. I am so glad you're alive." Gray Dove sank down into the arms of her grandmother and cried for the first time since the sickness took her family from her.

Pee-miss-a-quot-oquay (Flying Cloud Woman), sat and held her granddaughter in her arms; their tears flowed freely. She had heard from other Natives passing through that all her tribe had died, but she had held on to hope that someone had lived, and she had been waiting. The others wanted to move on, but Cloud had stubbornly refused. She held tightly to Gray Dove, her only living blood family she had.

Cloud's first husband, Nim-min-did, was killed in 1791 at the Miami River in northern Ohio, fighting against General St. Clare. They had been together for ten years before she had a son, Gray Dove's father. He was only five summers old when his father was killed. As was the custom in their tribe, she married Nims brother, Wolf Jaw, and became his second wife. Otherwise, Cloud Woman and her son may have starved to death. Sippy Quay (River Woman), Wolf Jaw's first wife and she got on fairly well. Wolf Jaw raised her son as his own, and he became a great warrior.

"My prayers have been answered," said Cloud. "We will need to send for your uncle, and then we will perform a ceremony for all those that perished, and to cleanse you. Now sit here at my side, and tell me everything. You are safe now. I have waited for you to come home."

CHAPTER 21
A WEDDING

Jean-Luc wearily climbed the stairs and entered the bedroom. He went over to where Glyn was sleeping off the previous night of merriment. He looked down at the sleeping man. They had become close, as close as brothers. He hated what he was about to do. He reached down and shook Glyn awake.

"Glyn, I received a letter this morning from a cousin in New Orleans. He wants me to come down and go with him to Mexico." Jean-Luc put as much enthusiasm as he could muster in his voice.

"Seems that a group of Americans are in a state in Mexico called Texas, next to Louisiana. They want to secede from Mexico and join the United States, but a General Santa Anna will not let them. My cousin says there are a lot of opportunities down there. He wants me to come down, maybe start a business with him, shipping cotton. He says land is cheap, and the ground fertile. If we go now, we will have a jump on everyone. He says Americans will flock to Texas if they are successful, and Texas becomes part of the United States. If we go now, we could make a fortune!"

Jean-Luc had received a letter that morning that the cousin had sent. It had been received right after he had left to fight in the militia early that spring. His mother had forgotten all about it until Jean had asked that morning if any mail had come for him while he had been away. The letter had taken months to reach Detroit from New Orleans.

Glyn jumped out of bed in a burst of enthusiasm. "That sounds like something I'd be right interested in. Now that I'm going to be marrying Maggie, I need something to do to make some money. We could go down there and help the Texans, get the lay of the land. Start making some money of our own. I know that Maggie wants me to work for your father, but I'd rather work on my own. Do you think Magdelaine would want to move down there? When are you leaving?"

As usual, Glyn was excited by the prospect of a new adventure, which was what Jean was counting on. He had been in conference with his father and mother all morning, with the village priest called in, too. They had come up with a plan, and Jean-Luc was putting it into effect.

"I was planning on leaving within the week. We can take a steamboat all the way to New Orleans. We can see what's going on, meet up with my cousin and go on to Texas. If we wait too long, all the fighting will be over, and all the opportunity will be gone. If you're sure you want to go, you had better talk to Magdelaine."

"We can put the wedding off until we come back. I'll get myself washed and dressed and go find Magdelaine to tell her the good news. She surely will be surprised. Maybe she can go and meet my folks, get to know them before we're wed."

"And I'll go find Maggie and tell her you want to talk to her. Then I'll go down to the docks and find out what sort of schedule they have for traveling out to the Atlantic and then down south. We may have to change boats several times, but it shouldn't take long for us to go to New Orleans. It may even be quicker to go overland to the Ohio River, and take a steamboat down the Mississippi. You fix things with Magdelaine, and I'll see you when I get back."

Jean-Luc went out into the hall, down the winding stairs and into the dining room, where they had been plotting all morning, and where his parents and Magdelaine were waiting.

"Everything is set, just the way we planned it. Glyn will be down in a few minutes. He thinks you should put the wedding off till we return. That can't happen. You need to convince him to marry you in the next couple of days and spend a week on a honeymoon.

"I'll set up our departure in about two weeks, time for you to marry and get with child, but not enough time for you to go and see his folks, or for them to come here. Then we'll go down to this Texas place and spend four to six months and be back. I hear him coming down the stairs. Go Maggie and convince him you can't live another day without being his wife." Jean-Luc bent down where Magdelaine was sitting and kissed her on the forehead. He turned to leave to make his way to the docks. Under his breath he said, "And may God forgive us."

CHAPTER 22

Gray Dove and Blue Bird

It was autumn, an especially busy time of year. Every morning one could hear the "thump, thump, thump" of someone pounding corn, or nuts used for flour (acorns, hickory nuts, beechnuts, walnuts, or hazelnuts) in a poodahgon, or stump pounder. At dark, the eerie sound of a lonely Indian flute, along with the call of the loon, carried across the water. At the Indian Camp, along with several more wigwams, a longhouse had been built as several Indian families planned on staying the winter.

Ash Leaf and Fox had brought what was left of their band. Storm had not been able to find any of his wife's family, so he and little Red Feather came to live at the Camp. Sickness had made traveling to Mackinac Island less appealing this year. Last winter's outbreak of smallpox across the northern regions and Asiatic cholera in the southern parts had exterminated whole villages and bands of the Natives. The ones left clung together. The once-proud race were now reduced to begging outside of forts and at the missions. The sickness seemed to carry off the able young adults, leaving the old and the children to fend for themselves. The adults left had become despondent; they could see the only way of life they knew fading away before them. Whiskey, at twenty-five cents a gallon, always a problem in the Native population had destroyed the very fabric of the Native culture and left a wretched existence for what had once been a proud people.

The settlement at the forks had grown over the summer with many immigrants making this their permanent home, and many more passing through. Some of the pioneers purchased lumber from sawmills near

Jackson and floated it downriver in scows, sometimes several in a row. Benjamin Knight was building a small store and warehouse in the center of the newly laid out town. Spicer's sawmill was up and running, and a grist mill was being constructed at the mouth of Spring Brook, now called Big Meadow Brook by the locals.

Mathew Gillett, a young farmer that lived outside the settlement, found a deposit of clay that was good for firing and made bricks for buildings and chimneys. Daniel Hosler was setting up a wagon shop, and James Strawn built a blacksmith shop. A stave mill, a harness shop, a tannery, and several asheries were planned.

Cloud took Gray Dove with her when Summer, Dawn, and she went to the trading post. "Olive, this is my grand-daughter, Gray Dove. The one I have told you about. She is very special to me. She gives my life meaning."

Gray Dove and Olive became good friends. Olive was especially impressed with the education Gray Dove had received at the mission schools.

One day Olive had a group of children from around the settlement at her table, trying to teach them their sums when Gray Dove came in to fetch some supplies for her grandmother. Several people were in the trading post. Gray Dove went over and picked up the crying baby and sat at the table with the children. "You go, I can sit with the children until you return. You look as though you could use some dream time."

"Yes, thank you, Gray Dove. It has been a trying day. The baby, I think is teething. I was up all night."

Gray Dove told a harried Olive to go wait on the customers. When Olive returned, the children were deeply engrossed in a Native American tale of how the world had come to be. The baby was sleeping and the children behaving, Olive asked Gray Dove to come every day to help her out. She could tell Gray Dove was a natural teacher. Olive went on to give Gray Dove more advanced lessons than she had received at the mission schools, and to encourage her to read the books Olive had brought from back east.

Gray Dove began to bring the children from the Camp to Olive's make-shift school so they could study since they wouldn't be going to a mission school that winter. One little girl, Blue Bird, was sickly. Gray Dove always made sure she came and had a place in the sun, or on cool days by the fire to stay warm. Olive and Simon soon became very fond of her. She had a sweet disposition, fitting her name. When she got too weak to walk all the way to their cabin, her father carried her every day and came for her in the afternoon. Then she stopped coming at all.

Blue Bird had missed a week of lessons. One warm sunny Sunday afternoon, Olive said to Simon, "Let's walk over to the Camp and see little Blue Bird. She must be worse off. I made some of the tarts she always liked and we can take them to her."

They walked to the Camp and found Blue Bird's father and mother sitting outside their wigwam beside a small hammock strung between two trees, with Blue Bird sleeping in it. Her father rose and walked over.

"Thank you for coming. We do not think she will last the day, and she will be with the Great Spirit. She always was happy at your cabin. Thank you for making her feel special."

"Here, take this basket. She always loved tarts with strawberries preserves," said Olive, who had tears in her eyes as she handed the basket to the young brave.

He took the basket without a word and sat back down beside the hammock. Everyone that lived at the Camp was there. One old man would start chanting, than another joined in. They had made a drum by stretching a piece of deer hide tightly across one end of a hollowed out log and pegging it in place. Two men sat and drummed to call the Spirit of the Great Father to come for Blue Bird so she wouldn't become lost. A small fire burned and smoked with herbs and sweet grass, tended to by the old women. Younger braves with bells tied below their knees danced around the fire.

With the smoke, the dancing, and the drumming, it seemed otherworldly, as though they were watching ghost-like images move among the trees. Olive and Simon were very moved by the way the Camp had turned out for Blue Bird and her parents.

The next morning when Olive and Simon woke, Blue Bird's father was sitting in front of their fireplace. He sat there in stony silence. They got up, dressed, and put breakfast on the table. Only then did the grieving father finally stand up and come over to Simon and Olive.

"Blue Bird is with the Great Spirit. Will you make a box for her?" he said as he drew a picture of a coffin on the floor with a stick. Olive wept.

Simon went out to a lean-to where they stored lumber. With the grieving father, Simon fashioned a crude box. Olive fetched one of her quilts to line the box with. They went back to the camp with the grieving father. They watched as the women of the tribe gently laid the little girl in the box. Simon went up and started to nail the lid down.

"No! No! Do not nail the top down. The spirit of Blue Bird has to be able to leave, to go with the Great Father. That is our belief," said one old man.

He went over to a beech tree and cut long strips of bark, and with this, he tied the lid of the crude box on. That way, her spirit would be free to leave.

Simon and Olive followed behind the band as they carried the coffin down to the O Washtenong and slipped into their canoes. They paddled up the river to their sacred site. It sat on high ground, on the east side of the river's bend, on the opposite shore from the Forks. It was an old oak grove, with tree trunks like mighty shafts holding up a canopy so thick and dense no sunlight could penetrate. It was bordered with giant beech trees whose limbs came to the ground, creating a natural auditorium. Here is where they performed sacred ceremonies and left their dead. Usually, the corpse was left in the sitting position on the ground, behind a crude fence, but Blue Bird's mother wanted her daughter buried in the manner of the French missionaries, in a box in the ground.

They lowered the coffin down into the cold, black earth, under giant trees that had stood there since time immemorial. After putting items she might need in the afterlife on top of the coffin, along with her favorite playthings and Olive's basket of tarts, everyone helped toss dirt back into the grave. After the ceremony, a somber party paddled their way back to the Camp.

CHAPTER 23
A LETTER FROM GLYN

A rider heading north along the river stopped with a bag of mail from Jackson. Little mail had come though since mid-summer. When the people around the settlement learned that mail had come to the trading post, everyone came, hoping for a letter from family back East, or maybe even a newspaper. There was no official post office yet, but the trading post served as the unofficial post office. People saved their pennies, for to receive their letter, they had to pay the twenty-five cent postage. Simon and Olive had been in charge of collecting postage and handing out letters since coming here and hoped to someday have the official post office at the trading post.

As Olive sorted the mail, she found a letter from Glyn that she put aside so she could read it to the family at supper. They had heard nothing from him since mid-summer when he had written to inform them that the Michigan Militia had disbanded, and he was working on a riverboat to make money. After the mail had been dispatched and customers served, Olive hurried to put a meal on the table.

Simon sat on the front stoop, reading aloud to a small crowd the newspaper that had come in from Detroit. Most, Olive knew, could hardly write their own names, let alone read a newspaper. Not that they had no schooling. Many came from different countries and could only read in their own language, and some had been schooled at home in only the most basic lessons.

As they sat around the table eating supper, Olive started to read her son's letter.

Dear Mother and Father,

Hope this letter finds you both well. As I said in my last letter, we fought the Ohioans until General Joseph W. Brown disbanded us. We were without any funds, so my friend from Detroit, Jean-Luc and I, worked on a riverboat on the Maumee, carting grain to Lake Erie. After that, we stayed for a couple of weeks at Jean-Luc's family's farm at Detroit, to rest up. I had all the intention of heading home after that. Then I decided to marry Jean-Luc's sister Magdelaine. She is real pretty and was educated in France. I know you will come to love her as I do, Mother. I wanted you and Father to come and meet her and her family and come for the wedding, but Jean-Luc received an urgent letter from a cousin in New Orleans, wanting him to come down to fight Mexico for the Texas Territory. Magdelaine and I were married yesterday and after a week, Jean-Luc and I are taking a steamship to New Orleans to meet up with his cousin and head to Texas. We think we can buy land down there and make our fortune. Please be happy for us.

Love, Glyn.

“What in tarnation has that boy gone and gotten himself into,” Simon shouted as he threw the fork down that he had been holding mid-air since Olive had read the part of marrying and going to Mexico.

“That fool boy has not an ounce of common sense, always running off without thinking. Marrying someone he's only known for a few weeks. Then going off to fight in Texas.”

“Where is Texas, Father, never heard of it. Can we go down and fight with Glyn?” asked Joseph.

“No! You're not going anywhere. Sit there and eat your supper. When did Glyn write that letter? I was reading in the newspaper that the fighting is all over down there. Gen. Santa Anna massacred everyone at a place called the Alamo. Then the Texas troops rallied and defeated the Mexican Army, and declared Texas its own country. I'm afraid Glyn has missed all the fighting.”

“Let me look to see if he dated it, "said Olive. "Yes, right here, August 30! Wonder where it's been all this time. I could have walked to Detroit and back twice by now. He never said what the girl’s family name is. We should go there and meet this girl and her parents. They must think we are a bunch of back-woodsmen.

“How could Glyn go off like this," continued Olive. "We need him here to help with the building of the new stagecoach stop. I figure that we will have enough money saved up so that the banks will loan us the rest of what we'll need, and by spring we should have all the lumber to start building."

Simon said, "Better write to the boys back east and have them sell the old place and head out here next spring. Sounds like you have everything planned out, and we'll need a lot of help. No telling what that fool Glyn will do, or when we'll see him again."

PART III- 1837

STATEHOOD - JANUARY 26, 1837

ᏟᏰ

CHAPTER 24
SPRING

Chief O-Ke-Monse

It had been a cold and wet winter; snow fell most every day. One day in early spring, Gray Dove brought her uncle, the old warrior chief, O-Ke-Monse, Chief of the Chippewa, to the Chatfield cabin to meet Olive and Simon. They were related in some way that only Indians understood. He was a short little man, no more than five-foot-four, but muscular and agile.

He was dressed in typical native garb: leather leggings and moccasins, a wa'mus with his large hunting knife, sacred pipe-hatchet, and a tomahawk stuck in his belt. He wore a turban around his head with some eagle feathers. Over the weeks, he came to love Olive's cooking, and frequently would visit the Chatfields at mealtime when he was in the area. Natives did not have a concept of privacy that the Americans had. If smoke came from the chimney, they would open the door and would simply walk in. Gray Dove had tried to explain that the American custom was to knock first. So now he would knock once and walk in and say, "see, now I American, I knock." The only way that the Natives would stay out was to put two sticks, crossed, leaning against the front entrance. This was their way to say that no one was home.

O-Ke-Monse was a story teller and loved telling the stories of his youth. Olive believed that this was a good teaching tool, and let her students listen at their dinner break. The children loved to listen, and he loved an audience.

Chief O-KE-MONSE spoke to a group of children:

"I was born around 1775 at Ketchewandaugoning *(Big Salt Lick)* on the Shiawassee. My father's uncle was Chief Kobekonoko, an Ottawa. My father was a fur trapper. My mother's father was Chief Manetogoboway, a Chippewa.

"I went on the war-path with my uncle, Chief Pontiac, at an early age and distinguished myself as a warrior. My totem is the bear. That makes me a brave and fearless fighter. I led my braves in war against General St Clair on the Miami River. That defeat of the American army even made General Washington take notice of me.

"He sent General "Mad" Anthony Wayne to rout us at Fallen Timbers. We later joined with the Ottawa and the Pottawatomie to defeat the Shawnees at Three Rivers. Then we went northwest, into Wisconsin and defeated the Chippewa. We were then at peace for a few years. We were able to settle down and raise our families as we had in the past. But it didn't last long until the British started to stir up trouble again. They were good at that.

"I then joined the 'Prophet,' Tecumseh's brother, to fight General William Henry Harrison at Tippecanoe in Indiana, along the Wabash River. We barely escaped with our lives. We joined the British and later fought in northeastern Ohio on the Seneca Plains, near Sandusky. We were slaughtered by the cavalry. I received a bad head wound." The old chief stopped and unwound his turban.

"See this," as he pointed an indention on his head. "Come here and look. I can put three fingers into it." The children gathered around.

"How did that happen," asked one little boy.

"We were crawling through the tall grass to attack the Americans when a heap of their cavalry charged. There was no time to reload our rifles; I stood up with my war club, and a soldier hit me with the butt of his rifle. Then he tried to ram his saber through me. I turned, and he struck a blow to my back. I remember my head feeling on fire as if a red hot poker had pierced it. I crawled to a swampy piece of the woods and buried myself in the leaves before I passed out. When I came to, days later, I knew I was badly injured. I crawled around the battlefield and found a cousin still alive, and then an old chief. All the other braves left were dead. With the help of the old chief, we dragged my cousin down to the Sandusky River. We found an old boat and lay in it, more dead than alive. We floated downstream. It was night when we floated past the American's army fort. We lay still at the bottom of the boat until we were past. The next day we came to a friendly Indian village. The women of the village took us in and kept us safe until we were healed.

My cousin was crippled the rest of his life from the wounds he received. I also still have the saber scars on my back.

"After many moons, I healed from my injuries. I went to General Godfrey, an Indian agent. He interceded with General Cass to make a peace offer. Our clan had always been loyal to the French until the end of their regime. Then we became the subjects of the British and remained true to them. Then their regime was over. We went to Detroit and presented ourselves at Fort Wayne. I said to the commanding officer, 'Now I make peace and fight no more. Chemokemon (white man) too much for Indians. Me fight plenty enough.' This promise I have kept faithfully.

"The soldiers made us prisoners until General Cass pardoned us. We were then sent to Ketchewandaugoning to live. They took all our land in the Treaty of Saginaw, except for certain reservations. We are supposed to have the right to hunt and fish."

O-Ke-Monse continued, "I moved my village to the Cedar River. We have dams on the rivers that we use for fishing and trapping. I once speared a twenty-eight pound muskellunge in one of the deep holes.

"The tribe clears trees and brush, and then we plant vegetables and corn. We 'cache' it in the fall by digging caves in the high sandy banks along the river. We line the caves with bark and leaves from the willow tree—that helps preserve food and repel the insects. We weave willow baskets with their dried leaves still attached to store our corn and vegetables, nuts from the trees, and dried meat, like venison, in the caves until the next planting season, the time when food could be scarce for us. We hide the entrance to the cache with brush and rocks so wolves and bears cannot get at it, then we leave and go to our winter camp.

"We return from our winter camp early in the spring in time to make maple sugar and maple candy. In the old days, my people would slash the trunks of trees and let the sap run into hollowed out log troughs and let it freeze overnight. In the morning they would break and remove the ice. Then they would heat stones red hot in a campfire and throw them into the sap trough to boil off the water. They would take the cooled stones out and reheat them, a slow, long process.

"Now we have large copper kettles that we trade furs for from the white men. We hang the brass pots over campfires, on wooden poles, and let the sap boil continuously. All day, young men with shoulder yokes, carry buckets of sap. They will trudge back and forth from the trees to the campfire. The women tend to the fires and stir the syrup to keep from burning. They fix food, and kept an eye on the children. On the last day, they hold a sugaring off party which everyone comes to. They have a large meal and finish off the syrup, making the last into maple candy and maple sugar. They stored the syrup in covered clay crocks; the sugar and candy we wrap in birch bark where it will keep for a year or more. The Indian people prefer the hard sugar, as it is easier to transport and use, breaking off chunks to add to food."

CHAPTER 25

THE SUGAR BUSH

Spring! Time to harvest the first crop of the season, maple syrup. The Native American Indians eagerly looked forward to this annual event. In the weeks leading up to it, they keep busy whittling spiels from large elderberry stems and making birch buckets to carry the sap in. Simon owned several hand bits and braces that they could use for drilling holes in the trees, as well as a few tin buckets and large copper kettles. The Indians knew of a large grove of sugar maples. Early on a fine, cold, sunny morning at the beginning of March, most all the people at the Forks and the Indian Camp, set out for the "sugar bush."

They crossed the still-frozen O Washtenong River and traveled several miles to the east. The land here was level. The settlers called it the Montgomery Plain for the man that owned a large tract of the land. Then they turned south and traveled to a knoll covered with huge maple trees.

The women and children set up the camp while the men started tapping the trees by drilling holes about as large as your finger and inserting a wooden spiel. The maples were so large that half a dozen spiels could be placed in each tree, always facing the warm, sunny south side of the tree where the sap is more likely to flow. The pails were hung, and the sap would begin to drip out of the spiel, filling the pails with sap. Firewood had to be cut, hauled and stacked by the campfire. When the boiling started, a fire had to be kept going under the cooper kettles day and night. Someone would have to stay up and stir the kettles so the syrup wouldn't burn. It took 40 gallons of sap to evaporate to make one gallon of syrup. The Natives set up several wigwams close to the campfire as a place to rest between turns at tending the fire and stirring the pot.

Simon, with the other men and boys, set out to bring more wood to the sugar bush. The snow was still deep enough in the forest to wear snowshoes—which were rather awkward but better than sinking to their knees with every step. A wind storm the summer before had brought down several tree tops not far from the knoll where the sugar-bush had been set up. The settlers had brought two oxen and two sleds with them. The Natives brought their nobugidabans *(toboggans)* pulled by their dogs.

One crew of men and boys worked on the tree tops, sawing and splitting, while the younger children loaded the sleds with firewood. Simon had been splitting wood and needed a rest, so he volunteered to take the next load of wood back to camp. He started his ox and sled moving through the snow when O-Ke-Monse jumped on the sled with him. They traveled in companionable silence for a ways, Simon stretched his shoulder and back to get the kinks out.

O-Ke-Monse started talking as the two old warriors looked straight ahead. "I was at the Battle of the Thames too. I was wounded in the shoulder but was able to escape into the woods while you fought with Tecumseh. I saw Tecumseh and you, heard Tecumseh curse you. Seen him cut your face. Saw you killed Tecumseh, the greatest warrior of our time.

"I saw how the soldiers cut strips of skin off my brothers to make belts, then bury the dead warriors like animals. I saw them desecrate the sacred site. I do not blame you. We are all in this wheel of life together. If we had sided with you Americans, instead of the British, we would have been better off. We are now a defeated people. We have to live with the choices our leaders made.

"The curse Tecumseh put on you is a blood curse, very bad. Part of his spirit is with you now and forever. It drives some men insane, having two spirits in one body. You need a ceremony for your spirit before you die, or your spirit will wander the Earth and never rest."

They were by now back in camp. The old chief jumped off the sled and started unloading the firewood while the children stacked it. Simon stared ahead and tried to shake the nightmare of memories out of his mind. A sharp pain pierced his chest as he heard a mocking laugh inside his head.

CHAPTER 26
FAMILIES ARRIVE

Olive and Gray Dove were cooking breakfast for the settlers, and the pioneers camped at the Forks. They had had a late, cold spring, but now the days were warming. Ice on the rivers had broken late, but now lumber was floating down to the settlement and beyond from sawmills that worked all winter providing much-needed building materials as more settlers poured into Michigan. Olive and Simon had 26 people who stayed there the night before. Most were camped outside; in tents, on the cabin stoop, or slept in or under their wagons. This was not unusual. Olive hired Gray Dove and the women who lived at the Indian Camp to come every day to help feed them.

Olive was visiting with a new neighbor in the settlement while she cooked ham and eggs, and toasted bread in the fireplace. A large pot of hominy bubbled away on the hearth. Mrs. Waldron had come into the trading post to buy supplies. They talked about future plans for the settlement.

“We really need the new tavern built as soon as we can," Olive said. "Now that Michigan is a state, a lot more people will be coming though. We have most all the lumber we need stacked up out back, drying. I know just how I want the floor plan. The tavern we had back in New York wasn't laid out to suit me. Always said that if I could build my own place, I knew just how I want it.

She continued, “My eldest son, Elmer, is a carpenter. Been building barns since he was 16. As soon as he and his brother, Joshua, arrive with their families, we can get started. They sold the old tavern we had and got a decent price for it, as it was right on the Erie Canal and was always busy. They're bringing the money with them. Simon told them not to trust any banks, not after what he heard the last time he went south and picked up supplies. The banks then would only take certain specie, and turned away paper money. Those red dog and wild cat banks that are springing up all over are crooked, and are cheating everyone out of their money."

Olive had invited Mrs. Waldron to stay for a cup of coffee. Olive wanted to be friends with the new women in the settlement. Mrs. Waldron, along with Mrs. Darling, Mrs. Conley, and their families had moved into their cabins in the settlement earlier in the spring. Mrs. Conley had broken her foot out on the trail. It had been sticking out from the wagon, and a tree came too close. A doctor in Jackson had set it, but she was to stay in bed until her child was born.

It was nice for Olive to talk to other women who understood the hardships of pioneer life. She boiled more coffee for them in the fire while keeping an eye on the ham she had in the reflector oven, while she slowly turned the spit. The outside was glazed in a maple syrup. Primitive but sturdy slab tables were set up in the backyard, with stumps for seats. Gray Dove was busy carrying out platters of hot bread, ham slices, and bowls of hominy to all those who wanted to buy their breakfast. Pots of coffee sat on the table, as well as crocks of freshly churned butter.

The two younger boys, James and Joseph, were in charge of cleaning the tables off and washing dirty dishes. They also kept hot water in the big brass kettle, so anyone who wanted a bucket of water could have it. It was a chore to keep clean on the frontier. Hot water, lye soap, and vinegar were about all they had.

Most of the trees were leafed out. By now, some of the dogwood were still blossomed, and the ground was covered in wildflowers. The birds were so loud and so numerous it was hard to hear a person talk if they weren't next to you. The sun would dim when huge flocks of migratory birds flew over on their way to the north country. Fresh Pigeon Pie was a staple this time of year when people were tired of eating corn, beans, and salt pork, three times a day. Men and boys would shoot into flocks of passenger pigeons and harvest enough birds for several meals. Netting was another way to catch the birds while they roosted in trees.

That afternoon, the two older boys, Elmer and Joshua, arrived with their wives, Harriet and Hannah, along with their four girls. They each drove four yoke of oxen with a Conestoga wagon packed full. Not only had they brought clothes, household items and assorted furniture from the old tavern, but had stopped on their way to the Forks at different trading posts, picking up needed supplies. The children were tired after the long trip and needed naps. Olive heard the commotion when they arrived. She ran around the side of the cabin just as Simon stepped off the front stoop. Everyone was talking at once.

"I'm so glad you're all finally here," Olive said as she climbed up on the first wagon and lifted a crying Daisy up, the youngest toddler. "My, Rebecca and Daisy have grown since we saw them last!"

"Mother Olive, we're the ones glad to see you. Thought for sure some of those wild Indians would get us. And the wolves! They would howl all night. I was sure they were following us through the woods," Hannah said as she lifted Rebecca up and gave her to Simon.

"I was sure we were lost. I have never seen a woods go on as long as this. The trail was nothing more than blaze marks on some crooked trees. Joshua said he knew the way, 'Gee off' at Jackson and 'Haw to' at Spicer's Mill. But when we left Jackson, I was sure we would never see another living person."

Elmer jumped off the wagon came up to his father. "Here we are, thanks to the grace of God. We made good time and had no surprises. Got all the supplies you wanted.

"Still not that much here, a few more shacks and a few more cabins than were here a couple of years ago," Elmer said as he looked around. Elmer never minced his words; he said what was on his mind.

"How did our cabin work out? Looks as though the roof held up. The fireplaces didn't smoke too bad, did they? I learned a new way of building them, called the Rumford fireplace, really popular back east. I brought some architectural drawings from some new books."

Elmer had been drawing and building things since he was a young lad. At twelve, he was at every barn and house raising in the neighborhood. At fourteen, crews were asking for his advice. At sixteen, he had his own crew that helped build houses and barns for the growing population. Elmer was very fussy and noticed any mistakes. You could see him walking around a half completed barn with his level and plumb, and he had better not catch any mistakes; his shouting could make the devil shake in his boots.

"Damn it, Elmer; it's good to see all of you again." Simon, never one to show much emotion, gave his eldest son a bear hug, and turned to Joshua and gave him one, too.

"Been almost two years. Too long for a family not to see each other, too long for a father not to see his sons."

Olive had been kissing and hugging Elmer's girls, Henrietta and Mabel, as well as Joshua's, all her grand-babies that she had missed so much were now here. Then she came over to hug and kiss her eldest boys. It had been hard being separated from them for so long.

After everyone had been hugged and introduced to all the locals, the crowd suddenly quieted down.

"Mother Olive, who is that?" Hannah asked.

Two men approached along the south trail on black horses. They both looked forlorn. They had on dark, dusty clothes and cowboy hats that shadowed their faces from the sun. One had a papoose in a cradle board on his back. Everyone stopped talking and watched as the horsemen silently made their way down the worn track.

"I don't rightly know. Somehow, they do look familiar," said Olive as she watched the horsemen approach. She put her hand up to shield her eyes from the bright, dappled glare from the sun shining through the trees. A cool wind picked up as a cloud passed overhead, throwing them in shadow.

"It's Glyn!" she said when she realized who the figure was. "Simon, Glyn has come home! Glory be, what a day of surprises."

They gathered around the horses as Glyn dismounted. He untied the cradle board with his sleeping infant. Simon rushed over to help Glyn slip off the shoulder straps and set the bottom of the board on the ground. Then Glyn untied the baby boy and smiling, handed him to his mother.

"Your youngest grandson, Mother." Glyn leaned down and kissed her cheek, and shook his father's hand.

"Well Father, I'm home for good. I see everyone else has arrived, too." He hugged his brothers and their wives, all of them talking at once, and then he started walking towards the cabin.

Olive cried out, "Glyn, don't walk away. What has happened to you? Where have you been for the past year? If this is your son, where is your wife, Magdelaine?"

Glyn stopped, looked back at his mother. She could see tears coming from red-rimmed eyes, running down his sunken cheeks and into his dusty black beard. He said nothing. He looked down and shook his head, turned and kept walking.

Jean-Luc wearily dismounted from his horse and gave a slight bow.

"If I may say something," Jean-Luc said, talking softly in his French-accented English.

"Let him go; he will explain later. He hasn't slept for a week or more, not since we arrived back in Detroit from Texas. We found Magdelaine had died, just the week before. She never recovered completely from giving birth and caught typhoid shortly after. I am Jean-Luc Marcotte, Madelaine's brother.

"You must be Olive, his mother, and you, his father." Jean-Luc took and kissed Olive's hand and shook Simon's hand. "Glyn always talks so warmly about you two that I feel we are old friends."

"Oh yes. You must forgive us our manners'" Olive stammered. "This is just so surprising to us. We had no idea Glyn was coming home, or that his wife was expecting."

She was still holding the baby close to her. "Does the baby have a name? Is the baby healthy, or is the baby sick, too? How did you two feed a baby on the trail? What is wrong with Glyn? Something more than fatigue."

"Aw yes, the baby's name is Xavier-Francis Girona Chatfield. It is a name Magdelaine chose. The baby was early. Magdelaine was afraid he would not live until Glyn came home, so she had him christened. Instead, it was she that died before Glyn made it home, and the baby thrives." Jean-Luc reached out with his finger to caress the baby's apple red cheek.

"Glyn received a letter from Magdelaine telling him that she was expecting a child. The letter took months to find us. We were doing business in Texas, buying land from the new government. We got in legal trouble. After we bought land, we found that there was no clear title. A noble Spanish family claimed they owned the land and took us to court. The court favored them. We had to counter sue the new government to get our money back. We ended up in jail. Long story. Thanks to the US Consulate, we were released. We received more land than we bargained for in our settlement, but in a different part of Texas than what we wanted.

"Now Glyn blames himself for Magdelaine's death. He thought he should have been home with her, and she would still be alive. He did truly love her with all his heart. He talked non-stop about the new life they were to have together. When we got back to Detroit, and when he found that she had died not a week before, he went crazy. He went out, got drunk and tried to throw himself into the Detroit River. Some Indians found him, fished him out and brought him home.

"After we sobered him up, we made him realize that he had his and Magdelaine's baby to take care of. Glyn insisted that he come back here. My family wanted him to stay in Detroit, or at least leave the baby there with them, but he insisted on bringing the baby back here. He wanted to come home, he said.

"As for feeding the little one, we French have found that goat milk is good for babies that the mother cannot provide for, as well as making the best cheese in the world. We had the goat tied behind us when a group of Indian children down the trail wanted to play with it." Jean-Luc turned and pointed back towards the Indian Camp.

"They promised Glyn they would bring it to the cabin later. He has not slept since we got back to Detroit, and I have not slept much, trying to keep Glyn alive. Now, tell me where to stable these horses, and I will sleep, too."

"James!, Joseph!" Simon turned and yelled, trying to find the boys in the crowd of people that surrounded them. The boys came pushing their way through the crowd. "Take these horses out back and hobble them by the cow shed. We still have Elmer and Joshua's oxen to take care of, and their wagons."

Simon turned to Jean-Luc, "We are very grateful to you for looking after Glyn and bringing him home. We will take care of the horses. You go and get some rest, too. Go to the cabin. I imagine Glyn is up in the sleeping loft. After you both get some sleep, we will talk more."

Olive, still holding the baby, walked over to Simon as they watched a weary Jean-Luc walk towards the cabin. "Now what? We have received our wish of having the whole family together again. Five grand babies, the five boys, two daughters-in-law, and our Sarah. Fifteen people, not counting Jean-Luc, in a two-room cabin. I think we had better start building the stage-coach stop and make it twice as big as we planned."

"Elmer has been talking about the new tavern since they arrived. He has already drawn up some plans to show you that he brought, as well as design books. He's out back, measuring our pile of lumber. He said we are woefully deficient. Joshua's been helping him figure out what more we'll need. By the way, they got over three thousand dollars for the old place. Elmer made false floors in both wagons, stashed the gold and silver coin between the floorboards," said Simon, laughing.

"We still have those old army tents that we brought with us. The boys can sleep in them. I better go and tend to the horses and unsaddle them. That Jean-Luc must have money. The horses and saddles are first rate, not like what we had in the militia, where when it rained, the saddles fell apart like paper."

The baby woke, and started crying. "Before you do anything, have someone go and fetch that goat! I sure hope someone knows how to milk one. Hurry before one of the Indians get an idea that she may taste good roasted."

-------#-------

Glyn slept for two days, curled up in the farthest corner of the loft. The noise of the family never penetrated his semiconscious state. Jean-Luc stayed by him. He also slept, but fitfully. Jean kept dreaming of his dead sister, and of the letter she had left for him.

Jean-Luc

If you are reading this, then I am dead. I write to you to tell you I received a letter from my baby's grandfather, Count Pontchartrain. My Xavier was killed in battle, fighting to put Don Carlos back on the throne of Spain. His wife's father, the Spanish Count of Girona, was also killed in battle, a few months before, so the family title went to Xavier. There is no other heir. Xavier's wife, the Countess, being the last of a long line, also died in childbirth, along with the child. So my child will inherit the title.

Xavier's father knew all about our love affair and our lovechild, and will testify in the Spanish court for his inheritance. I am sick and don't care if I live. It would be better if I did not, as I have found that, even though Glyn is twice the man that Xavier was, I still love Xavier. Look out for my son, the new Count of Girona. I have told no one else.

Magdelaine

Glyn slowly woke and became aware of his dim surroundings. He closed his eyes and gave his head a shake. Where was he? Memories started flooding back. He tried to shut them out. The room slowly came into focus. Then he remembered, marrying Magdelaine, spending the most magical week of his life in her arms, in a small hotel in Detroit. Hardly leaving the room, except when hunger drove them to a small cafe next door. He knew pure bliss that week, then the tearful farewell.

He remembered the Texas jail cell they put Jean-Luc and him in.

Hot, stinking, rat infested. They had no money. It had been taken from them when they were arrested. If they wanted to eat, they had to pay, and no one remembered taking their personal items from them. He recalled being released after ten days to find the bogus charges against them dropped, and that their case had been won in court. And worst of all, coming back to Detroit to find his Magdelaine had been ill since the birth of their son and had died the week before. Now he was back home, with a baby boy with a foreign sounding name on the frontier of Michigan. He wept silent tears for a dream that would never be.

Finally, Glyn got hold of himself and looked around. Jean-Luc was snoring, wrapped in a bearskin robe, one thin, naked leg sticking out. Glyn dressed and climbed down the ladder from the loft. He heard people talking and children playing. It made quite the commotion out on the back stoop and out in the yard. He wasn't ready yet to face his family and all their questions. He washed his face in the white enamel bowl and pitcher by the door and combed his hair. He spied a pot of coffee in the fireplace and found a tin cup that he filled to the brim. He headed out the front door.

Gray Dove was coming up the steps, his little papoose on her back in the cradle board. She was holding Sarah in one arm, singing to her in Ojibwa, with a small birch bark pail, half full of fresh goat milk, in the other. She stopped and smiled at Glyn. He felt an odd stirring in his body, like fresh air blowing out the old dust and cobwebs from his battered soul.

"Hello, you must be Glyn. I milked that rotten animal you brought. She kicked me and dumped the pail over. If she belonged to me, she would be tonight's supper. I was able to save enough milk for the baby. Xavier? I think is the name." She had a smudge of dirt on one cheek, a few blades of grass in her messed hair.

Glyn laughed for the first time in weeks, "Here, let me have him, I call him Frankie." He took his little papoose out of the cradle board and sat down. "Do you have the feeder? I've gotten quite good at this, believe it or not."

"It's inside. Watch Sarah. I know where it is. Where did this cradle board come from? I have never seen bead work like this before," Gray Dove said as she unfastened the cradle board and propped it against the wall.

"When I received my wife's letter, when she told me she was with child, I was in Texas. I bought the cradle board from the Indians down there; Paiutes, I think they were called. I had hoped that Magdelaine would have liked it." Glyn said with tearful eyes.

Gray Dove reached down and gently hugged Glyn. She turned and went inside. Her long gray homespun cotton dress swished past him.

"My Sarah, you have grown so since I saw you last, do you remember me? I'm your brother, Glyn. I remember when you were no bigger than Frankie here. I used to rock you, just like I'm rocking Frankie. I've been gone a long time. I was in the militia. Then I went down south to a place called Texas where it's hot all the time."

Sarah, who usually was not shy around strangers, looked at the floor, holding her straw doll. Then she reached up and wiped Glyn's tears away.

"Here it is," Gray Dove said. "It was washed out and sitting on the dry-sink. It's a wonder I found it, with all the people walking through the cabin." She handed the feeder filled with goat milk to Glyn.

"Thank you, you look so familiar. I never caught your name. And thank you for looking out after Frankie and milking the goat. Her name, by the way, is Madame Marie-Therese." Glyn said as he fed Frankie. "She cost me a lot of money. The family in Detroit that owned her told me they were very fond of her and didn't want to sell, but her milk is the only thing that didn't make the baby sick. But I think I was taken for a fool. With Therese's personality, I believe that they were plenty glad to see her go!"

Gray Dove laughed, "My name is Gray Dove, and it has been no work at all taking care of Frankie. He is a joyful little boy."

She paused and looked at Glyn. "We have met before. Here at the trading post the first summer your family moved here. And do you remember the night in the woods? When you stole your horse back. You were leading the horse across the stream. We met in the middle of it." Her face blushed at the thought.

"Yes... don't tell me," Glyn laughed in surprise. "That was you! At first I thought you were a goddess, so beautiful, standing in the moonlight. Then I was sure you would kill me! I was so scared you could hear my knees knock."

"I was afraid you would kill me, too. After you turned and left, I thought you were so brave and thought it would make my brother so mad, you stealing his horse back."

"Is he still mad, your brother? That I stole his horse that he stole from us," Glyn said, laughing.

Suddenly the smile on Gray Dove's face was gone, replaced with a far-away stony look. "That winter, my whole tribe died. My mother, my father, my brother, all the children I grew up with. The white man's smallpox killed almost everyone I knew. My grandmother, Cloud Woman, stayed here at the Camp that winter. She is the only person I have left. After I became well, I came and found her.

"I have been living here since. Grandmother brought me to meet your mother, and now I come every day to help at the trading post. Your mother is teaching all the children in the settlement and the surrounding farms, as well as the children at our camp. I help her as I can, and she helps me with my learning, too. I went to the missionary schools at Mackinac Island. But I have learned so much from her. She and your father are very kind."

Jean-Luc stumbled out the door, and in French said. "Here you are. My God, how long have I slept? I woke up and thought a bear had me in its clutches! Is there anything that resembles coffee in this place? I see Frankie is nursing. Who was the lucky one to milk Madame Therese?"

"Jean-Luc, may I present Miss Gray Dove, milk maid, and a goddess I met one night in the middle of a river. Miss Gray Dove, my friend and brother-in-law, who has seen me through thick and thin. Had my back in the militia, but because of him, we almost starved to death in a Mexican jail," said Glyn, who by now spoke French almost as well as Jean-Luc.

"By the time we graced those cells, it was actually a Texas jail." Jean-Luc said and nodded toward Gray Dove.

"You are one brave soul to take on Therese. French goats are notorious for their disposition. Now, do you know where our saddle bags would be? I need to bathe and shave," said Jean-Luc as he picked up Glyn's coffee cup and drained it.

"Yes I do," said Gray Dove pointing over the men's heads. "Your father hung them over a rafter here on the stoop to keep the children out of them. You two go on, and when you come back, I'll have something for you to eat, and some fresh coffee waiting. Give me the baby; I'll look after him. Come on Sarah, let's go fix your brother and his friend a meal."

"Get our saddle bags, and I'll show you our special bathtub. The French call it 'le Grand'. And you're in luck, looks as though the ice is gone," Glyn said to Jean-Luc, as he winked at Gray Dove.

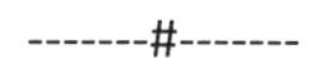

One night after supper, Gray Dove and Jean-Luc were sitting on the front stoop. Glyn had gone inside to bath a sleepy Frankie and put him to bed.

"Tell me," said Gray Dove in French. "What was your sister like? Glyn must have liked her very much."

"Yes, Glyn was very much in love with my sister. He had known her only for a few weeks when he knew he wanted to marry her. They were only together as husband and wife for a week before we left for Texas. We were gone longer than we thought we would be. And they never saw each other again.

"Glyn is very upset, very angry with himself. He is a good, caring man. He blames himself for what has happened. It is not his fault. No one blames Glyn. Not me, or my family. Everything that could have been done was. She would have died whether Glyn was there or not. I hope he can find a woman to love again. A beautiful, loving woman. Like you."

Gray Dove put her head down to hide her blush. "I notice you did not answer my question. What was Magdelaine like?"

"You do ask hard questions. Magdelaine always looked out for Magdelaine. She was a beautiful woman. And she usually got what she wanted. When she didn't, she made sure that she came out on top, anyway. No, she did not love Glyn, not the way that Glyn loved her, although she was very fond of him. I shall tell you the truth. The man she loved lived in France and was killed fighting in Spain. I think she died more of a broken heart. Glyn never knew that, and it would kill him if he found out."

Jean-Luc stayed for several weeks. He was anxious to go back to Texas, where he and Glyn had purchased over two thousand acres of land. Magdelaine had given Glyn all her dowry money to invest in their new home. He and Jean-Luc bought the land together, and now that Glyn had decided to stay in Michigan, Jean was going back to Texas to manage it.

Everyone in the settlement came to send Jean-Luc off. He had become quite the character in and around the Forks. Olive hugged him as if he was one of her own sons. Simon and the boys all shook hands and slapped each other on the back, the way men do.

Glyn rode out with Jean-Luc a ways, talking of old times and what would come. They promised to write. Jean promised to say hello to his parents and brothers and sisters for Glyn and to stay out of jail in Texas. They rode up beside each other, facing one another and shook hands.

Jean-Luc pulled Glyn close and hugged him, saying, "You are more than a friend, I love you like a brother now. I know how badly

Magdelaine's death weighs upon you. You have to keep strong for my little nephew. You will have to find a good woman to marry, so my nephew can have a mother, and you can be happy again. A man needs a woman to love. So long, my brother. We will see each other again; I promise you."

They parted, with unshed tears in their eyes, both knowing that in this uncertain world, this could very well be the last time they would ever see one another.

Glyn rode back to the settlement subdued. The crews were back at work. He joined them and worked hard all day. That night, after putting Frankie to bed, he slipped out to where the young men camped, to gamble and drink, and to forget.

CHAPTER 27
THE TAVERN

Work commenced on the tavern/stagecoach stop as soon as everyone in the family had a chance to rest and settle in. Elmer ordered more lumber from Spicer's Mill. Instead of the five-bay, two-story building Olive thought would be large enough; the boys envisioned doubling the size to a ten-bay, two-story, square building. It would be build right over the old two-room cabin.

They would still have room for a lane behind the tavern and beyond that for a livery stable, the necessary house, and a laundry. Large oak and maple timbers, some sixty feet long, for the building's post and beams, had already been delivered. They would have to be constructed on the ground first, mortise and tendons cut, numbered with Roman numerals and put together like a large jigsaw puzzle. After the holes had been drilled and pegs whittled, whole sections would be put together. Then with the help of pulleys and ropes, and crews of mules and men, the walls would start to go up.

But first the footings had to be dug, along with a shallow basement. Because the water table was so high, a proper English basement was impossible. Digging down further than four feet and water would fill the hole. Olive would have liked the kitchen and laundry in the basement, but Cloud Woman told of stories of spring flooding when the water could get to be two or three foot high where the tavern was to stand.

Elmer had left behind a highly trained crew back east. One that knew what his hand signals meant and could anticipate what needed to be done before they were told. He put together this new crew with a few volunteer settlers, some immigrant stragglers passing through, and men from the band of Pottawatomie. The Indians knew that they had to start adopting the ways of the Americans. A few were eager to learn, but some of the settlers did not want anything to do with them.

Indians were blamed if a cow came up missing or an item was stolen from a house or barn. The Native Americans did like a good joke, and would sometimes tell a man that they would trade a pony for his wife or daughter. They had learned bawdy jokes and salty language from the French voyageurs, which offended some of these straight-laced, church-going New Englanders, who did not appreciate their humor.

The Reverend Jack signed on to be part of the crew. Elmer quickly saw his potential and it wasn't long before old Jack was a valued part of his team.

Amos Spicer wanted to build a second sawmill at the mouth of Spring Brook, as well as a much-needed gristmill. It was decided that the gristmill would come first. It wasn't long before men, having heard that work could be had, came pouring into the settlement.

Cash was scarce since most of the wildcat banks had closed, making their paper money useless. Many men had lost their life savings. Simon and Olive had the hard cash to pay, thanks to Elmer and Joshua's excellent bargaining skills in selling the old tavern back east. And in securing gold and silver coins and successfully transporting them to Michigan beneath the false floorboards of the wagons.

Elmer happened to come to the state at a time when an experienced builder was much in demand. He was hired to plan and build the larger buildings around the settlement. Farmers came to help so that Elmer would go out to their farms in return, to supervise the building of their own house and barns, now that proper lumber was at hand.

Peter Moe and John Boody from Motown had come to help raise the stage-coach stop. In turn Elmer and Joshua took a crew out to their farms, about three miles to the west of Spicer's Mill, and raised their houses and barns. Elmer liked the looks of the country in those parts and decided to stake out a claim by them.

Joshua liked the land he had seen out by Israel Allyn's when they raised his barn. He lived about two miles to the south of Spicer's Mill, off the old Clinton Trail, not quite halfway between Spicer's Mill and Charlesworth. Joshua bought land out there.

Simon knew how to construct the dirt-scrapers that mules pulled to dig the basements from his days working on the machinery at the Erie

Canal. It wasn't long before they had the foundation for the tavern underway. They dug the dirt and rocks and used that as fill to level the road in front.

The Indians at first were leery of the huge mules that were brought in to work, but soon learned how to drive them. In no time, Simon had the best mule bosses around. As soon as the basement foundations were dug, rocks from the river were loaded onto stone boats and hauled to the site where Jack’s crew quickly laid them up. Then the crew that worked on the post and beam walls was ready to assemble and raise them.

Many of the giant old trees had been cut down to make way for roads and buildings. Olive remembered where the Native American women held the ceremony for Sarah shortly after she was born. She often went out to that tree when she was troubled, or one of the children was sick. She would simply sit beneath it on the thick moss and lichen to think and pray. It made her feel better, as though she had been comforted by an old friend. Her troubles always seemed lighter.

“Simon, you know where my tree is. Lucky for us it's right near the edge of our claim, or we would have to buy more land. I want you to be sure to leave that tree alone. After the stable is built, it will be a nice shade tree for the stable-yard and laundry. And I want you to leave as many of the old trees as you can. I know we need the lumber, but I love those trees.”

“Yes, the men have asked me why there is a red scarf around that tree. I told them if anyone touched that tree, they would have you to deal with.”

PART IV – 1838

ଓ

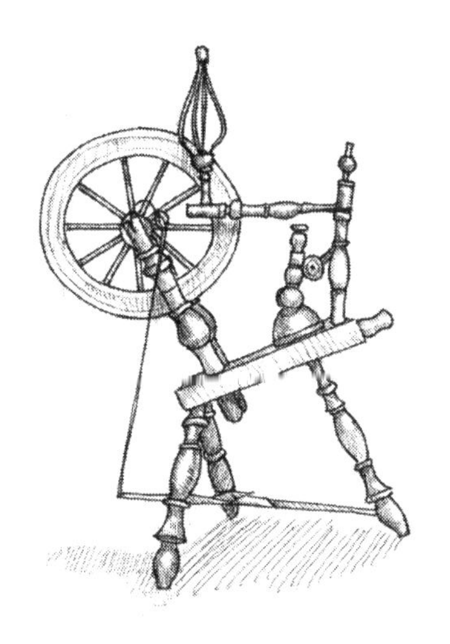

CHAPTER 28
THE SETTLEMENT

The first Eaton Township town hall meeting was held at Spicer's Mill. The whole county had been divided into three townships, Bellevue, Eaton, and Vermontville, in February by a legislative act. Organized as a township, it was still a toss-up where any villages would be. Spicer's Mill and the Forks, at this time, had about the same number of people. William W. Craine was elected as Supervisor; W. McQuean, Town Clerk; and J. Montgomery as the Justice of the Peace.

Michigan had finally become a state, and mass meetings were taking place to elect representatives to the state legislature. The first meeting in this area was held at Johnson Montgomery's farm. A free dinner and speakers from other states brought in many people from surrounding counties. Tables were set up that were eight rods long and held eight roasted hogs.

The first county convention was held at a log house that belonged to Levi Wheaten. The law was that elections were to be held on the first Monday of April. Some wanted to hold a democratic convention, but because so few people lived in Eaton, it was decided nominations would be made. Then a vote was required to be canvassed at the country seat. At that time the county seat was only a stake driven in the center of an Indian prairie. No buildings were there, and no one was sure where the stake had been driven. So they met under a burr oak tree in what became known as the "seminary" lot, being close enough to the center of the prairie. Afterward, they went to J. Searls' house to have dinner where they discussed politics and the elections that were to be held in November.

After a few months, the tavern was completed on the outside, although there was much work on the inside yet to do. They built around the old cabin and kept that as the south-west corner of the structure. The living quarters of the old cabin, with its huge stone fireplace, became the kitchen. The old trading post section became the family parlor. The roof and the rafters of the old cabin were removed so the ceilings could be raised to ten feet, in keeping with the rest of the structure, and with nine-foot ceilings on the second floor. In front of the family parlor was another room, the "good parlor" for company, and then a hall with a private front door for family that led out the front to the trail, and with a C-shaped walnut staircase leading to the four family bedrooms above.

Beside the kitchen were the workrooms any busy tavern needed. There was a larder for food storage, a scullery that had two zinc dry sinks for prep work, a storeroom for dry goods and a pantry to store dishes, which also had a zinc dry sink for cleaning up. A back stairway led to the guest rooms above. Along the front of the building, they had a public dining room and a large parlor for guests. Then the reception hall, with the front desk, a hallway leading back to the two large guest bedrooms and two suites, and a wide staircase that swept up to the ten small guest bedrooms.

Spicer's Mill sawed forty foot long maple boards, three feet wide for the floors downstairs, and white ash for the bedrooms upstairs. The walls would someday be plastered, but for now, horizontal basswood boards were nailed to the post and beam walls with square nails. Doors and windows were built by hand, but most of the windows only had wooden shutters, and the inside doors had blankets covering them for privacy. Windows panes were the most expensive article in buildings since glass had to be shipped from the east coast.

Olive wanted the woodwork to be in simple ash, nothing fancy. Elmer argued that the woodwork in the public rooms needed to be nice, and wanted walnut and cherry. The outside was covered with wooden lap siding and roofed with cedar shakes. Fireplaces were in all the major rooms. Even in these primitive conditions, it wasn't unusual to have fifteen to twenty paying guests at night. After living in a covered wagon, riding a mule for days on end, or floating down river in a flat-bottomed scull, the tavern was a haven in the wilderness.

Most people had no hard cash with which to pay. With the banks failing, it was hard times. Guests either bartered or promised to work to pay for their room and board. Some just spent a night or two as they were passing through; others stayed at the tavern until their homes in the settlement or township were completed.

Benjamin Knight built a store and warehouse in what was becoming the center of settlement, north of the tavern, and C. C. Darling had put up a small trading post to sell supplies and whiskey south of them. Elmer was working hard on the grist mill that Spicer was building at the mouth of Spring Brook; it should be up and running by fall. The huge millstones had been delivered and were piled up across from the tavern.

Olive and Simon decided to do away with the trading post business and concentrate instead on the tavern and livery stable. Olive hired local Chippewa women to help in the tavern, and Simon trained the men to work at the blacksmith and livery. A slab shanty had been built across from the Native Camp, and Gray Dove taught all the local children there. It was about eighteen-feet by twenty-four feet. Holes cut into the walls were hung with oiled paper to let a little light in. A fireplace provided the heat. Slabs of wood on legs were constructed for desks and chairs.

At this time on the frontier, it was normal to have around three to four months of school out of the year. As children worked on the farms, school was taught at the times when the children were not needed as much. Starting in late November or early December and running until the first good spring weather.

Most of the Indian families had, by this time, built themselves small cabins to live in. The number of pioneers had slowed with the bank failures, but people were still coming through. These were better educated and more business-minded than those who had come before.

Wolf Jaw, husband of River Woman and second husband of Cloud Woman, went to the Great Spirit in the early spring, after never fully recovering from his bout of lung fever. The Chatfield boys built Wolf Jaw a small cabin, thinking that a fireplace, instead of the open fire in the center of their wigwam, would help the old warrior breathe. Nothing helped. His wives knew that with the changing of their way of life, the old warrior did not cherish life any longer.

The boys were all living at the tavern and called it their home. Elmer and Harriet bought 80 acres out past Motown, very reasonable because most of it was a huge, snake-inhabited, cedar and tamarack swamp that only the lynx called home.

Elmer wanted the trees for the lumber and roof shakes. Cedar and tamarack wood resisted rot, and he thought the lumber would come in useful in building around the rivers. He never planned on building a house out there as it was seven miles from town. It would take all day to travel to town and back.

Joshua and Hannah bought 80 acres a few miles to the south of Spicer's Mill and he had already started cutting lumber for his house and barn. He hoped to have his family moved in by fall. He still helped his brother in the building trade and Hannah helped as she could at the tavern. She was expecting their next child by the end of summer. Joshua had always wanted to try his hand at farming and had purchased some nice rolling land that drained well.

CHAPTER 29

THE PATRIOT WAR

The great Patriot War of Canada started in the fall of 1837 when citizens of Canada decided to throw off the iron yoke of British rule. Canadian Patriots stole the US steamship, The Caroline, to smuggle arms to Naval Island in the Niagara River in December of 1837. The British Navy intercepted the ship, killing one black American seaman, Amos Durfee. Then they set the ship afire and sent it over the Niagara Falls.

December 29, 1837- "Gentlemen! Gentlemen! If I can have your attention, please! Gentlemen! Please quiet down!" Mr. Henry Hendy and Dr. Edward Theller were in Detroit giving speeches to raise arms and men for the Canadian Cause. Glyn was in Detroit to see Madelaine's family. They wrote and invited him for the holidays, and to sign some legal papers that Jean-Luc had sent from Texas. One of Jean-Luc's younger brothers, Adrian, had invited Glyn to go to the meeting with him. It was held at the large Opera House.

Afterward, they went to a tavern to eat and drink. Jean-Luc's brother was interested in signing up. At first, Glyn was skeptical, but after a few more drinks, he got more enthused. By the next morning, Glyn and Adrian were signed up with the Counsel of War, formed by Judge Orange Butler, a member of the Michigan House of Representative.

Men from all over the northeastern United States came to serve. The first mission was to raid the Detroit Jail and steal four hundred muskets, then the Office of the US Marshall for two hundred more. Then they sailed on the schooner Ann to Fort Malden in Amherstburg, Canada.

January 8, 1838- "I can't believe I'm doing this, I have a little boy back home. I should be there with him. Not running from the Brits." said Glyn, while rowing a boat on the cold, rough lake.

Their ship, Ann, after being chased by the British, ran aground and beached. Glyn, along with Adrian and a handful of lucky sailors, escaped in a rowboat, the rest of the crew were captured.

February 24, 1838- "Soon as we get to shore, I'm taking you home. Then I'm going back where I belong, out in the backwoods, not out here on the lake, escaping from the US military."

"Come on Glyn; we almost made it to Fighting Island this time. If the US Navy hadn't shown up, we would have run the Brits out. I don't know why the US government doesn't want us fighting with the Patriots. Wasn't that long ago they were fighting with the British over Michigan. Wonder what the Navy will do with four hundred prisoners. They won't hang them, will they?"

"No, they will have to sign a paper saying they will go home and not fight anymore. If they catch the leaders, now that will be a different story. They probably will be handed over to the British and hanged for treason."

February 27, 1838- "I told you, after this, we are going home," said Glyn to Adrian as they sailed from Watertown, New York, heading to Hickory Island.

"We won't lose this time, you just wait and see. General vanRensselaer is the best general we have. We're meeting up with another regiment, and marching to Quebec. This will be the largest battle to date. We'll show the Brits. They ran the French out once, but we're going to show them this time. We will run them back across the sea."

March 3, 1838- "I'm telling you, Glyn, if the generals hadn't disagreed on strategies and disbanded our units, the war would be over by now. All we need to do is be more like a single fighting force, and quit squabbling among ourselves. This is the one; I know it will be. I heard the generals planning this morning. We're going to Pelee Island in Lake Erie. The Brits have no idea we're coming. We'll capture the island, and use that as our base of command.

"Oh crap, are those US. battleships heading this way?"

April 29, 1838- "I told you that if we ever got out of that brig alive, I was taking you home, no more excuses. I was in jail with your brother down in Texas. Never wanted to go through that again. At least this time, we got food and water."

"Ah, come on Glyn, it was only for a month. They let us out and told us to go home. Feel sorry for the Canadians being handed over to the British Navy; those men may never see daylight again. Now, the plan is, we are going to dress up like Indians like they did at the Boston Tea Party. We take over the steamship, and sail it back to headquarters."

"Have they told you where headquarters is yet?"

"No, haven't told me. Probably in case some of us are captured."

"If we sail anywhere near Detroit, we're getting off, and I'm taking you home. I'm going to tell your Mother and Father that I'm no longer responsible for you, and I'm going home. Should have been home months ago. Frankie is going to be all grown up by the time I get back. I sure hope Mother and Gray Dove are taking good care of him. He must look like your family. He doesn't look like Madelaine, or me, at least not yet. Maybe he will as he gets older."

"OK, this is it, this is Wells Island. You got your Indian paint on? Good," said Adrian. "There should be only a skeleton crew on board. Just the one ship, in for routine maintenance. The crew is on shore leave. The other ships are out to sea."

"Why did I let you talk me into this?"

Twenty men, dressed as Indian fighters, were able to board the ship easily. They roused the crew from sleep and marched them off the ship with muskets pointing at their heads. Empty storage sheds were used to imprison the sailors. After they had been tied up and gagged, the doors were chained shut. The Patriots were able to walk on board, ready to cast off. They brought several ex-Navy men with them to operate and sail the steamship.

"We have a problem, Glyn. The boilers are apart, below deck. No way to fire them up. Maintenance crews have been working on them. They are inoperable. We have been told to abandon the ship and go home. Nothing more we can do. We did capture the crew!"

"There is no way that this is going to be a failure. I am not going home like this! Where is General McLeod? I have a plan. We set it afire, right here at dock-side. If we're lucky, not only the ship but the docks will burn, too. It'll cause the Brits a big mess. They won't be able to use the island as a port anymore. We'll go home and tell everyone that was our plan from the beginning. We may not be heroes, but at least we will be able to hold our heads up. And we have the British sailors as our prisoners."

The one big success of the Patriot War was when a group of men disguised as Native Americans boarded the British Steamer, Sir Robert

Peel, at Wells Island and set it afire.

Although Glen went home after burning the Sir Robert Peele, the last battle wasn't fought until the Battle of Winston, on December 4, 1838, which the Patriots lost after capturing the steamer Thames and setting it afire. In the end, 93 Americans and 58 Canadians were taken prisoner by the Brits and transported to a penal colony in Australia. Four Patriot leaders, Lucius Bierce, EJ Roberts, Thomas Jefferson Sutherland, and Dr. Theller all escaped to Detroit, then went on to settle in the interior of Michigan.

In 1842, the US Secretary of State, Daniel Webster, signed the Webster-Ashburton Treaty with Great Britain, bringing hostility between the two countries to an end for the last time.

CHAPTER 30

Reverend Johnston

One morning as Amos Spicer and Benjamin Knight were eating breakfast in the tavern's dining room, Chief O-Ke-Monse walked in with a young man, went over and sat at their table.

"This man here is the new preacher at the Shimnecon," said O-Ke-Monse. "He wants to build a church in the village and needs lumber." Shimnecon, or "Peaceful Valley" was an Indian village thirty miles or so downstream from their summer camp on the Cedar River, by a large bend in the O Washtenong River.

The young man, still standing, reached over to shake hands. "How do you do? My name is Reverend Stanley Johnston, and as the Chief here said, I'm the new preacher at the Indian church in Shimnecon."

"Hello, I'm Amos Spicer, and this is Ben Knight. Pull up a chair and tell us what we can do for you."

Gray Dove walked up with a coffee pot. "Hello Uncle, would you like some coffee? And something to eat?"

O-Ke-Monse said, "This is my niece, Gray Dove. This is the new preacher at the Shimnecon church, Stanley Johnston. Yes, I am hunger. We just paddled all the way from the summer camp. Give me lots to eat!"

"Oh, Uncle. I never knew when you were not hungry. Here is a cup of coffee for you and your friend. And it's nice to meet you, Reverend Johnston. I'll go and get you both a big plate of grits with some ham and gravy, and a some of Olive's biscuits."

Gray Dove, helping out on a Saturday, turned and left, her head held high, her back straight, and her hair in a single braid that she had coiled on her head, under her bonnet.

"My Lord, who was that enchanting being? I've never seen a more lovely creature," said Reverend Johnston. "That woman is an Indian? I don't believe it. She is a good head taller than you are Chief."

"Her grandmother's clan always took up with the Frenchman. My clan always stayed true and married only our own, never took up with the French."

Spicer and Knight both looked at each other and smiled. Everyone had heard stories about the lusty Chief.

"Well, gentlemen, why don't we get back to business," said Spicer. "There must be some reason for the two of you to came all this way?"

"Yes, as the Chief has said, we are building a new church. The long house we are using now is old and needs to be replaced. We have been to see the owner of the sawmill at the river along the ledges. His price is quite high, and so we came to see you, to see if we can make a bargain. This is for a church, a very worthy cause." said Johnston.

Knight said, "Well gentlemen, it's been a pleasure, but I need to get back to my store. Rev. Johnston, good luck trying to deal with this man. He's been known to squeeze a penny twice before letting go." Knight was still laughing as he left.

After they had talked for a time, they settled on a price for a certain amount of board feet of lumber, and then Spicer left. Gray Dove came in from the kitchen to pick up the last of the dishes.

"Do you work here every day?" Johnston wanted to know.

"No, I used to. When I first came here, I helped out wherever I could. When Mrs. Chatfield found out I attended classes at the missionary school at Mackinac Island, she asked me to help with the children. She was teaching them herself, as well as running the old trading post.

"We were finally able to build a small school house, down by the Camp. It's just a small slab shack for now, good enough for us. We are hoping to receive financing from the state to build a better schoolhouse. Since Mrs. Chatfield is very busy here, she asked me to take over teaching the children. They pay me $2.25 a month, but I would do it for nothing, I love teaching the children. We don't hold school on Saturday or Sunday, so I come here to help out if I'm needed."

"Tell me," asked Johnston. "Do you work all day here, or are you free for supper?"

O-Ke-Monse went to the camp to talk with friends and family. Someone always asked him to stay the night, and they would go back to their village in the morning. Johnston made supper plans with Gray Dove. He would meet her in the dining room at seven, after the supper crowd. He walked in just as the mantel clock struck seven. Gray Dove was already sitting at a table near the back. She was able to look at him closely as he walked up.

He was just about her height, but he was wearing boots with heels. He did not have the muscle tone of a man who had done physical labor every day. He was narrow through the shoulders and wide in the hips. His short, dirty blond hair was greased back, which showed a receding hairline. He was near-sighted, so even with glasses on, his watery blue eyes seemed to bulge out slightly. He smiled when he saw her. His lips were thin and seemed to disappear, which showed off his tobacco-stained, crooked teeth. But he could talk an ear off; he was a preacher after all.

In the family parlor, Glyn and Simon were reading books. Glyn had Frankie on his lap; Simon had Sarah. Sarah loved being read to every night, and she was full of questions. Frankie just liked sitting on his father's lap. The two youngest boys, Joseph and James, were studying their lessons as well. Tomorrow was the Sabbath when only the Bible could be read.

Simon said, "I thought Gray Dove would be here tonight, I saw her in the kitchen. But I saw O-Ke-Monse earlier, too. Maybe she's visiting with her family tonight."

"No," said Olive. "She is still in the dining room. She told me that a preacher man from Shimnecon had asked her to supper. She said she would wash up afterward. I thought it was nice for her to see someone other than us all the time. Her people are used to traveling every season and go to festivals, pow-wows, where they meet up with family and different tribes. They don't have that anymore."

"Wonder what she is seeing a preacher man for?" said Glyn. "She's the one always preaching to me to spend more time with Frankie before he grows up."

"I don't rightly know. She told me the preacher, a Rev. Johnston, came with the Chief today to buy lumber from Amos Spicer for a new church at Shimnecon. He then asked her to supper. I think that was sweet."

Glyn said, "Good way to get a free supper if you ask me. He's probably tired of eating Indian stew all the time. What do you say we go over and meet this preacher man?"

"No, Glyn," said Olive. "If she wants to bring him over to meet us, she will. Otherwise, leave them alone. If she needed a chaperone, O-Ke-Monse or Cloud would be there."

"Alright, I don't have the time to go visiting with a preacher man anyway. So, Father, you want to read first tonight, or do want me to?" Glyn said, a little brusquely.

Simon looked over and gave Olive a knowing smile. "Why don't you go first."

CHAPTER 31
THE FALL DANCE

It was late in the fall. The farmers had their crops in. There had been several husking bees in the neighborhood. Glyn went to a couple of them. If a person found a red cob of corn, they could choose someone to kiss. He noticed that the young men always gave their kisses to Gray Dove, to the chagrin of the other young ladies.

Simon and Olive decided to have a dance at the tavern for everyone in and around the county. Back East, it was a tradition to celebrate the end of harvest season. They had several men lined up to play the fiddle. Even Simon and Glyn would play a little. The night of the Harvest Celebration, Gray Dove had the school children come in and decorate it with paper chains hanging from the tables and walls. The center of the dining room was cleared out for dancing, the tables all pushed to the walls. The women cooked all day and the tables groaned under the weight of food.

Glyn wanted the first dance with Gray Dove. When the music started, he began to look for her. He found Chief O-Ke-Monse and Cloud with several other Natives in a corner watching and asked if they knew where Gray Dove was. They pointed her out on the dance floor.

She looked ravishing, a vision of gray and green. Her black hair shone in the candlelight, her dark eyes sparkled. The simple dress would have looked plain on another woman, but on Gray Dove's tall, slender form, it was as fashionable as a Worth gown from Paris. Glyn couldn't tear his eyes away. Until he saw whom she was dancing with. Glyn never got on with the Reverend Johnston. There was something about him; Glyn didn't know what, that reminded him of something slimy, like a snake from the swamp. The Reverend had made a habit of coming to the tavern every couple of weeks to have supper with Gray Dove. He said he was checking on his lumber. He talked to Gray Dove about the people in Shimnecon and his sermons, and the different parishes where he had served.

Olive had helped Gray Dove cut the pattern and sew the dress. She had never been to a white man's dance before. Olive thought the style would probably be out of date back east, but here on the frontier, she would be the best-dressed girl on the floor. Gray Dove had wanted to keep the dress a secret until the night of the dance, in case she lost her nerve to come. She still did not feel entirely comfortable socializing with white people she did not know.

Olive, along with Hannah and Harriett, had helped Gray Dove sew the dress of soft gray and dark green stripe. Hemlines of skirts were longer now; they came to the floor. Dresses were tightly corseted, with large sleeve puffs. The hairstyle was for elaborate chignons, but Gray Dove chose to wear hers in a simple braided coil. They also taught Gray Dove the popular dances. Although the scandalous waltz was all the rage on the East Coast, the gallop, and the polka would be danced here tonight.

Gray Dove had all the young men, and some of the older ones, waiting to dance with her. She thought it felt good to be the center of attention, something she had not experienced before. But all she wanted was for Glyn to ask her to dance.

Every time she was free, she turned around to find Glyn, and the Reverend would be there at her side. She finally saw Glyn. He was playing the fiddle with the other men, but she noticed he watched her constantly. She did not know how to decline a dance without seeming rude, so she stayed on the dance floor all night. And Glyn kept playing the fiddle.

When the dancing was over, Gray Dove's feet ached. She tried to find Glyn, but to no avail. Supper was served, and when she wanted to help the other women, they told her no, she was in demand at the table. Again she tried to find Glyn, but he seemed to have disappeared. The good Reverend stayed by her side.

Finally, it was time to leave. Gray Dove wanted to go back to her cabin, kick her shoes off and get out of the corset she had borrowed. Reverend Johnston was at her side.

"Please allow me to escort you home, Miss. I have had the best time tonight."

"All right, since you are staying at the Camp tonight, too, with the

Chief. We can walk together."

Gray Dove was so disappointed. She had sewn the dress especially for Glyn, and she felt he ignored her all night. So if this Reverend Johnston wanted to court her like a proper lady, why not?

"Well Stanley, what are you waiting for. Let's go back to the Camp," Gray Dove said, smiling.

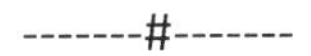

As the dance ended and supper commenced, Glyn still felt bereft. Everything that mattered to him in his life was in shambles. The death of Magdelaine had left his soul shattered. Gray Dove made him feel whole again. Being around her every day felt most natural. Why did he not show her more of how he felt? Why did he not tell her how much he appreciated all she did for Frankie?

Whenever Frankie fussed so much that even Olive was unable to quiet him down, all Gray Dove had to do was to pick him up and sing one of her Indian lullabies, and Frankie would settle down and usually go to sleep. When he thought of Gray Dove in a romantic way, Madelaine's memory was always there, casting a dark shadow over him.

He had made his mind up things would be different at the dance. He would face his devil. He could no longer let the guilt he felt over Magdelaine rule his life. If he didn't act tonight, it might just be too late. He had been sitting in his room, not wanting to talk to or see anyone. Frankie was with him, sleeping in the crib that he had made for him. Glyn got up and went downstairs.

He walked into the chaotic kitchen, "Mother, have you seen Gray Dove?"

"Not since we finished eating. I hope you complimented her on her dress. She worked a long time on it. Always, 'You think Glyn will like this, You think Glyn will like that.' Glad this party is over. I'm about tuckered out. Come to think of it; I never saw you dance with her. Now, you go find her and take her home. She must be dead on her feet."

Glyn walked out and through to the dining room. Not seeing her there, he walked into the big guest parlor where people congregated in small groups. O-Ke-Monse was holding court in one corner, telling war stories to a few young men.

"Chief, I'm looking for Gray Dove, to take her back to her cabin, have you seen her?"

"You're too late for that. The Reverend Stanley, that little sniveling excuse for a man, left with her. Did you know, he promised to pay for that lumber for his church he ordered two months ago? Said he had the money from donations from his big church back in the East where he and his wife lived. He has never paid for it. Tonight he said he now wants the tribe to beg money for it from the white men around here. No new church this year. The one we have is good enough, I always said."

The chief was still talking, but Glyn had turned and run out of the door. He had a sick feeling in the pit of his stomach. He ran down the trail towards the camp.

-------#-------

Gray Dove had pulled her cape and bonnet on. It was a cool night. Almost to the camp, she stumbled over a rut in the trail, and the Reverend grabbed her elbow to steady her and held on.

"Careful, wouldn't want you to fall now, and ruin that pretty dress of yours."

"Thank you, Stanley, but you can let go. I am all right now."

Stanley put his arm around her. "Now you know that I'm pretty drawn to you, Gray Dove. Don't go playing all coy on me, like some proper white woman. You've been giving me hints all night. Now give me what you know we both want. Give me a little sugar, Indian bitch!"

The Reverend jerked her to him and wrapped her in a bear hug, trying to kiss her. She screamed. There had not been anything alcoholic to drink tonight, but Gray Dove could smell whiskey on his putrid breath. He must have brought a flask of his own. She kneed him in the groin and pushed him away. The Reverend seemed to jerk backward as he held hold of the shoulders of her dress, ripping the bodice. Gray Dove never looked back. She kicked her shoes off, picked up the hem of her ruined dress, and ran like a streak to her cabin. She ran in and slammed the door shut. Cloud and Rain were sitting by the fire, gossiping about the nights' festivities.

Cloud and Rain, both startled, rose up and rushed over. "What happened? You get chased by a bear or a wolf? Your pretty dress is ripped. What happened, child?"

"That new reverend! He attacked me! He tore my dress! I kneed him in the groin and ran!" Gray Dove choked out the words. She was breathing heavily; the corset was still tightly binding her, making it hard to take a deep breath. Tears ran down her cheeks. Not in fear, but in frustration of a special night ruined.

Rain walked over to the fireplace and picked up two large butchering knives. She handed one to Cloud. "Stay here," she said to Gray Dove.

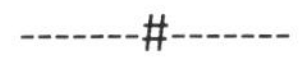

As Glyn ran down the trail, he could see two figures ahead. Then he heard shouting. He reached them just as Johnston reeled back. Glyn grabbed him by the shoulder and spun him around. He heard fabric rip; Johnston's glasses flew off. Glyn gave a good left hook to his opponents' face. He saw a flash of Gray Dove as she turned and ran and he was happy. Johnston went down on his knees, but grabbed Glyn by the legs and threw him to the ground backward, knocking the wind out of him. Johnston was standing over Glyn as he pulled a knife out of his boot.

"You're not so tough now. Bushwhacking me from behind. I'm going to carve you up and feed you to the bears. Then I'm going to have that Injun squaw that thinks she a white woman, and after that, I'm going to feed her to the wolves," hissed Johnston as blood dripped from his nose.

Glyn laughed, "You're such a poor excuse for a man." Quickly he lifted both legs and kicked Johnston in the stomach, knocking backward. Glyn jumped up as Johnston stumbled, regained his balance, and came charging forward, his knife held in front of him.

Both were hunched over in the traditional fighting pose, circling each other like a wolf circling a wounded bear. Johnston lunged with his knife. Glyn ducked, then lightning fast, grabbed Johnston's arm while tripping him. Johnston fell on his hands and knees. Glyn kicked him in the buttocks, which flattened Johnston to the ground. Johnston rolled over as Glyn jumped on top of him and grabbed the arm holding the knife. Using a trick picked up from the Indians, Glyn pressed on a nerve in the arm that paralyzed the hand, and the knife dropped harmlessly to the ground. Johnston punched Glyn in the face and rolled on top. He got a few punches in, then with both hands, tried to strangle Glyn. Glyn blocked most of the punches, then returned with a kidney punch, and managed to sock Johnston in the right temple. Johnston tumbled to the left. Now Glyn was on top. After a couple more punches, Johnston lay in a daze.

Glyn tried to stand, several hands reached out to help. He looked around, confused. The grandmothers were both standing there, holding knives, as was the Chief, holding his tomahawk. Gray Dove stepped out from behind the grandmothers. She had hastily slipped on her buckskin dress. She slid her hunting knife back into her belt.

"Come, lean on me. We'll get you to the cabin."

"What about this piece of crap?" asked Glyn, through swollen lips.

"I will take care of him. I am the one who brought this plague to our Camp," said the Chief.

Johnston was never seen again.

PART V - 1839

CHAPTER 32

Glyn was dreaming of dancing with Magdelaine in the hall of her parents' home. She wore the same ball gown she was wearing on their wedding day. But then, they were no longer dancing in the Marcotte home. They were in the dark woods and stood in a stream of water. Wet black hair glistened in a moonbeam against naked skin, water dripped from bared breast, slowly sliding down long dusty legs...

Glyn woke with a start. After a night of drinking corn whiskey and gambling with the men who worked in the settlement, he wished whoever was beating the drum inside his head would stop. His stomach felt on fire. He had been asleep on the filthy ground, and someone had thrown a flea infected bear robe over him as he lay beside a smoldering fire. He must have passed out as he couldn't remember what day it was, or how long he had been here. He still had his clothes on and boots on his feet, so he must not have done too bad at gambling.

It was dark, but he knew where he was, even if he couldn't remember how he got there. The old Indian longhouse at the Camp. It smelled like some men relieved themselves against the walls, too drunk to make it outside. Families had long since moved out into cabins of their own. Only a few young men and those old men with no families, both white and Native American, stayed there. Every night, the drinking and gambling went on. Loose women came and went. The women of the Camp threatened to burn the place.

Glyn needed to relieve himself. He needed to go home. He needed to wash and shave, and take care of his son. His mother was looking after Frankie. He and Sarah shared a bedroom. Olive looked after

Frankie like one of her own. Glyn tried to be there as much as possible, to milk the goat and to feed and change Frankie when he could.

He stumbled around the long house, tripped over dogs that growled and men who cursed until he found a doorway to the outside. It was still winter, though spring was not far off. The air still had a cold sting to it. The sun was not yet up. A false dawn lit the southeastern sky, light enough to make his way to a cluster of bushes and stunted trees to answer the call of nature.

On his way back, Gray Dove was suddenly in front of him; anger burned in her eyes. “Why are you not home with Frankie? Your mother works hard all day. You need to be there more to help her with your son. I have watched you. You drink every night, gamble away all your money. That will not bring your dead wife back! You have a son to look after.”

Glyn bent over, clutched his burning stomach and vomited. He fell to his knees and was sick some more. Gray Dove was disgusted with him. She has seen before what whiskey can do to people's lives.

She turned to leave, picking her skirts up out of the mess. She needed to go to the school house to start a fire, to take the chill off the little shanty before her students came for class.

“Gray Dove, please don't leave. I know you are disgusted with me, and I'm sorry. I'm disgusted and ashamed of myself. I do appreciate all you do for Frankie.” She turned back to Glyn and saw the haunted and desperate look in his hollowed eyes. He tried to stand on shaky legs.

“Please understand, if I don't drink every night I can't sleep. I have nightmares. I walk the floor. I come here to forget. Don't you understand? I killed my wife by not being there. I killed my son's mother, my Magdelaine!”

Once more he sank to his knees in front of Gray Dove, hot tears ran down his cheeks, making rivulets through the greasy dirt and stubble that covered his face. He was shaking. Gray Dove couldn't tell if it was from his weeping, the whiskey, or the cold. She helped him stand, put her arm around him and took him to her cabin. Once inside, she called Cloud to bring hot herbal tea. She eased Glyn down on a blanket in front of the fire.

“Grandmother, watch over Glyn. He has the whiskey disease and has been sick. He's been staying at the longhouse again. I'm going to burn that vile place! See what you can do for him.”

Gray Dove knew exactly what needed to be done for Glyn. She went out to find the old wigwam that her uncle, Chief O-Ke-Monse, slept in. He had arrived the day before from his village, Shimnecon. He and his family came to help with the sugar bush. The cooking fire in front of his wigwam was burning bright, a sign that the family was up. She ducked through the doorway and found them around the small fire inside, eating their morning meal.

"Good morning, Uncle. Please come to my Grandmother's cabin. Glyn is there and is sick. He blames himself for his wife's death. He tries to drink away his demons every night. He has a little boy to raise, if his self-loathing doesn't kill him. Please come and help him. He is a good man, even if he is an American."

"My daughter, you are distressed. Are you sure you are not the one that is sick, maybe love sickness?" O-Ke-Monse laughed. "I know about Glyn, Simon's son. Simon talked to me about him when I was here last. He was worried about him then. He must be worse. I will come. There are a few things I must prepare first. You go and wait at your Grandmother's. I will be there."

Gray Dove went back to the cabin. River and Cloud Woman had cleaned Glyn up a bit, dosed him with herbal tea to settle his stomach and had left him to sleep. Cloud said that she and River would go up to the tavern and tell his family not to worry, that Glyn was with the Chief and would be home when he was better. They left, and O-Ke-Monse arrived with his medicine pouch. He told Gray Dove to go, that he would look after Glyn.

She went to the school. The children had already started the fire and filled the water bucket by this time and were outside playing. She called to them to come in and start their lessons.

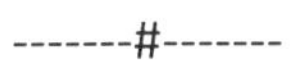

Two weeks passed before a thin and pale Glyn showed up at the tavern. O-Ke-Monse had taken him to stay in a sweat lodge, with nothing but water and teas to drink. A special herb blend burned continuously in the lodge. His head felt clearer. The alcohol poison had been leeched from his body. He thought that he could finally find a path for his life to follow. He had finally, for the last time, put Magdelaine to rest. The chief had stayed with him the whole time and with his help, Glyn had excised her ghost from his soul.

He walked in as the family was sitting down at the dinner table. After greeting everyone, Glyn sat but merely pushed his food around on his plate, still having no appetite. Afterward, they all sat in the parlor.

Sarah looked through an old picture book with Simon, and the two young boys played a game of jacks.

Glyn had Frankie on his lap. "I've missed you so much, little Count. I do believe you've grown."

"Why do you always call him your little Count?" asked Sarah.

"Jean-Luc's nickname for him. I don't remember why we started calling him that. The name just stuck." He turned to his father. "I have decided to study law, the way you did. I want to be able to help people, maybe go into politics."

Simon was taken aback. "What's put this notion into your head? I went to Yale and studied before being accepted at the Litchfield Law School. It would have been another 14 months of study. I only went for about a year before dropping out and going into the military. But if I had finished, I still would have had to clerk with a lawyer. Then read law for a couple of years before taking the bar exam to get a license to practice."

"I know that I will never be able to go back to school the way you did, Father. But you have already taught me so much about what you learned at Yale. I want to study your notes that you have in those bound leather volumes you have kept all these years."

"I kept those volumes in case I ever would need to study up on the law again," said Simon. "They are based on Blackstone's Commentaries; they were the best at the time. I've been meaning to dust them off and catch up on some things. Why don't we start tomorrow night after supper? Hamlin and Knight have been after me to be more involved in local politics. We will see how you like it. Maybe after a year or so, you could go and clerk with a lawyer and then take your bar exam."

Simon knew that his son had been deeply troubled since returning from Texas. He had tried to help and guide him but wasn't able to stop his slide into an emotional hell. Maybe this would turn his attention to something that would soothe the loss of his wife. Simon always thought that helping others was the best way to forget one's own troubles. It would be tough for Glyn as he had never liked school that much, although he was bright enough when he put his mind to. Olive and Simon had always tried to teach all their children the love of learning. Maybe they had listened after all.

CHAPTER 33

Sarah

Sarah had four older nieces. And Frankie, her nephew, who was younger than she by a year or so. But he was still a baby. As she was now a big girl, she tagged along with the other big girls wherever they went. Henrietta was the oldest. They called her Henni. Sarah thought she was awfully bossy; that was probably because she was always put in charge, being the oldest. Henni's little sister was Mabel. Their parents were Sarah's eldest brother Elmer and his wife, Harriett. Brother Joshua and his wife Hannah's girls were Daisy and Rebecca, whom Sarah called Beck. She was closest to Sarah's age.

They all lived at the tavern. They had such fun playing in and around the big building, and its many rooms and staircases. They all had their chores to do in the mornings. After helping with breakfast, the beds of guests had to be stripped and remade; floors swept, and the furniture dusted.

Sarah would follow them to school in the little slab-shack down by the Indian Camp. Gray Dove, their teacher, didn't mind the youngest of children attending school. The Indians thought teaching should begin as soon as one could walk. She gave Sarah simple tasks to do. But Sarah was bright and a fast learner. She soon joined the older ones.

At recess, they played with a couple of Native boys who were about the same age as Henni and Daisy. The older students played stick ball and thought they were too young to play. So the younger children sat and watched, and played with their jacks or marbles. Red Feather and Owl had told the girls about hunting for morels the day before. The whole tribe had ventured out and found so many they needed several blankets to carry them all back.

"I bet if we went out, we could find lots, too." Red Feather told the girls. "I am real good at finding morels. You have to know just where to look for them. My father taught me."

"When we go home from school, we can look by the path to see if we can find some," said Henni. "Then we can take them home and have them at supper. Grandma will be surprised."

Sarah said, "Mummy told me to come home after school, not wander about."

"We'll look on the way home. It won't take any longer since Red knows where to look!"

Red Feather, boasting, said, "I am the best morel hunter around. I'll find us lots."

Gray Dove began ringing the school bell. All the children started running for the schoolhouse. One by one, everyone lined up and stopped to drink from the gourd cup kept by the birch bark water bucket; then they took their seats on blankets under the trees. It was the middle of May and the last few days had been warm and muggy. Gray Dove taught outside when she could. The light was so much better, and a cool breeze blew through the trees.

The last two hours went by quickly. Gray Dove released her students.

"Come on," cried Henni. "Don't dawdle. You all need to stay with us. We can use our dinner pails to carry all the morels home."

They looked and looked along the path and under the umbrella-shaped may-apples and found not a single morel.

"Red Feather, where are all the morels? You said you knew where they were," said Henni.

Red Feather was embarrassed. He had bragged about his morel hunting prowess, and they were coming up empty-handed. "I know! Lets' go over nearer the brook. Sometimes they grow along the river bank."

So they ran over to the brook and started looking. Daisy found one, then Mabel did, so they looked some more. They all began to find one or two, so they went farther along the brook, away from the settlement. It was exciting to see who would find the next morel, so they kept going. They came to a large tree which had fallen over the water.

Owl said, "Come on, let's go across. There are sure to be lots over there."

Sarah and Beck weren't so sure about crossing on a log, so they all held hands and passed over.

"You see that knoll over there," said Red. "I bet there are lots over there, so many we won't be able to carry them all home."

They reached the knoll and looked, but found nothing. Sarah saw some pretty wildflowers over on the next hill.

"We can't get over there. The swamp is full of water," said Owl. "We will have to go down that way, then circle around."

Off they all went on their merry adventure. After a time of exploring, picking wild flowers and finding pretty rocks, Beck said, "I'm getting hungry. Let's go home. Mommy will be looking for us."

They turned around and started back.

"Are you sure this is the way, Owl?" asked Henni, looking around. "I don't remember the land being so hilly. We should have turned around when we could still see the brook. I don't see it anywhere."

"Yes, if we go in a straight line, and we will come up on it. Should be right over that next hill," said Red Feather.

"Wait," said Owl, pointing, " there's a bear with cubs down in that ravine, coming this way. Come on; everyone stay close together. We'll circle around that hill, and come out behind them, then run to the brook. Never mess with a sow bear with cubs. Come on, let's go before she gets wind of us."

The children all ran. But either they ran the wrong way, or the bears turned around. When they ran around the hill and came out into the open, there were the bears. The old sow smelled the children, stood up on her hind legs and roared. She stood a good seven feet tall. She was old, her fur had a cinnamon tint, and the paws she waved in the air were at least a foot long, not counting her claws.

The children stood transfixed by the giant before them.

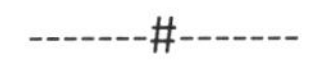

Back at the Forks, James and Joseph came home from school and went about their chores. Wood needed to be split, and pails of water hauled to the tavern. Harriett came out from the laundry.

"Have you boys seen where them girls have got off to? I haven't seen them, and they need to get home. I have sheets and towels to be carried upstairs to the linen closet. My goodness gracious, my feet are swelling up in this heat. Been on them all day, ironing. You two go find them. Tell 'em if they don't come home right now, I'm getting the switch out. They're probably down playing at the Camp. Go on, get to finding them!"

The boys went up the path to the Camp and asked around if anyone had seen the girls. No one had. Owl's mother came out of their cabin.

"Owl and Red Feather haven't been home since school either. They often play with the girls. Red's father went up to the school just now to look for them."

Storm, Red's father, came walking into Camp with Gray Dove.

"No one has seen them since school was let out," said Storm. He had got his name from his quick temper and the way his face would turn dark when he was angry, which he was.

Mani and Shing, the two boys who were best friends with James and Joseph and lived with their grandfather, came up to the group.

"We saw them after school. They were looking for something on the ground, and they all went down by the brook, then went upstream, to the south. I think they were looking for morels; I heard Red telling everyone about finding some yesterday."

"We can go find the ponies and go look for them," said Mani, who rode whenever he could, and was the best horseman of the boys.

Storm said, "You go find them and bring them home. They should not have taken the little girls out without telling anyone. Red is always running off. He thinks he is older than he is. He is going to be in trouble. The ponies are grazing over by the river. I heard their bells."

The four boys ran, found the bridles, then went down to the river to catch four ponies. The Indians always attached ropes, with bells, to their ponies' necks so that they could be easily found. Hearing pony bells was just one thing people took for granted on the Michigan frontier, along with stump pounders and the cry of the whip-poor-will.

The boys found and bridled their favorite ponies and took off down the trail. James and Joseph had no ponies of their own. They did ride the oxen sometimes, but riding the Indian ponies was a favorite pastime for them. As they cantered up the path, Glyn came riding down on his black mare.

"Heard the girls were missing. Anyone seen them?" asked Glyn as his horse skidded to a stop in a cloud of dust.

"Hello, Glyn! Yes, they were seen along Spring Brook. We're headed there now!" called James. "Come and help us. We'll cover more ground that way."

The boys liked their Uncle and loved spending time with him. All five of them galloped to the brook and started riding along side it, looking for clues. It didn't take long for them to find the trail.

"Look there! They crossed over the brook on that log," shouted Shing.

They found a place to cross the water, but they had to be careful. The brook was known for its muddy river bottom where a horse could easily be mired in the mud. But Mani and Shing soon found a safe place with a gravel bottom to cross. They trotted across and looked for more clues of where the children could be. The two Indian boys found the track in no time and led them to the hill and around to the ravine. Mani and Shing stopped.

"Look there," pointed Mani to the muddy trail. "A bear with cubs passed through here sometime recent. When a sow has cubs, she can be real nasty, especially this time of year when the cubs are so young. Keep your eyes open and hope she stays away. If she sees all of us, she should take her cubs and run, but you never know."

Just then they heard the scream of a little girl.

Glyn and the boys heard the scream, coming from just over the hill. Like a well-trained cavalry, they turned in unison and galloped up and over the hill.

The bear sensed danger to her cubs: the smell of humans. She reared up on her hind legs and roared out a warning. Then she came down on all four legs and reached out to grasp the closest obstacle in front of her before she turned to run, leading her cubs from danger.

Sarah screamed as the giant bear came down in front of her. Before she knew what was happening, the bear grabbed her by her skirt and petticoats and picked Sarah up like a rag doll in her huge mouth. Sarah looked up, and she could see the reddish looking eyes, glazed over in fear, and could feel the bear's breath on her face.

Red Feather, holding a walking stick in his hand, ran to the bear and smacked her in the head. The other children picked up stones and sticks, hurling them at the monster.

"Let go of her!" screamed Red Feather as he beat the bear over the head.

The bear reached out and swatted Red as if he were a pesky fly. Red tried to jump out of the way, but the bears' claw caught him on the shoulder and sent him spinning backward.

Glyn and the boys came riding over the hill at a full gallop. The boys yelled and hollered like braves on the War Path. Glyn had his rifle out and shot. The shot went wild and only grazed the bear's back.

The sound of the rifle, the sting on her back, and the sight of the horse and ponies rushing towards her and her cubs made the old sow roar with anger, dropping Sarah, forgotten, in the grass. The sow and her cubs ran off into the brush and trees, the old bear still roaring in fury.

Glyn rode over and jumped off his mare where Sarah lay, expecting the worst. She was curled up in the fetal position, with her arms protecting her face.

"Sarah! Sarah! My God, Sarah, talk to me!" screamed Glyn, picking her up in his arms. "Sarah, are you hurt bad? Tell me, how badly did that bear hurt you. Oh Sarah, talk to me!"

Sarah suddenly looked up into Glyn's' eyes and burst into tears, her little arms encircling his head.

Sobbing, Sarah said, "I'm not hurt. The bear had me by my skirts. I'm just scared. I wasn't at first. I just played dead. But now I'm so scared."

Sarah cried and cried. Glyn had tears of relief in his eyes, too, as he held onto Sarah, holding and rocking her until she stopped shaking and crying.

The other children crowded around, all talking at once. Glyn looked up and saw Red holding his shoulder, blood dripping through his fingers.

"James, Joseph, you boys come over here and hold on to Sarah until she quiets down. Is there anyone who was with you that is missing? Is everyone here that you started out with?" He handed Sarah over to the boys and went over to Red. The children looked around and nodded that yes, everyone was here.

"Looks like the bear got you. Does it hurt bad?" Glyn gently took Red and set him down on the grass. "Now let's take this shirt off and look at your shoulder. It'll be all right, there now. I got the shirt off. Now let's take a look at your shoulder. All I see are a couple of short, but deep cuts. Can you move your arm and shoulder without a lot of pain going down your arm?"

"I'm all right," Red said as he flexed his arm and shoulder. "That bear just nicked me with her claws. My arm don't hurt none, just where she got me. That's a lot of blood. Am I going to bleed to death?" Red asked in a low voice.

"No, you're not," said Glyn with authority. "This is a superficial wound, but they can bleed a lot at first. I'll wrap my shirt around it to stop the bleeding. When we get back to Camp, Cloud will fix you up in no time. Don't you worry.

"My father is going to be so mad at me. His face turns red, and he beats me with a switch unless I run away and stay with Cloud and Rain. If he has been drinking fire water, he won't listen to anyone. I try to tell myself to be brave and take the beating. But I'm afraid of him. More afraid of him than of the bear."

"You have my word that your father will not beat you for this. I am sure that he loves you very much. Now listen to me Red, I'm taking you home to Cloud. She will take care of you and see that your father is not angry.

"And the bear didn't hurt Sarah none either. The bear had Sarah by her dress, so she's fine, just shook up, like you are. Here, hold my shirt here, over the wound. I'm going to tear your shirt into strips, and I'll have you bandaged up and back home. I saw you charge that old bear. That was brave of you."

They rode back to Camp. Glyn carried Red and Sarah on his horse in front of him so he could hold on to them, and watch them for shock. The others all piggy-backed with the boys on their ponies. Glyn took Red and Sarah to Cloud's cabin and sent the rest home. Storm met them and gently lifted Red off the mare and carried him to Cloud.

Storm came back out to thank Glyn.

"Your boy was very brave. He tried to fight a bear off with a stick to save Sarah. I would be very proud to have him for a son. The other boys, Mani and Shing, were a great help, too. This could have turned out much different." Glyn lowered his voice, "Red told me you get drunk and beat him. If I ever hear of you beating that little boy again, I'll give you a beating you will never forget. If you want to fight, come to me and we will fight each other. But never lay a hand on him again. He is a good boy, and you should be proud of him. Go see O-Ke-Monse, he may be able to help you." Glyn reached down and gave Storm an Indian style handshake

Glyn took Sarah back to the settlement. Everyone came out and gathered around. The older children had already told their story of what had happened with them and the bear.

Olive ran over to Glyn as he rode up. He picked Sarah up and gently handed her down to Olive. Sarah burst out in new tears at the sight of her mother and wrapped her arms tightly around her mother's neck.

Glyn said, "She says she is fine. You should take her in and check her over good just to be sure. That bear had her picked right up in her mouth, but Sarah said she only had a hold of her dress. That was close. So close."

Later that night, as Olive was tucking Sarah into bed, Simon and Glyn came in to say goodnight. As they were turning to leave, Sarah said, "Do you know what the worst thing about today was?"

"No honey, what was the worst thing for you?"

"Well, it was pretty scary, the bear and all. And I was afraid the other kids would be hurt too. But the worst thing is, we left all our morels there. We didn't get to bring any home!"

CHAPTER 34

Red Feather

The next day at school, the children were lectured about going into the woods by themselves. By now, everyone had heard about the bear attack. Red Feather was treated like a hero for charging the bear and getting hurt. He was all smiles at first, but by the last recess, he asked Gray Dove if he could go home because he wasn't feeling well.

After school, Sarah asked the girls if they wanted to walk down to the Camp and visit Red. When they went to his cabin, no one was home. An old man sitting by a cooking fire said they were at Clouds' cabin. They went over. The door was open, and they were told to come in. Red Feather lay on the bed. His father, Storm stood by him.

Red had been stripped down to his breechcloth. River Woman was bathing him with cool water from the artesian spring. Cloud had removed the bandage and was applying a hot compress to the infected claw marks on his shoulder. The wounds were red, festering, and swollen. Red streaks ran down his arm. The children came over to the bedside.

"Red, what's wrong? Are you sick?" asked Hanni.

Red replied, "I don't feel very good. I'm awfully hot, then cold. My shoulder and arm feel like they are on fire. I think I want to sleep." Red closed his eyes.

Cloud said, "Red has bad medicine in the wounds from the bear. He is very sick. You girls go home. Red won't be well for a long time."

The girls took the trail and went home. There would be no morel hunting today. Sarah was very quiet, thinking about her friend Red.

When they were home, they were given chores to do, the best way of keeping children out of trouble. Sarah went to her mother.

"Mummy, I'm worried about Red. Cloud said he is very sick. I've never seen Cloud act so serious before. Can I go down and stay with Red for awhile? I can help Cloud and River take care of him.

"Storm is there, too. He scares me. He is always scowling. I feel bad that Red got hurt." Sarah started to cry silently.

Olive gathered Sarah up in her arms, "I don't know what you could do there, besides be in the way. Gray Dove is there to help, too, after school. And I'm sure if Cloud needed help, the whole tribe would be there, to offer any assistance.

"Why don't the both of us walk down to the Camp, and we'll ask Cloud if there is something you could do. Come on, dry those tears. Red Feather wouldn't want to see you so upset. He was brave yesterday, and you need to be brave for him, all right?" Olive knew Sarah was feeling guilt over the bear attack and was blaming herself for Red Feather's wound.

Sarah said that would be strong for Red Feather. Olive gathered up a few items in a basket she thought Cloud could use, clean cloth bandages, a pint of medicinal whiskey, a gallon jug of vinegar, and they set off. When they came to Clouds' cabin, more of the tribe had gathered outside. A cooking fire had been lit and someone had put fragrant herbs on it. The old men were drumming. The Native Americans were trying to adopt the ways of the white man, but many old customs lingered. A sick child brought out the whole tribe. Nothing was more serious to them than the welfare of their children.

Olive and Sarah went into the cabin. Red had a large compress on his shoulder, and he was covered with a blanket. Olive went over and gave Cloud the basket and asked about Red.

"He is in a bad way. His shoulder is full of poison, and it is traveling down his arm. I have done all I can. I sent for Chief O-Ke-Monse. He may know of something or of someone who could help. The arm might have to come off. Red is resting now. We have to wait. Is there any white man medicine that would help him?"

"I don't think so, but when I get back to the house, I'll send Glyn to find the closest doctor. Sarah wanted to stay here to help. I know she can't do much, but she wanted to be here for Red Feather." Olive knew that in cases of infection, very little could be done. The arm would have to come off, so the infection didn't travel into the rest of the body. Even then, the prognosis was not good.

Storm came up behind Olive and said, “Yes, I would like her to stay. It will be good for Red.”

So Sarah stayed.

CHAPTER 35
THE SWEAT LODGE

Glyn rode to Bellevue, then to Battle Creek to find a doctor. When the doctors found out it was for an Indian child, they all refused to come, saying they were too busy. When Chief O-Ke-Monse was found, he came right away and brought a healer from Shimnecon. The two of them conferred with Cloud Woman on a treatment. A Sweat Lodge would be constructed.

Sarah stayed that night, sleeping on the floor beside Red. She kept waking up to his delirious moaning. He ran a high fever. The women took turns watching over him, bathing him in the cool spring water.

In the morning, Red Feather was carried out to the Sweat Lodge. It was a wickiup, constructed with slender withes of aspen and willow, about ten feet in diameter and round in shape, with a pit dug in the center. Covered in bear hides, it had a pole in front about three paces in front of the entrance, which faced to the west. The pole had a bear skull on it. This stood in front of a fire where stones were being heated.

Men lined up at the entrance and were purified with a smudge of sweetgrass, cedar, and sage before crawling in, sun-wise, and seating themselves along the wall, cross-legged. Storm carried Red in as he was unconscious, and sat in the east, holding Red across his lap. Sarah stood outside watching until Storm motioned for her to follow him. Women, especially girls, were usually not permitted inside the sacred sweat lodge.

After everyone had been seated, Chief O-Ke-Monse closed the entrance flap, throwing the wickiup into darkness. Prayers for Red were said, and O-Ke-Monse passed around the scared Chanunpa, or medicine pipe, filled with a sacred tobacco and herb mix. Then the chief motioned for the fire-keepers to bring in the heated stones. They were dusted off with cedar branches first to cleanse them. Then they were put into the pit that had been dug, in a careful ceremony, east, west, south, and north. Each time a stone was brought in and placed in the pit, a gourd dipper of clean artesian spring water was slowly pored over it. The steam hissed and rose in the air. When the pit was filled, and the flap was shut, more spring water was pored over the hot stones.

The sweat lodge was dark. Sarah, sitting next to Storm and Red, could not see anything. It was hot. The steam was so thick she could hardly breathe. Men seated in the sacred circle said prayers and passed around the sacred Chanunpa. Sarah could hear the women outside, chanting and beating drums. Sarah closed her eyes. The heat of the steam, the smoke from the pipe, and the chanting and drumming from outside made her feel strangely weak and dizzy.

She felt herself slowly floating above the men in the Lodge, floating far away. She looked down and could see what looked like herself, only more grown up, in a class with boys about her age. They were gathered in a large circle, listening to a man in a suit, who had on a white apron. When she looked down, the man in the apron had a knife and was cutting open a little boy. A boy that looked like Red Feather!

That vision changed into one where she and other boys were seated together in a large room. They were dressed funny, all had on black robes and wore funny hats. They were being called to the front, one by one, and given a rolled up piece of paper. She looked for Red, but couldn't find him.

Then another scene appeared. She must be all grown up now, as she wore her hair like her mother, and had on a dirty gray dress. It looked like it had been white at one time. Now it was splattered in blood. She held a small saw in one hand, and a needle and thread in the other. She was in a tent, and tables were lined up, tables that stretched to eternity. The tables dripped with blood. There were men on the tables. Some of the men had holes in their bodies or their heads. Some were missing arms or legs. They all gushed blood. Blood covered everything. There could not be so much blood in the world. She looked down. She was standing in it, and the blood was slowly rising. Men kept carrying in more bodies, wheeling more tables in. She could hear explosions outside the tent, could see bullets as they tore through the fabric of the tent. A hand came up and grabbed her arm. It was Red, and he said, in Ojibwa, "Thank you, thank you, thank you." Then all was dark...

Sarah woke, the only light came from the fireplace. She looked around. She was sleeping on a bed in Cloud Woman's cabin. Red lay beside her. He had a large bandage on his shoulder but seemed to be sleeping quietly. She sat up and looked for Red's arm. It was still there. The swelling had gone down, and the red streaks were gone.

"Go back to sleep, Sarah. Red is through the worst. We think he will heal now. All the bad medicine from that bear is gone, from both of you." Gray Dove had been sitting up with the two children, watching over them during the night. Sarah crawled out of bed and went over to Gray Dove and climbed into her lap.

"I'm glad Red is going to be all right. I had dreams, really strange dreams like I was looking down at myself and Red."

Gray Dove hugged Sarah, "Sounds like you had a vision. Remember your visions always, if it wasn't important, you wouldn't have been given the gift."

Sarah and Gray Dove talked deep into the night.

The next morning, Red asked for something to eat, then complained that he had to stay in bed. He said he felt strong enough to walk around. Storm came and carried Red to a chair beside the table so he could eat. Afterward, he, Sarah, and Owl played jacks until Red said he was tired and wanted to lie down again. He soon fell asleep. Storm stayed with Red while Cloud took Sarah back to the tavern.

Later that night, as Olive was tucking Sarah into bed, Sarah said to her mother, "Gray Dove said I had a vision while I was in the sweat lodge with Red."

"Oh, how exciting. What was your vision about? Did you see yourself playing with all your friends?"

"No. I saw myself cutting open men and sewing them up. I think I'm going to be a healer, like Cloud!"

CHAPTER 36
END OF AN ERA

Business at the tavern slowed considerably. People were still coming into the state, but the flood of immigrants had declined with the worsening economy. Simon and Olive had a cash reserve on hand, so they were still in good shape financially. The same could not be said for many of the other homesteaders.

The windows were by now installed in the tavern for the coming winter, and so were the doors. Elmer installed fancy black walnut and cherry woodwork in all the public rooms and used the cheaper ash in the rest. He personally handcrafted the woodwork from premium heartwood he obtained from Amos Spicer. Everyone thought it breathtaking. More furniture was still needed, but they had enough to get by. The stable in back was finished and floored in the plentiful trash walnut that would last for years, with room for a couple milk cows and the goat.

Joshua and Hannah had moved into their new farmhouse in the summer. Hannah gave birth to a healthy little girl that autumn, but she wanted to stay close to Mother Olive for the winter months. The closest neighbor to their farm was three miles away. Joshua still helped his brother build new structures, but he was itching to start farming.

Elmer and Harriet still lived at the Eaton House. Elmer had staked a claim for two different lots in town, one on each side of the river. The people in the settlement had petitioned the state for funding to build a bridge across the Grand, but that had not yet been successful. Elmer and Harriet weren't sure which lot they wanted to build on. A lot would depend on the bridge. And there was no hurry the way the economy was. Besides, Olive loved having the grandchildren close by.

Simon and Glyn studied the volumes of Blackstone's Commentaries every night after supper. Most important in being a lawyer was speaking, so every night one would present an oral argument for or against a topic the other had chosen. Olive and Sarah would listen while they sewed or knitted, and would ask questions and decide if their arguments had merit. Sometimes Gray Dove would join them for supper and stay for the arguments.

One night in the early fall, Simon came into the tavern from doing the night chores and called Olive outside.

"Do you hear that commotion going on at the Indian Camp? What's going on up there? Is this one of their festivals? Never heard so much racket coming from them. Ever since someone burned down that long house, things have been quiet there."

Olive said, "Let's walk over and see. Maybe something is wrong. Cloud and River didn't say anything when they were here today."

When they reached the Camp, they could see the tribe was in deep distress. The women were crying, some men were seated in a circle in deep discussion, others were drumming and dancing. Gray Dove ran up to them, with tears in her eyes. "Have you heard the news? The army is at Marshall. This morning they went to Bellevue and Olivet and took all the Indian people from those Camps. They will be here in a day or two to remove all of us. We have to travel west, to the Mississippi. We were supposed to have land here, for farms and to hunt on. Men who said they were our chiefs signed treaties and took money. Now we all have to leave our homes. How will we live? Who will look after our dead? There are too few of us to fight the army any more. We have been living in peace with the Americans. Now we are being forced to move to a strange land to live beside our longtime enemies."

Gray Dove was crying, and Olive took her in her arms. "I don't know, but there has to be something we can do. When we go back to the settlement, we will see if the other people there will band with us and try to talk some sense into what the army wants to do. There must be some way that you all can stay here."

Gray Dove, talking through her tears, said. "We have lost so much. We never wanted anything from the Americans except to be left alone. You forced us to worship your gods, to live like you do; you never respected our way of life."

Gray Dove pointed to the setting sun, blood-red, resting on the treetops in the west. "I remember sitting on my grandmother's lap as a child, and she told stories about why the sun goes down every night and rises in the morning. I'll never be able to see the sun rise again in this very spot. They are ripping away our very spirit, everything we know and love, and yes, we love our land. Our people have lived here and called this home for a hundred generations. This land is who we are, it's where we were born, it's where we lay our dead. They are sending us to a strange land, with strange people we do not know. They are sending us to our deaths!"

Gray Dove turned and walked away with tears streaming down her high cheekbones, tall and proud, even though she knew this was the end of her life as she had always known it.

-------#-------

Simon and Olive raced back to the tavern. They sent James and Joseph out to all the houses, cabins, and shacks in the settlement to announce an emergency community meeting in the tavern's dining room at ten o'clock the next morning. Simon, Glyn, and Elmer rode out to the farms on the outskirts of the settlement to pass on the news about the meeting and about the Indians that were being forced off their land and moved west of the Mississippi.

A large crowd showed up the next morning, Olive and Harriett had pots of coffee ready, as well as rolls and biscuits on the table.

Simon stood and spoke after everyone quieted down. "I called everyone here today because the army is forcing the Indians to move west of the Mississippi. The Indians are very upset about having to go. This has always been their home. They have always been an asset to us. What can we do to keep them here?"

"Keep them here?" One farmer stood up. "I thought this meeting was about getting rid of them flea-bitten savages. Why one day when I was out in the field, and my wife was poorly, three squaws came into the house and demanded bread. When she told them she was sick and to leave, they cussed her out."

"Yes." Another man stood up. "I had a bushel of wheat, and three chickens come up missing. Someone said they seen a couple of those thieving bastards in the area that same day."

One person stood, "That's why no one comes here to settle like they used to. They see that God-awful Indian Camp at the edge of town. No one wants to live around them savages; you can't trust them. Why they look right in your eye and steal you blind. As bad as Gypsies."

One of the settlement founders stood up. "That's why we sent a petition to the Governor's office, to get rid of them low-life savages. You know they carry diseases. They need to either be moved or put down like a rabid dog. We all know that you and your Quaker family coddle them something awful. You even got one of them teaching our children. A savage, teaching our God-fearing children who-knows-what about their heathen ways. We just can't let this go on any further."

Glyn spoke up. "Think of all the good they have done. When we first came here, they helped my mother deliver her baby when she was by herself. They have helped all of us when we needed it. They are helping us build our town. They will become more like us, like all the other immigrants that come here, if we encourage them, and give them time. Besides, the treaties that were signed promised them land for farms and land to hunt on."

Someone else spoke out, "We don't need them anymore. They signed the treaties, got their money, now they need to go. We will all sleep better knowing we won't be scalped in the middle of the night by some drunken savage."

"Hear, hear!" A shout went up.

Simon could not believe what he was hearing. His friends and neighbors had begun a petition to send the Indians away. He had thought that with the Native Americans building cabins, and working alongside white men, they would be accepted into the community. Yes, at first he was prejudiced against them, too, but living in close proximity to them had taught him they were just as decent and kind as anyone he had met before. They were just different. As they all were.

Simon stood. "The meeting is over. I can see that all your minds are made up."

Everyone rose up to leave, crowding out the door and slapping each other on the back. A job well done. When most everyone had left, there were two or three men that came over and told Simon that they, too, felt like he did. That the Indians were an asset and they hated to see them go. Phineas Phelps' brother, Alpheus, told how his family would have starved to death the first year if the local Natives had not fed them. Another told how one of the women nursed his daughter after his wife died in childbirth.

Olive and Harriet came into the dining room to clear the tables. The noontime dinner guests would be arriving soon. Olive walked over to where Simon was standing. "I heard, now what are we going to do. Almost everyone wants the Indians gone. Why are they all so darn bull-headed and set in their ways? Most of them have worked side by side with the Indian men and have seen how hard-working they can be. Just because they're different, they hate them."

"Let's go down to the Camp and see what we can do," said Simon.

"I have to stay here. It's almost noon. Elmer will be bringing his work crew in for dinner. Neither Cloud nor River came in to help today and Harriet took the baby and children upstairs. Frankie is teething, and the others needed a nap. They've been snapping at each other like a bunch of tomcats!"

"I'll take Glyn, have you seen him?"

"No, I haven't."

The two young boys came running in with a catch of fish.

"See what we caught for you, Mother? You can fix fish for supper," said James.

Joseph said, "Yeah, been fishing all morning, and we divided the fish up between all us boys. They were really biting today! And we killed two massasaugas, too, but Billy took them home. He said his father is making a belt out of their hides for him."

Olive said, "What do you mean you've been fishing and killing snakes all morning! Why didn't you go to school like you were supposed to? Gray Dove is going to be mighty angry with you boys for skipping class, and so am I."

"But we went to school, and Gray Dove never came. We waited for an hour. When she didn't come, all us boys left to go fishing. The girls stayed at the school, said they would study by themselves. How dumb! So we thought we would do some fishing," James said as he proudly held up his fish, grinning.

Olive said to Simon, "This is not like Gray Dove. Something is wrong. And with Cloud and River not showing up; have you seen any of the Indians today? I haven't, come to think of it."

Elmer and Joshua came in the door, and Elmer thundered, "Here I was talking about how reliable the Indians are, and none of them showed up to work today. Left us terribly short- handed."

"No one has seen any Indians today. Something must be wrong," Simon told Elmer.

"You boys see anything of Glyn when you came in from fishing?"

"Yes, he was going down the trail to the Indian Camp. We hollered at him to show him our fish, but he was in such a hurry, he didn't even stop," said Joseph.

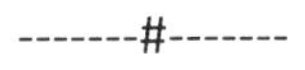

Glyn was full out running towards the Native Camp. The closer he got, the more he could feel that something was wrong. No smoke came from the cooking fires, no dogs barked, and no young children were shouting. When he realized during the meeting that the army was going to come for the Indians and that there was nothing he or his family could do, he knew he had to finally tell Gray Dove how he felt about her.

He arrived at the camp to find it was completely deserted. He had never felt a place that was so desolate. The campfires had gone cold, no meals were cooking, the doors hung open on the cabins, slowly swinging in the wind. There were no children laughing. No women singing Indian lullabies to babies in cradleboards or old men gambling under the trees. No thump, thump, thump of stump pounders grinding flour, or the luring music of the Indian flute. All he heard was the lonely wind blowing through the trees and the water of the rushing river.

Glyn ran over to check the cabin that Gray Dove shared with her grandmothers. Finding it just as empty as the rest of the Camp, he ran back towards the settlement. Olive and Simon were heading down the path to the Camp as Glyn came upon to them.

"They're gone. The Camp is abandoned! All the Indians have disappeared! I've got to find Gray Dove!" Glyn said, bent over with his hands on his knees, gasping for breath. "Mother, you talk to the grandmothers every day. Where would they go?"

Olive tried to think, "The band is so small now, I doubt if they could head to Canada by themselves. Maybe another village, to meet up with others?"

"O-Ke-Monse!" said Simon. "I bet they've gone to the summer village of Chief O-Ke-Monse. He goes to Canada to visit family and pick up their yearly annuity from the British Government, so he knows the way."

"Do you know where that is, did O-Ke-Monse ever say?" Glyn needed to know.

"I'm not sure. You go down the O Washtenong to Biddle town, then go up the Cedar River for a ways. That's their summer camp. Can't be too far. He used to come here and said it only took him half a day."

Glyn turned towards the river. "I'll leave now. I should be able to find someone along the river that has seen them, or knows where the summer village is!"

"Glyn, stop for a minute. You can't just go off without thinking. Come back to the tavern and pack some provisions. You don't even have a rifle with you or any coins." Olive took her son by the shoulders. "I know you have feelings for Gray Dove, and I know she has feelings for you, too.

"They must have left at sunrise, so they are probably already there if that's where they're headed. As long as you find them before they leave for Canada, you'll be able to talk to her. Now come on back with us. We'll round up what you'll need and get you set off."

CHAPTER 37
THE BLESSING

Gray Dove was asleep, dreaming of a starry night many moons before. She was standing knee deep in a cold stream. Glyn was beside her; they were both naked. Drops of water ran in rivulets down Glyn's chest; his pale skin glowed in the moonlight. He ran his fingertips down her cheek and on down to her breast. Glyn reached out to pull her to him...

"Gray Dove, wake up." Her grandmother, Cloud Woman, was shaking her awake. "Granddaughter, wake up! The council has decided. The tribe will pack and travel to Chief O-Ke-Monse. We will have him guide us to Canada. We will not be forced off our land to go west to our enemies, to be slaughtered like rabbits. Gray Dove, you must wake up!"

"I'm awake, Grandmother. I must have fallen asleep waiting for the council. Have you decided then? We will go before the army forces us to leave. I am glad. I have packed up most everything already. There is some good stew left in the spider by the fire. We shall eat, then get ready to leave. Where is River?"

"She is helping Ojeeg gather possessions from his wigwam. She may not be living with us much longer. He and Wolf were childhood friends. He has no family left and is lonely. River has a daughter in Canada. She has been talking of going to them to live. We shall see. She has been a good sister to me. I wish her happiness."

This startled Gray Dove, for as long as she could remember, her grandmothers had always squabbled.

The canoes were packed as the sun rose in the east. The tribe assembled on the banks of the O Washtenong, their medicine-women chanting a sacred blessing, facing the morning sun. Her arms raised, Gray Dove had tears in her eyes. She was thinking of all the morning suns she had seen here, on the banks of this river. Even when the tribe traveled, this spot was always home for her, where her most precious memories were. And this would be the last time. But by leaving, she at least would be alive to remember and tell the stories to her grandchildren. She glanced over to her grandmother and could see the hot tears on her wrinkled cheeks, on the faces of all her people that stood there that morning. Afterward, they pushed off in their canoes for the last time, paddling towards their freedom.

They reached the summer village of Chief O-Ke-Monse in the early afternoon. A swift messenger had been sent ahead, and the village was anticipating them. Runners had been sent out to other villages, with the news that the army was coming to remove the Native American from their land. Families packed their belonging to flee the area. Some were coming to the village to seek guidance or look for family. By the time Gray Dove and her band reached the summer village, a council was already in progress. The Elders hurried off to the council house. Gray Dove set up a campfire around which people gathered to rest and await further news.

It was decided some would travel down river to Lake Michigan, and follow the shore to Mackinac Island. From there, they would cross into Canada. O-Ke-Monse would lead this group of old people and children. Another group, led by Chief Tuckamin would go cross country. Many thought that going north to Saginaw Bay would be the best route to take. And they all thought that it would be a good idea to separate into smaller bands, and to stay far away from Detroit and the fort there. Scouts were sent to watch the river, in case the army came before the village was ready to leave. They would all be gone before the next dawn.

Gray Dove settled down by their campfire to catch some sleep before the arduous journey the next day. Both old grandmothers and Ojeeg would be leaving with her on their flight to Canada, with Chief O-Ke-Monse. Almost asleep, she heard a commotion from the river. Two braves were loudly shouting. Had the army found them?

She heard someone shout, "Gray Dove! Gray Dove!" Then fighting, and silence.

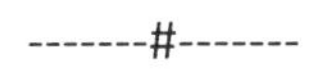

Glyn slowly regained consciousness. His head throbbed something awful. His head was also lying on something soft. Something cool and wet was on his forehead. He didn't want to open his eyes. He knew it was going to be painful. Slowly he opened his eyes a tiny fraction and could see a campfire. Then he opened his eyes a little more. He could see three bleary, old and wrinkled, Indian faces staring back at him. He quickly snapped his eyes shut again. Then he felt a finger prying one of his eyelids open. He opened his eyes once again. As his vision cleared, he recognized the grandmothers.

"Gray Dove," Glyn said hoarsely as he tried to rise. "I need to find Gray Dove. I came to find Gray Dove, to keep her from leaving. To tell her how I feel about her. I need her to stay here, with Frankie and me. If she will. I need her. I don't think I can live without her. Please, tell me where Gray Dove is. Don't tell me she's already gone!"

Two hands from above gently pushed him back down.

"I'm right here, Glyn. Stay quiet; you have a nasty bump. You slipped and fell, and hit your head on a rock at the edge of the river. The scouts thought you were army and tried to jump you," said Gray Dove as she eased his head back down onto her lap. "I already miss Frankie and your family, and it hasn't been a day yet. And I have dreamed of you since that night we met in the middle of the river, so many moons ago. But you see, I can't leave my grandmother again. She is the only blood relative I have left. I am truly sorry," she softly wept. Salty tears ran down her face and dripped on Glyn's lips.

"Gray Dove! I love you. I've loved you since that night we met in the middle of that stream, so long ago. Marry me and I will protect your whole tribe with my life if that's what you want. Just stay with me." Glyn reached up, held on to her hands, and softly kissed her palms.

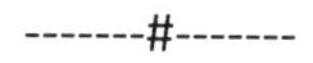

-------#-------

Glyn stayed at the summer village, helping everyone to pack quickly and leave. Mani and Shing came by and asked him to tell James and Joseph to keep the ponies for them until they came back. Glyn promised that they would take good care of them. He did not say that he didn't think they would ever be back.

Storm and Red Feather walked to where he was. Red hugged him. "I'm going to miss you and Sarah."

Red took a rawhide thong from around his neck. "This is my lucky talisman. I wore it when the bear attacked us. That is why she didn't eat us all, and why I still have my arm. Give it to Sarah for me. Tell her not to forget her Red brother."

Glyn took the talisman. "I'll give it to her. I'm sure she will always keep it. You take care, and stay away from bears, Morel Hunter."

Red Feather grinned as he reached up and hugged Glyn.

Storm shook hands with Glyn, "Thank you for protecting my boy that day. And thank you for showing me how to be a good father. I have been in misery since Red's mother died. Chief O-Ke-Monse has helped me find the path that I want to follow. To be a good father."

"Are you going with O-Ke-Monse?"

"No," said Storm. "We are going across to Saginaw Bay. I can help Tuckamin with our group."

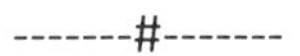

Around noon, Glyn left the deserted town. Gray Dove sat in the front of the canoe, with Glyn paddling in the back. Cloud Woman was seated in the middle. After a tearful farewell, River Woman stayed with Ogeej and would travel to Canada with Chief O-Ke-Monse. She and Ogeej would find and live with her daughter.

The Cedar River was strangely quiet. They came to and paddled up the O Washtenong. Even then, river traffic was slow, a few flat-bottomed scows full of lumber. They did meet two different Indian families fleeing to the north. Gray Dove and Cloud talked and told them how to find O-Ke-Monse, that he was leading the People out to Lake Michigan, and where they could likely be found.

Dusk was on them when they reached the Forks. Two young boys were innocently fishing along the bank until they spied the canoe and waved them to shore.

"Quick," whispered James, just slightly lower than a shout. "The army is at the tavern. Mother sent us to keep watch for you. You have to hide Cloud and Gray Dove until they leave. They have about a dozen captured Indians with them. Mostly women and children. They had them tied to their ponies. They put them in the cabins at the Indian Camp, under guard. Mother told the soldiers they could eat at the tavern, as long as she could feed their captives."

"Father said to go to Joshua's," said Joseph. "Stay there until he sends for you. I'll tell him you have Gray Dove and Cloud Woman. Take Spring Brook up to Bradford's Mill. You can paddle up that far, and you'll be about a mile or so from Joshua's place."

As quick as lighting, the boys had their fishing gear picked up and were heading back to the tavern. The laughed loudly and were joking with one another. They did this to cover any noise the canoe made as it slid away.

CHAPTER 38

Runaways

It was after midnight before the three reached Joshua and Hannah's farmhouse. Cloud Woman made the walk without any complaints. Glyn thought she was far more agile than most men half her age. They hid their canoe with all the women's earthly belongings in a group of willows along the stream. Glyn would retrieve the bundles in the morning.

Glyn tried the back door of the farmhouse, but it was locked. He went around to his brother's bedroom window and softly knocked on the glass, not wanting to wake the children. The window quickly opened, Josh stuck his head out, started to say something, and stopped. "What are you doing here? Wasn't expecting you, thought it was someone else."

"The army came. They're at the tavern now. They had about a dozen Indian captives and locked them in at the cabins at the Indian Camp," said Glyn. "Father said to come here to hide out until they go. I have Gray Dove and Cloud with me. The rest of the Camp was able to escape."

"Tonight is not the best of nights...," said Josh, yawning.

"Who are you talking to?" Hannah came and stuck her head out. "For Pete's sake, Josh, go unlock the kitchen door and bring them in! Get yourself around the side of the house, Glyn. You say you have Gray Dove and Cloud? Well, hurry and bring them all in. It's a bit nippy out tonight."

The door opened, and Joshua motioned them in, and after looking around outside, closed and locked the door. Hannah came into the kitchen, pulling a wrapper around her night clothes.

"Josh, stir that fire up and pull some chairs up close to it. Do any of you need a blanket to get warm? What you all need is something hot to drink. Let me get some cups."

"You said you weren't expecting us; who were you expecting at this hour of the night?" said Glyn to his brother.

"Look, you all have had a hard day. We'll talk about this in the morning. You were the last person I expected to be pounding on my window in the middle of the night, but you are always welcome here, anytime, little brother. You know that."

Hannah passed around steaming cups of herb tea. The women both said they were quite warm enough without blankets, with the walking they had done. All they wanted was to curl up in front of the fire and sleep. Hannah stated that the three of them would sleep in her feather bed, and the two men could sleep on the floor in front of the fireplace.

The next morning when Glyn woke, the women were already busy in the kitchen. He was told that his brother was outside, hitching the mules to the wagon. He went out to help and guided the back of the wagon up to the basement door. It was stacked full of lumber.

"The lumber stay here? Do you want me to unload it?" asked Glyn.

"No, I'm delivering it to Alpheus Phelps. He asked me to. Said I would. Let's go in and eat breakfast. Father said for you to stay here, but I see no reason you shouldn't come into the settlement with me and act like it's any other day. Gray Dove and Cloud can stay here for as long as they want. Nobody passes by here. As long as we are watchful, there is no reason anyone should be suspicious. Now, let's go in and eat, so we can get going. Elmer is already going to be short-handed today, with the Indian men gone."

As soon as they came in to eat, Hannah said she had to go down into the root cellar to retrieve some potatoes for dinner. Glyn noticed she had two large baskets with her, but he didn't think much about it. He attacked his grits and eggs. After a few minutes, Hannah rushed back up the stairs.

"Cloud! Gray Dove! I need your help." Hannah turned and said to Joshua, "You might as well tell Glyn. The slave girl that was with child is not going to wait any longer to have it. Thank God Cloud is here! I think she's going to have a rough time with it. She can't be much more than eleven or twelve." The three women disappeared down the steps.

"Tell me what?" asked Glyn. "Why do you have a slave girl having a baby in your cellar?"

"I am sorry, Glyn. The last thing I wanted to do is to get you involved with this, with everything you've been going though. We thought it best to keep you out of it. The Quakers back East are helping runaway slaves find their freedom in Canada. We have routes set up, with safe houses along the way for slaves to stay. We provide a place to rest, get food and clothes if they need them. Then we help them so they can go to the next safe house.

"When we sold the tavern back East and moved here, we helped set up a safe route through these parts. We don't get a lot of runaways this far north; most try to cross near Detroit. Depends on how close the authorities are watching. Right now, we are getting a few every day. Someone told the authorities about a couple of safe houses down by the state border, between Chicago and Detroit, so they're coming farther north, up this way, and crossing at Port Huron. Usually, they follow the Mississippi up, then the Ohio and cross over to Chicago and on to Detroit, and freedom in Canada."

"Why didn't I know any of this? You kept this part of your life a secret from me? Father and Mother know what you're doing?"

"Look Glyn, the fewer people know about this, the better. The authorities are starting to crack down on this. They used to just look the other way. Now Congress is passing stricter federal laws, with jail time and fines. There was nothing you could do to help, but now I'm afraid you are involved. Yes, mother and father know a little about what we do. They don't ask many questions. Being in the settlement with people around, they need to be careful. But they have more than once provided shelter. Word was out among the Indians that if they find any slaves in the woods, to secretly bring them to Mother or Father and they would be rewarded. A lot of the runaways stay with the Indians, the way River did. Now with the Indians gone, it's going to be much harder for the slaves to find their way.

"When they get here, most of them have been on the run for weeks. They're beat up and misused. The girl down in the cellar now, she's no more than a skinny little thing. Her brother is with her, helping her to escape. The baby, she says, belongs to the overseer of her master. The overseer's wife told her she was going to drown the baby as soon as it was whelped. That's why she ran away.

"The brother is a big strong lad, about fifteen or sixteen. They'll be looking for him. I would think he would be worth a lot. They've been here for two days now. The girl thought she would be strong enough to start running again. Hannah was afraid she might go into labor, and she's no midwife. It was a blessing you all came last night. I thought you were slave hunters when you came knocking on my window.

"There are five more runaways staying. Erastus Hussey from Marshall brought two in yesterday morning. If the women think it's safe for us to leave them, we should try to get the men moved to the next safe house. If you're done eating, let's go down and see what they think."

They went down into the dirt-floored root cellar. The house was shaped like a "T," with the top bar facing the road. That part contained the parlor, front hall and two bedrooms, one for Joshua and Hannah and one for the girls. The back had the dining room, kitchen, pantry, and workrooms. Stairs in the pantry led down to the root cellar beneath the kitchen and dining room, and a set of stairs led from the cellar to the outside, where Glyn and Joshua had backed the wagon earlier. Joshua had built a wall of shelves filled with crocks and jugs and garden produce across the opposite wall, and Glyn noticed that a small section of this wall had been pulled open, with a secret opening going into the long section of the basement beneath the parlor and bedrooms.

They entered this room, and a strong metallic smell of blood and embryonic fluid engulfed them. Several Betty lamps were lit around one of the cots. The women were all gathered around it, as well as the men who looked on helplessly.

"One more push, little one, give me one more big push," said Cloud to the little girl she was kneeling in front of. Gray Dove was behind her, holding her shoulders up. The girl had a stick between her teeth that she had almost chewed through. The girl gave one more push with something between a growl and a scream, as though something was being torn from her.

Cloud took the baby and handed it to Hannah who wrapped her in a towel, shaking her head. "Gray Dove, let her down slowly, then prop her hips and legs up with some blankets. She's bleeding bad. Hannah, put the baby to her breast, sometimes that helps stop the bleeding. Glyn, you need to go now and get my pouches from the canoe. I have medicine in them that might help. Hurry! Don't stand there! Go! Now!"

Glyn and Joshua turned and ran out at the same time, up the stairs and outside. They quickly unharnessed the two mules, bridled them, and off they went. They raced down through the woods and swamp, found the canoe hidden in the willows, and gathered up all the leather pouches, baskets and anything that looked like medicine.

As fast as they could make the mules run, they went back to the farm house. But as fast as they went, it was not fast enough. When they got back, both the baby and mother were silent and turning cold beneath a white sheet. The brother was holding his sister's hand, saying a prayer, tears spilling down his face. The other men were standing in a protective circle around them, quietly singing an old-time gospel hymn. Joshua went over to clasp a red-eyed Hannah in a bear hug. Glyn turned and made his way outside.

Gray Dove followed and walked up behind Glyn. "We all did everything we could for her and the baby. Even if Grandmother had all her medicines with her, I think the girl would have died. She wasn't old enough to have babies. And the child was too small to live on its own; it wasn't ready to be born yet. But it had got too big for her to carry it any longer. The girl, I don't even know her name, she lost too much blood. She started bleeding and having pains in the night, and never told anyone, the poor child."

Glyn turned around, and they fell into each other's arms.

"Why is this world so cruel?" said Glyn. "We try so hard, and in a blink of an eye, our lives can change. If it was just the bad people, the sinners, that were hurt, I could understand. But that poor little girl and her baby? They done nothing to deserve to die like that, in a dirt-floored cellar surrounded by strangers."

"She may have been surrounded by strangers, but they were strangers that cared for her, and tried to help her. I think she knew that. And her brother was with her at the end."

"I love you so much, Gray Dove. I'm so afraid something will happen to you. Please, promise me you will never leave me, and I promise you that I will be at your side forever."

CHAPTER 39

Grace

The six runaway slave men, along with Glyn and Joshua, dug a grave for the dead girl and her baby at the edge of the woods in back of the house. With shovels, picks, and with the help of axes to chop the tree roots, they made short work of it. Hannah rode one of the mules into the settlement and found Reverend Jack. Knowing she could trust him, she brought him back to perform a Christian burial for the girl, whose name, the brother said, was Lucy, and he named the newborn baby Lucy, too. The women had wrapped them in clean sheets, a child mother holding her dead baby to her cold breast. A make-shift coffin was put together, and the eight men carried the small, light coffin to the grave where it was gently lowered down while the good Reverend spoke a short sermon.

Back at the house, Reverend Jack asked Glyn what plans Cloud and Gray Dove had.

"Well, Jack," said Glyn, "before her tribe fled north, Gray Dove and I had their medicine women, and Chief O-Ke-Monse bless our union, so in the eyes of Gray Dove's people, we are married."

"Congratulations, Glyn. I thought the two of you would someday be together. But in the eyes of our government, you're not married, and the army could still take her away. Let me marry you now. We can fill out the papers later; then you will never have to worry about your legal standing. Gray Dove told me once that she was baptized on Mackinac Island at the Presbyterian Mission, so that's not a problem."

"You would do that for us, Jack? That would be great. Most Reverends won't marry Indians and whites, or Negroes either. That is so wrong. Ministers marry Germans and English, or Dutch and Irish and no one even blinks at that. But if a white man marries an Indian or a Negro, they become not only society outcasts, but law-breakers and criminals, too."

Glyn and Gray Dove talked it over, then asked Cloud Woman's opinion. "You are already husband and wife in the eyes of the Great Spirit. If being married in a Christian ceremony will protect you from being hunted down by the US government, why would you not?"

Glyn knew then that Cloud deserved to be called a true wise woman. The only wiser person he knew was his own mother. It was a fine day, so they had the ceremony in the yard by the house. Glyn wished his mother and father were there, but these were trying times, and he did have his brother Joshua to stand witness for him, and Hannah stood with Gray Dove.

Reverend Jack said before the ceremony, "We need a Christian name for Gray Dove, to put on the certificate so no one will ever question it. Do you have a name you would like to use? Or, does Glyn have a special name for you?"

"No, I never thought of having any other name. Glyn, what would you like to call me?"

Glyn smiled, "It never occurred to me to call you anything but mine. Let's think what makes sense. Gray Dove, Gray Dove, mmm...how about Grace? They sound alike."

"What about a middle name? Even an initial would do," asked Jack.

"Grace, what would go with Grace? What about C? Or, we could spell it Ce. We could call her Grace Ce!" said Glyn.

"How about a last name? Gray Dove, does your tribe, or family have a last name or something that separates you from others?" said Jack.

Cloud spoke up. "Our clan has always been known as, how do you say it, Sand Hill Cranes, the big birds that stay in the wet meadows. Because we are a tall people, but shy."

Glyn thought about what he knew of Gray Dove's family when they lived at the Camp. He never thought of them as shy!

The Reverend said, "Grace Ce Sand Hill, Grace Ce Crane. Let's go with Crane. Sounds more European. You will be known as Grace Ce Crane. What nationality should we put down? Maybe someday you could correct it, but for now let's put something from Europe."

Glyn said, "I've noticed a lot of Germans coming into the area. Some of the Prussians are darker than Gray Dove, with black hair and big black eyes. Go with German, Prussian; no one will argue with that. And Gray Dove talks better than they do, with their thick accents."

So history shows that Glyn Chatfield married Grace Crane, recently from Germany, with his brother and sister-in-law as witnesses, by the Reverend Jack, on an autumn day in 1839. What it does not show is that Grace was a Native American running from the US government, had helped birth, and then bury, a runaway slave and her baby, and was helping fugitive slaves on the underground railroad on that same autumn wedding day.

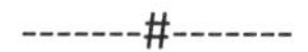

While the men helped the women strip the bedding from the cots in the cellar, it was decided that Glyn and Joshua would take the fugitive slaves to their next stop. The women were boiling the bedding and the men washed the room out with vinegar and water. They opened all the doors and vents to help dry the cellar out. Hot, boiling vinegar had been used since the middle ages as a cheap disinfectant. Housewives cleaned their floors and furniture with vinegar. Hannah was deathly afraid that some of the slaves might be carrying disease that could infect her girls. The cellar where the slaves stayed was always thoroughly cleaned and aired after a group left. Hannah had been orphaned after a smallpox epidemic. She hoped it would be a couple of days before any more slaves would come, but they never knew for sure.

Glyn and Josh would drop the runaways off and go to the settlement to find out if the army was still in the area. Joshua showed Glyn that the wagon of lumber had small hoops in the center, like those on a covered wagon, and the lumber was stacked around and over the hoops. Six to eight adults could sit and hide in the center of the wagon and not be detected. The tailgate looked to be solidly built to the wagon frame, but could actually be lifted up so the run-a-ways could crawl inside. A trap door in the floor could be slid open for fresh air or as an escape route.

Glyn said, "How did you ever come up with that idea? A person would never know you were hauling anything except lumber."

"Back East, it was an old trick, first used to smuggle whiskey out of the mountains. They started using it for slaves when the government started enforcing the fugitive slave laws. That's where our idea came from to put shallow false bottoms in the wagons to haul the gold and silver coins from the sale of the tavern and our houses when we moved out here. The banks were all closing so you couldn't trust them. It would have taken several large trunks to hold all that cash. The risk of being robbed was just too great. But it worked perfectly."

Joshua opened the tailgate, and one by one the men came up the basement stairs and crawled in. Hannah and Gray Dove had several baskets of food and crockery jugs full of water for the trip. The women said goodbye to the slave men as they handed them the food and water, and wished them a safe journey to freedom. The tailgate was closed, and they set off for Alpheus Phelps' farm, which was about a mile past the turn-off to the settlement. But because of the lack of bridges, impregnable swamps, and poor to non-existing roads, it would take several hours to reach their destination which was about four miles as a crow flies.

They pulled into Alpheus' barn late in the afternoon and let the runaways out. Alpheus said to the men, "Stay in the barn with the doors closed until it gets dark. Then come up to the house, my wife will have supper for you."

Lucy's brother thanked them for all their help. He knew how hard they had tried to save Lucy and her baby.

Joshua said, "We will put a headstone on her grave, so if you ever come through these parts again, you can stop and see it."

"Thank you, sir. But you see, neither Lucy or I could read, so no use putting no headstone on her grave. But she shore liked flowers. When Lucy was little, she would sneak into the Master's garden and pick the Missus' flowers. She caught hell for that, yes she did. But she would sneak right back out there and do it again. She loved her flowers. If you could plant some flowers on her grave, well, she would like that. I don't have no plans on coming back through these parts, no sir. But it would be right kind of you to put flowers on her grave. Mighty kind."

They left Alpheus and traveled to the tavern, arriving just as the family was ready to sit down to supper.

Glyn picked up Frankie, "Come and sit on my lap. I'm going to hold on to you until you fall asleep. I've missed you so much."

Olive asked, "Glyn, did you make it to Joshua's with Cloud and Gray Dove the other night alright? The army left this morning. They sent the fugitive Indians that they captured back to Marshall with a small regiment. The rest went north. They had been told by some settlers where several of the Indian villages were and went to capture and remove them. I heard them talking this morning. They know that the

Indians will try to go north to Canada, and they're going to try to capture them before they do."

"Mother, why does the army want to capture the Indians when they're trying to leave anyway?" asked Joseph.

"Because they think the Indians will just come back in the spring, like they always have, and cause trouble for the settlers. So they want to move them as far away as possible."

"Does that mean I'll never see my friends again? They always leave, then come back again. They always do! Then we play together and hold races. I can almost run as fast as my best friend."

"Oh Joseph, they may not come back again. You might not ever see them. It's not that they don't want to, but because they're not able to. Remember what good friends they were. Maybe when your grown up, things will change, and you will be able to see each other again."

"That reminds me of something," said Glyn as he stood, walked over to and knelt at Sarah's chair. "I talked to Red Feather before he left. He asked me to give you his lucky talisman." Glyn pulled the leather thong from his pocket and placed it around Sarah's neck

"He said it was to keep you safe, but I think he wanted you to remember him by it."

Sarah looked at the talisman and held it in her hand. It was a single bear claw, curled, but would have been six inches long stretched out.

"Well, Mother, you might just ask Glyn here what he's been up to," said Joshua.

"Lord in heaven, I'm almost afraid to ask."

Glyn replied, "Oh, not much. After I left here, I was jumped by some Indian scouts, hit my head on some rocks and was knocked out. Then I found Gray Dove and married her twice. Once in front of the tribe by their medicine woman and Chief O-Ke-Monse, and again in front of Reverend Jack. Hid out from the army, found that my brother leads a double life, went to a funeral, and delivered a load of lumber. That's about it, for the other day."

"Good Lord, whose funeral did you go to? I haven't heard of anyone passing, but Elmer mentioned that Jack couldn't be found today."

"One of the men helping with the lumber," said Josh. "His sister died in childbirth. We all did all we could, but even Cloud couldn't save her." All the grown-ups involved knew what "lumber" or "lumber men" meant. The children were told only what they had to know, not that they would intentionally tell the wrong person, but children tend to talk.

Olive said, "Now, what's this about you getting married, Glyn. I wasn't invited to go to your first wedding. I thought you would have invited your parents to your second or third one!"

"Mother," Glyn said, "I wanted you and Father there, all three times, in the worst way. Gray Dove did, too. There wasn't time for you all to come to Detroit when I married Magdelaine. The second time, the tribe was fleeing, and the last time, we needed to make sure everything was legal so the army couldn't take Gray Dove."

"Glyn," said Simon, "Your mother knows that you did what you had to, she's giving you a rough time, is all. I'm glad, no, we're all glad, you married Gray Dove. But you know how people feel about the Indians; they don't want them around. And they look down on anyone who marries one. You won't ever be invited anywhere; no white man will have anything to do with you. Are you prepared for that?"

"Yes, I am. She was always there for me, even at my lowest point in life. Whatever comes our way, we will have each other. And our family. Jack changed her name on the marriage certificate. She is now, legally, the former Grace Ce Crane from Germany."

"Are you and Gray Dove going to come back and live here at the tavern?" asked Elmer. "We built a small cabin out by the cedar swamp. Thought that it might be needed for the "lumber men" at some point, but it's never been used. It's small, and it's rough, but it's built solid and has a good fireplace. It's there if you and Gray Dove ever need a place to stay. It would be out of every one's sight. Then if you ever decide to come back, you and "Grace," I doubt if anyone would remember Gray Dove, her just being an Indian. I've noticed people don't stay around long. They're here for awhile and then move on."

"Thank you for the offer, Elmer. We're going back to Joshua's farm tonight. I'll talk to Gray Dove and see what she thinks."

Night had fallen by the time Glyn and Joshua reached the farm. Gray Dove met them at the door. "I was afraid that you two might have decided to spend the night at the tavern. I'm so glad you came home. Have you eaten yet?"

"Yes," said Josh. "We had a good meal with the family. I'll go and find Hannah. I'm sure you two will want some time to yourselves." Josh winked at his little brother and left.

Glyn smiled. Gray Dove said, "Good. Hannah and I have worked all day on a surprise."

Gray Dove took Glyn by the hand and led him to the hallway and up the stairs. "You know that the four upstairs bedrooms were never finished since Joshua and Hannah have no need of them yet, although Hannah told me they plan to fill them with babies. We cleared the extra lumber out one of the rooms."

Gray Dove opened a door to a room. A warm, romantic fire was lit in the fireplace, and a bed made up on the floor. "Hannah didn't think it was very good. She said we need a proper bed, but I told her it was everything we would need." Glyn smiled as he closed the door behind them.

CHAPTER 40
A PASSEL OF PIGS

The sun streamed in through the east-facing windows. Glyn lay on his back on the bed that Gray Dove had made up on the floor. She was curled up next to him, half lying on him, her long black hair spread over them. The room smelled of new wood. Glyn was softly humming the Native lullaby that Gray Dove sang to Frankie. He watched as the dust motes slowly danced in a draft of air in the sunshine.

The room was a bit chilly. Glyn got up and put several sticks of wood in the Rumford fireplace. The dry oak quickly caught, casting warmth throughout the room. Glyn put a couple of logs on the fire, then he sat and watched the fire, his arms around his knees. After a few minutes, he stood and went to lay back down. Gray Dove's dark brown eyes were watching him.

"Sorry if I woke you. The room was cold."

"Don't be sorry; I love just watching you. What were thinking about, just now?"

"Just that I'm the happiest man alive. I've been through Hell and back, and God gave me you and Frankie. I feel that I'm truly a blessed man."

Glyn snuggled under the heavy feather quilt next to Gray Dove, "If we were at a fancy hotel in a big city, we could have room service sent up, and we wouldn't have to get up."

"That would just be a distraction; I'm not ready to get up."

Later, when they did come downstairs, they found a note from Joshua and Hannah. They, and the girls had gone to the tavern, Josh to help Elmer, and Hannah to spend the day with Olive. They wouldn't be back till dark. Glyn and Gray Dove found Cloud out in the garden. She was husking the last of the corn, so when it was brought into to the house, it could be strung on a rope on the rafters in the kitchen to dry. After the corn was dried, it would be shelled, bagged, and taken to the gristmill to be milled into cornmeal. Except for the best kernels. They would be bagged separate and kept dry in a closet for popped-corn. She already had several bags full, as well as baskets of potatoes and onions.

Glyn carried all the bags to the house while the women brought in the baskets. Then they stopped to eat.

"Elmer asked me yesterday where we would live. He said that he had built a small cabin on his property out past Moetown. It was going to be for runaways, but it has never been used. He said we could live there as long as we wanted. It's far from any roads or neighbors. We could lie low there through the winter, or as long as we want."

Cloud said, "I know the land there, big cedar swamp. If the snow gets deep, the deer stay there to eat the trees. Not good in the summer. Too many mosquitoes and flies, too many snakes. There are several high hills around there with springs, where we camped."

Gray Dove said, "I will gather supplies, and we can go out there in the morning if Joshua can show us the way."

Glyn smiled. He knew that Joshua and Hannah wouldn't mind giving supplies to them. He had tried to explain to Gray Dove that white men thought differently about their possessions than the Indians did. The Native Americans believed that all things were communal. Everyone helped for the good of the tribe. If you shot a deer, the whole tribe shared. If you needed clothes, all the women would share buckskins and help sew. All the food gathered in the woods, or grown in the fields was communal. Everyone shared what they had. No one took more than they needed. If the children were hungry, none of the adults ate. If any person was sick, others would see to his family. It was just the way of the People.

The next day was warm and sunny for fall, muggy even. Cloud said they must be having a big storm someplace, because of the unusual heat and humidity. Joshua said he would take them out to the cabin by the cedar swamp, that even Cloud would not be able to find it.

"Don't know why you all would even want to move to that little cabin," said Josh to Glyn, as they rode along in the wagon with Gray Dove and Cloud. "Hannah and I both told you that you should stay with us, at least until next spring. We have more than enough room."

"We do really appreciate the offer. Gray Dove wants to take a look. I think she just wants a place of her own."

Gray Dove said, "I have lived in a wigwam most of my life. Your house is too large!"

"I've been inside longhouses before; they were quite large inside."

"Yes, but many families shared a long house. Ten Indian families could share your house, and still have room for visitors."

"Well, here we are. We'll go around this pond-hole, and the cabin is just beyond those old cedar trees."

The mules suddenly started to shy. Joshua had a hard time holding them still. The usually passive animals were trying to turn and bolt. He finally them calmed down.

"What's wrong with these mules, they've never acted this way. Come on girls, calm down. I'll have to tie them up here. We can walk the rest of the way, the cabin is just on the other side of that pond, in back of those big cedars." said Joshua.

Glyn jumped out and helped settle the mules down, and tied them to a small tree. They all started walking, with Josh showing the way. When they came close to a small pond, Cloud pointed. In the swamp oaks that surrounded the pond, hung large black water snakes. Cloud said, "Told you this land was known for its snakes. Being warm out, they are just catching the sun before they go into the ground for the winter, which will not be long now. Those black water snakes might bite if you get too close, but they will not kill you. They eat rats and mice, and small birds if they can catch them. Watch where you walk."

They steered around the pond and trees and came out close to the cabin. Not only big black snakes but long blue racers and garter snakes were hanging off the rafters of the cabin, sunning themselves. Milk snakes slithered across the stone step to the door. A big Massasaugas coiled up beside the cabin, raised his huge head, and looked at them. Then he slowly uncoiled and slithered under the cabin, as if saying, "Come into my den if you dare."

Cloud said, "We need to find some hogs, they will take care of the snakes in no time. When can we move in?"

Gray Dove said, "We're not. We'll stay with Joshua and Hannah for now. I remember one summer when the snakes kept sticking their heads up through the sleeping mats. We would wake up, and one would be watching you, the firelight reflected in its eyes. No, I have changed my mind. I would rather stay in a house this winter."

Glyn said, "When we first moved into our old cabin, we had snakes coming up between the floor boards. Mother was not impressed. But we got a passel of pigs, and let them sleep under the cabin for a while, never had a problem after that."

Cloud said, "All we need is some hogs, problem solved. The snakes are thick now because they are getting ready to sleep."

"Yes, and where do you think they are going to sleep? In and under the cabin. Any time the cabin warms up, the snakes will come out. No, we will stay in a house this winter, and find a large passel of pigs next spring to let loose in the swamp, then we'll see what happens," said Gray Dove.

They all turned and gingerly made their way back to the wagon.

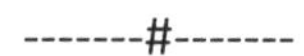

A wooden washtub stood in front of the fireplace in the simple bedroom they shared at Josh and Hannah's' farm. Glyn was soaping himself up with the lye "soft soap", the universal cleaner on the frontier. It had been a hard day of work, helping raise the new grist mill for Amos Spicer at the mouth of Spring Brook. Glyn was covered in sweat and the sawdust was making him itch. Gray Dove came into their bed chamber with a stack of clean and freshly ironed clothes and bed linens in one arm and a bucket of water in the other. Another bucket of water sat and warmed by the fireplace. Even though it was only lukewarm because fire smoldered during the day, it was better than breaking the ice to swim in the brook on a cold December day.

"Grandmother is still talking about moving into the cabin in the swamp. She gets this twinkle in her eyes when she talks about it. She never had a place she could call her own. She went from her parents to her first husband's wigwam, to his brother's, then she shared the cabin with River." Whenever Glyn and Gray Dove were alone, they always spoke in French.

"Do you want to move there, too?"

"No, we should move back with your folks at the tavern. We are legally married. They cannot force me to leave, your father said so. Cloud should stay here for the winter. She loves the girls, and she gets along well with Hannah. The baby has been a little peaked and Hannah worries about the winter, about what would happen if they were snowed in and the baby was sick. With Cloud here, she wouldn't have to worry so. Cloud can cure about anything that sickens a baby. Just look at Sarah. She was no bigger than a baby possum, according to your father, when she was born, and now she is bigger than her cousins."

"And sassier, too," Glyn added. He loved his little sister, but she could out talk and out sass anyone. She talked more like a grown-up, and she preferred grown-ups' company to children her own age.

"I want to continue teaching, and you need to study with your father more at night. Then you will have to read law with a real lawyer. Your mother said that with the county seat being in, what did your mother call it? Charlotte, where the Peoples big cornfields were, that that is where the lawyers will be. She said she heard that a tavern is being built there. It was to be a steam-powered gristmill, but now will be a tavern and courthouse. How does steam from a tea kettle turn a mill?

"I'm not sure. The big paddle boats on the lakes are powered by steam. Maybe someone is going to try to bring one of those big boat's steam-engine and power a grist mill with it, instead of water, the way we do.

"I worry about how people will treat you if we move back to the settlement. They already said that they don't want an Indian teaching their children. I won't have anyone talking down to you."

"The most important thing is for you to learn to be a lawyer and pass the bar. Then we won't have to worry about people. Your father said if you can get into politics, you will be able to pass laws, to protect others from being treated badly. That would be a noble thing to do."

Glyn stood and reached for the warm bucket of water to rinse off the soap.

Gray Dove reached over, "Here, let me help you." She picked up a bucket and poured it over Glyn's head.

"Oh damn!" Glyn said, along with some other French swear words. "That water is c-cold!"

"I'm sorry, I picked up the wrong bucket, the one I brought in just now from the well." Gray Dove picked up the warm bucket and poured it over Glyn and wrapped him a towel.

"I'm sorry, I was talking and wasn't paying attention to which bucket I picked up."

"That's all right, my love. It startled me, is all. Come here and warm me up." Glyn stepped out of the wooden wash tub and picked her up. He carried Gray Dove over to the bed and lay next to her.

"Are you sure moving back to the settlement is what you want? We can leave Cloud here to help Hannah. We can come back here as often as you like. Joshua would appreciate the help in clearing the fields and Mother would appreciate all the help at the tavern. We can see how the settlers react to you. They might accept you now that we are married.

I'll look to find a lawyer I can read under. Are you sure this is what you want?"

"Yes," Gray Dove said. "This is what I want to do. This will be best for both of us, and our children."

CHAPTER 41
SARAH'S BIRTHDAY

Olive was fixing breakfast for Simon and herself in the tavern's kitchen, at the same stone fireplace that had been in the original log cabin. The fireplace was all that remained of that small cabin which so much of their lives had taken place over the past five years. The room now boasted fine six-over-six double-hung glass windows, plaster walls above tulip wood and ash wainscoting, and a smooth maple floor. She and Simon woke early every morning to eat their first meal of the day together. The two of them would sit at the table in front of a west window that looked out over the Spring Brook marsh.

The sun was just beginning to brighten the eastern sky. Fog had rolled in during the night as the temperature dropped. Simon came in from the woodshed with a load of kindling and split firewood.

"Any coffee ready? It's right cold out. I'm going to have to dig my gloves and heavy coat out of the trunk." Simon laid the wood beside the fireplace and went over to where Olive was placing the last loaves of bread dough in the bee-hive bake oven, hugged her from behind, kissing her neck.

"Lord, your hands are freezing," said Olive as she wrapped her small, warm hands around Simon's.

"I love you more today than I ever have. Never thought that would be possible. I was thinking while I was out chopping wood, about when our Sarah was born. I was away. You were here alone, with only the boys. Cloud and Rain came and helped. We were lucky to have the Indians Camp so close. Without them, things might have turned out so different."

Olive turned from the fireplace and into Simon's embrace. "If it wasn't for Cloud and Rain and Dawn. Well, there is no use thinking about what may have happened. The good Lord, or The Great Spirit, or just luck, brought us all together. I love you too, Mr. Chatfield, and am proud to be your wife."

Olive gave Simon a kiss. "The coffee smells about ready; it's boiled. I pulled it off a couple of minutes ago. Would you get me a cup, too? I have to turn the ham slices and put the eggs on, and turn the toast, and then we'll sit down. The girls should be here in half an hour to start breakfast for the guests.

"I say, these new farm girls are easier to train than the Indian girls were, but my Indian girls were far better workers. They didn't need anyone to watch over them."

Small footsteps were heard coming down the stairs. Sarah came into the kitchen in her long flannel nightgown; loose strands from her dark auburn hair stuck out from a long braid under her nightcap. She clutched the corn-husk doll Cloud had made for her when they were at Josh and Hannah's husking bee. She hummed an old Native lullaby Gray Dove always sang to her.

"Good morning, darling! How's my little possum?"

"Oh, Daddy! I'm not a possum; I'm a girl."

"You'll always be my little possum!" Simon still stood straight and tall, with a military bearing. He bent and scooped her up in a bear hug. Sarah shrieked in laughter as her father tickled her neck and face with his gray beard.

"You two settle down, the guests will think wild Indians are attacking us." Olive laughed. "Come over here and take this platter of toast over to the table. Wash your hands and smooth your hair down. Then sit down with us and eat some breakfast."

The children usually ate later, either with the hired girls, after helping them serve the guests breakfast and washing up afterward, or with their own parents.

"Do you know what day this is?"

"Yes'm," Sarah said, still chuckling while taking the platter to the table. "Today is my birthday. Beck said I might get a cake at supper tonight!"

"Would you like that? I've asked the whole family to come and have an early supper with us."

"Yes'm. I miss Glyn and Gray Dove, with them living out on Josh's farm. And I miss Frankie, too, but don't tell him I said so. School will be starting soon. Will Gray Dove be our teacher this year?"

"I'm not sure," said Olive as she brought over the platter filled with eggs and ham. "If she doesn't want to, I will. With the Indian children gone, there won't be so many to teach. I might have them meet here at the tavern."

"Come with me, Sarah," said Simon as he went to the back door and opened it.

"Where are we going? Aren't we going to eat? Mummy said to sit down to eat."

"Yes, just come here, I want to show you something."

Sarah went to the open door and looked out. The clear morning sun just cleared the top of the trees.

"Look at the frost sparkle!" Sarah clapped her hands. "It looks like feathers on all the trees and bushes. Cloud would say this was a birthday gift from the Great Spirit."

"You two come in and close the door. Breakfast is on the table, and it'll be getting cold."

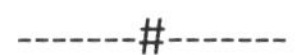

The day grew cloudy around noon and snow fell thickly by two o'clock. Two wagons of homesteaders came and stopped at the tavern for the night; settlers headed for the Grand Rapids area. They pulled their wagons along the side of the tavern. The oxen were bedded down in the stable with plenty of wild meadow hay from the rick. The herd of Indian ponies James and Joseph inherited from the Natives stayed close to the Forks. They nibbled from the hay-ricks when the snow got deep and drank from the artesian springs that never froze. They were tough creatures that braved the snow and cold.

The whole family gathered that afternoon at the tavern. The women cooked up a special birthday meal, with all of Sarah's favorites. At four o'clock the family assembled at one of the long tables in the public dining room. A warm fire burned in the fireplace. The large mirror above the mantel reflected the black-walnut woodwork around the doors and windows. The new plaster on the walls would take another year to thoroughly dry. Olive left the off-white plastered walls alone for now, but she did stencil flowers and vines on the walls, around the ceiling, and along the wainscoting. No heavy drapes would hang at the large windows. The material would absorb cooking odors. Instead, full-length interior shutters made of black walnut folded back into side-pockets in the wall and could be closed against the night.

The table was set with Sarah's favorite dishes. Simon had surprised Olive on her last birthday by having the dishes shipped from the East coast. It was the same pattern Olive had admired all those years ago at the VanCort mansion. Still popular, the flow blue tableware in the Manilla pattern and made by the British company Podmore, Walker, & Co., looked lovely with the pure white linen table-cloth and napkins. Olive only used the deep blue and white dishes on special occasions.

The family held hands and the traditional moment of silence was observed. Then Sarah's birthday supper began.

"Gray Dove," asked Sarah, as she passed a platter of corn bread. "Will you be teaching us when school starts again? I sure hope you will. Mama said she would if you don't."

"Yes, Sarah," answered Gray Dove. "We have decided to move back here to the tavern for the winter."

"If that's all right?" asked Glyn.

"Of course," said Olive. "We would love to have you all back. What changed your mind? I thought you were determined to stay out to Josh and Hannah's for the winter."

"Well," said Glyn. "I found someone to read law with. A lawyer named Wilkinson. He's staying in Charlotte at the new tavern, the Eagle House. They're using it as a courthouse until they build one. He said I could come and clerk with him and read law. It's close enough that I can come home when court's not in session. He said I could bunk with him since rooms there are scarce."

"And I want to teach the children this winter," said Gray Dove, "because by next year, I should be too busy, with a child of our own." She placed her hands on her still slim waist and smiled at Glyn.

Olive rose from the table and went over to where Gray Dove and Glyn were seated and hugged both of them. She bent down and kissed Gray Dove on the cheek.

"I am so happy. We all will be here for you. Our family watches out for each other." She kissed the top of Glyn's head and sat back down.

"Knowing you the way I do, a new papoose shouldn't slow you down none," said Simon as he picked up his handle-less cup in a salute to Gray Dove and Glyn.

"I hope so," said Gray Dove. "With Glyn staying in Charlotte and Frankie walking, climbing, and getting into everything, I just don't want to take on more than I should. Yesterday, I found Frankie out in the corral with the mules. And not a stitch of clothes on."

"I can remember when you took care of both Sarah and Frankie, when I first came back from Texas, and milked Madame Therese, too. You shouldn't worry so. And you'll have Sarah to help with Frankie, won't she," Glyn said, looking at Sarah with a smile.

Sarah smiled and nodded.

Cloud said, "I told Gray Dove that I will be here for the birth. Even if I have to dress in white women's clothes and wear a white woman's bonnet to be able to live in the settlement. No one will keep me away from birthing my great-grandchild." Olive and Simon both broke into laughter at the thought of Cloud dressed as a proper white woman.

Cloud continued, "My son, Gray Dove's father, and her mother, would be so proud of her. She has been through many trials, but they have made her a stronger woman." It was the first time anyone heard Cloud discuss Gray Dove's parents. The Natives thought it brought bad luck to speak of the dead.

Olive said while passing the salt cellar, "It will be so nice to have you back here at the Forks, Cloud. I miss the long talks we used to have, while we sewed and talked out on the back stoop. I miss Rain and Dawn, too. I hope they made it to Canada and found a warm place to live this winter."

"Cloud is going to teach me to be a healer like she is," said Sarah. "When I was with Red in the sweat lodge, in my dream, I was taking care of sick and wounded people. Gray Dove said that meant I would be a healer like Cloud. I need to learn everything she knows. I wish Chief O-Ke-Monse would come back. He knew things. Red told me he could see things other people couldn't. I wish he would teach me how to do that!"

"Yes, I can vouch that the old Chief knew things that no one else did," said Simon. "Learn everything you can from them. We Americans think we know more and are better than the Indians. That's not true. Their vast knowledge came from living with nature."

Elmer handed the vegetable bowl of mashed potatoes to Harriet and said, "I heard old man Hosler say just the other day that the woods aren't the same without the Indians. Use to be, if you needed help, there was always an Indian around to lend you a hand. I think some are regretting the Indians being removed. And some think the bear population is going to explode. The settlers don't care much for bear meat; they think it's too gamy and tough. They will only eat it if they have to. The Indians hunted them regularly, and that kept their numbers in check. Farmers aren't going to be able to let their hogs out to fatten up on the mast. It'll be the bears fattening up on the hogs."

"I worry about the wolves," said Hannah as she passed the fried fish. "We had a pack of them up by the smokehouse; we found their tracks. They tried to get in, too. Chewed and clawed the side of the door something awful. Good thing Josh made that door with double thick planks or all our hams would've been gone."

They heard the tavern's front door open and the bell at the desk ring. Laughter from one of the hired girls rang out, as well as a husky chuckle.

"I wonder who is out in this weather?" said Harriet. "Everyone knows supper is set at six, though I doubt any guests except those staying will be out on a night like this. Maybe someone got lost in the storm."

The double doors that separate the dining room from the guest parlor burst open.

"Ah, so this is where you all are hiding! I rode all this way to wish Miss Sarah a Happy Birthday!"

"Jean-Luc!" cried Glyn as he jumped from his seat and ran over to his brother-in-law. "You're the last person in this world I expected to see walk through these doors. How come you're here and not down in Texas?"

"I took the last bales of cotton for the season to New Orleans to sell and wanted to come back to Detroit to see the family. Then I had to come and see my other family, here in the forest."

"You haven't changed a bit, Jean-Luc! Still uglier than a three-legged pole-cat." Both men grinned and gave each other a bear hug, then stood looking at one another. "Nope, I can't believe you're standing here in front of me."

"I came all this way, at least let me sit and eat. But first, I hear from my mother that congratulations are in order, that you and Gray Dove have married."

Jean-Luc turned to where Gray Dove stood and gave her a big hug and in French said, "We are all happy that you two finally married. My mother and my father, all my brothers and sisters, wanted me to tell you all we are glad you and Glyn are together. And now, Frankie has a good mother who will take care of him."

Gray Dove said softly, "We are having a little one of our own. But do not worry about Frankie. I couldn't love him any more if he were mine. I always have, since that first day you two rode in with Frankie on Glyn's back, and finding out that Frankie's mother had died."

Jean-Luc said, "Thank you." And hugged her again.

Jean-Luc bent down next to Frankie, "Ah, the little count, Xavier-

Francis Girona Chatfield. You do not remember me. I am your uncle, Jean-Luc. You have grown. You resemble your mother. I can see it in your eyes."

Frankie surprised Jean-Luc by saying in good, passable French, "Comment allezvous, Monsieur?"

Jean-Luc laughed, hugged the small boy back and started talking in rapid French. Frankie's eyes grew large.

"I'm afraid, Jean-Luc, that's the only phrase in French he knows," said Gray Dove. "We try to teach him, but he prefers English. We'll keep teaching him and he'll soon catch on."

"I am sure he will," Switching back to English, Jean-Luc said, "And now, Sarah. You have grown, too."

"Did you really come all this way because it was my birthday?"

"Yes, of course I did. Well, I would have, if I had known. The lovely young girl that greeted me at the desk said you all were in here, celebrating Miss Sarah's birthday. So, I will sit down and we can continue the celebration, and you can tell me everything that has happened since I left."

Olive placed dishes and silverware from the sideboard in front of Jean-Luc, "Miss Olive, thank you. And Simon. I must say when I rode in, your inn is most impressive. Not since I left Detroit have I seen such a nice building."

"And you must tell us about your life in Texas. We have heard from your folks that you are doing quite well, they are proud of you," said Olive as she put a cup of cider in front of him.

"Yes. One reason I am here is to try to talk Glyn into coming back to Texas with me. But first, let's toast. To the past, and to the future and to family, the ones we can count on."

Everyone stood, lifted their mugs, and toasted, "To the past, the future, and to family."

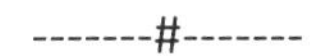

The early snow continued throughout the afternoon. It was agreed that, because of the storm, everyone would stay the night. After the meal, the family gathered in the guest parlor and talked, seated around the fireplace, while the wind blew sleet against the window panes.

Olive said, "I've been thinking about a name for this place. Everyone calls us Chatfield's tavern at the Forks. With the way the settlement is growing, it won't be long before someone else opens a tavern here. Then what are people going to call us, the new tavern and the old tavern? People need to know about our nice rooms, our public dining, the church services of Reverend Jack's, and our Friends meetings. Since this is Eaton Township, in Eaton county, I was thinking of Eaton Tavern."

"That sounds good," said Simon. "A real simple way for people to remember us."

"I would like something more European sounding," commented Jean-Luc. "Something more sophisticated, like Eaton House Inn. You have the nicest tavern between Detroit and Chicago. Even the one in Marshall don't compare with what Elmer has done here. You will someday be a destination; this beautiful settlement will be a place that people will want to come to see."

"I can't think why anyone would ever want come here to visit," laughed Olive. "Most of the guests we have are just people passing through, on their way to a better life. But I do like Eaton House Inn. Anyone else have suggestions for a name?"

"I like it," Simon said. "It has a nice ring to it, sounds pleasant to the ear. People will start to come here to live, what with the mills being built and the businesses going up along the river. But come here just to visit?"

"Good," said Olive, rising gracefully from her chair. "If you girls would like to help, we'll go and bring in the birthday cake and have it in here."

After the cake and syllabub, a frothy treat made for special occasions, had been eaten, and presents given to Sarah, Simon got his fiddle out and accompanied Olive on the pianoforte. The others joined in a night of singing and merriment.

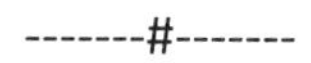

Later in the evening, after the children and most of the adults went off to bed, Glyn and Jean-Luc sat talking around the fireplace.

"We had a good crop of cotton this year. The ranch will support two families quite well if you and Gray Dove should decide to come down. And I could really use the help. I hate making management decisions without your opinion. It takes months to get a letter to you and receive an answer back."

"I trust you completely, Jean-Luc. I know you'll make the right decisions. We talked this over before. Plow all the profits back into the ranch, after you take your share."

"We're making enough now that I thought we should share the profits. Each of us take twenty-five percent and put the other fifty back into the ranch. There are five hundred acres next to ours I think we could buy cheap. The current owners have no water to irrigate. The river runs through our land. We would just have to run our irrigation ditches over there, and we'll have five hundred more acres of the best cotton land in Texas. The hill country starts beyond that. If we bought land there, we could graze cattle up there someday. Texas is growing fast, just like Michigan."

Glyn and Jean-Luc shook hands, sealing the deal for Jean-Luc to buy more land to expand the cotton and cattle ranch in Texas.

Jean-Luc stood beside Frankie's bed and looked down at the sleeping three-year-old. Firelight played on the walls, making the shadows dance.

"My little nephew, Count Xavier-Francis Girona Chatfield. The riches that awaited you. Duchies in both France and Spain, subjects that would have bent down at their knees and called you sire. If only Don Carlos hadn't been defeated and fled the county.

"But who knows what the future may be, little count. You have wonderful parents and a family that loves you. You live in a land of changing opportunity. You do not know it yet, but the world awaits you.

"And I have a lovely young lady waiting for me downstairs. I am going to teach her to play chess. Wish me luck, Count Girona."

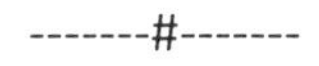

While Jean Luc conversed with a sleeping Frankie, Simon was seated at his secretary in their bedroom. His law books were on the shelves above, along with the ledgers and receipt books for the Eaton House Inn. Under the desk and above the first drawer was a secret drawer, no more than six inches high. By pressing a hidden latch, the drawer could then be opened. Inside Simon kept a small pistol, the remaining gold and silver coins from the sale of the old tavern on the Erie Canal and the obsidian ceremonial dagger that killed Tecumseh. Simon sat in the semi-darkness of the room and held the dagger. His palms burned. Simon could feel the scar below his eye pulse.

He told Chief O-Ke-Monse he still had the dagger in his possession. The old chief had given him a leather scabbard to keep it in. On it was a lightning bolt design made from porcupine quills and trade-beads. He withdrew the dagger and held it to the firelight. The obsidian shimmied and glowed. Colors seemed to dance within the dark blade. He would often hold the dagger, late at night when he couldn't sleep, and let the voices of those who had held it in the past, talk.

Tecumseh had him put the dagger back into the scabbard and placed it back into the secret drawer. “Not yet, Simon, not yet.” Simon stood, blew the candle out, and got into bed.

Simon rolled onto his side and pulled Olive to him in a hug. He still needed to be close to Olive to sleep well. "How does it feel to have all the family under one roof again? I thought by this time they would all be scattered to the wind."

Olive took his hand and pressed it to her chest. "I'm so glad we have stayed a close family. Mrs. Waldon told me that she hasn't heard from half of her kids in years and the other half she can't get to leave. We are truly blessed on this night.

"I was talking with Harriet today. Did you know they're planning on building a house on the lot they have along the river next summer? Guess I always knew that someday they would have a place of their own, but I just hate the thought of the girls leaving. I know they will be within hollering distance, but I'll still miss them.

"Hannah asked Cloud and I if we thought she had waited long enough since little Minnie was born to start thinking about having another baby. I told her I thought she and Josh could go back to being close, but she should wait another couple of years before they try to have another child. The last two babies were pretty close together, and she had a rough time getting back on her feet after Minnie."

Her worried comments were met with Simon's snores.

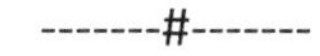

-------#-------

Down the hall, Harriet was in bed, reading the missionary literature she had received. Elmer was also sitting up in bed, going over plans for their new house.

"I'm just saying you should have waited until after the first of the year to tell Mother about the new house," said Elmer. "You know how attached she's got to the girls. I just don't want her fretting."

"And the girls are attached to her, too. But we'll be right down the trail from here. Actually, we will almost be across from each other. And it'll be a year before the house will be ready for us to move into. I don't like keeping such things from people.

"Did you ever think about doing missionary work? I've always wanted to. Maybe after the girls are grown. Something for you to think about. You could build cabins or Meeting houses for the Indians out west, or we could go to the Dark Continent."

"I thought you were doing work for the abolitionist. Ever since that William Lambert and John Brown fellows came through on their anti-slavery circuit in the summer, you've been wanting to set up an underground railroad here."

"When the new house is built, we need to be sure to have a place for runaways, the way Josh and Hannah have.

"The baby is waking up. Time for her to nurse. I just love having a baby to care for."

Elmer put away his drawings and blew out his candle. He loved his daughters, he truly did. But if they could just be blessed with a boy. A son he could pass his knowledge to, of building houses and barns and mills. Then he thought his life would be complete.

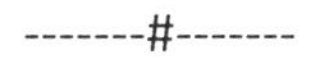

Because of the snowstorm, Joshua and Hannah had bedded down in the room they used when they stayed in town. "Wish we didn't have to stay over," said Joshua. "I worry about the livestock in this weather. They should be all right until tomorrow. But I would feel better if I was there to check on them."

Hannah said, "I don't like leaving the house empty either. I'm sure everything will be fine, but what if some runaways show up and need a place to stay? Mr. Hussey knows where we hide the key to the cellar door, but what if he's not with them?"

"They can always stay in the barn until we're back. At least they would be dry and out of the wind."

"Jean-Luc coming tonight, out of the blue, was sure a surprise though," said Hannah. "I heard him talking to Glyn about going back to Texas. Do you think Glyn will go?"

"No. Gray Dove isn't ever going to leave these parts, and Glyn will never leave Gray Dove. Besides, he has his heart set on being a lawyer."

"Josh."

"Yes? Something wrong?"

"No, nothing's wrong. It's been seven months since baby Minnie was born. I talked with Cloud and asked Mother Olive for advice. They both said I should be alright now. I know the doctor said not to try to have any more children for a year. But I've never felt better, and I miss you so much."

"Hannah! That's great news! We said we would fill those extra bedrooms with children someday." Josh hugged Hannah.

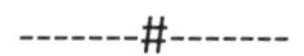

In the next room, Glyn and Gray Dove were asleep in each other's arms, completely exhausted and at peace with one another and the world. Both had smiles on their lips. Both were dreaming about a chance encounter one night in the middle of a moonlit stream.

A NOTE FROM THE AUTHOR

I am delighted you made the decision to read about the early settlers of Eaton Rapids, as seen through my imagination. If you found this novel an enjoyable read, please consider leaving an on-line review of the book.

This book has gone through several edits for content and grammar, but if you catch a spelling error or grammatical mistake, please let the publisher know at islandcitypublishing@gmail.com.

Please note that while the places and events used in the story are based on real events and locations, this is a work of historical fiction where most of what is conveyed is creative supposition on my part. Island City Publishing LLC assumes no liability for the content of this publication.

HISTORIC GLOSSARY

ASHERIES—
The lumber industry had not yet started, so when farmers cut down huge trees, the lumber they didn't use, they burned and took the wagon loads of ash to Asheries to sell for money. The Asheries took the ash and made it into lye for soap making, gunpowder, the chemical leavening saleratus, or baking soda. Pot ash was used for bleaching cloth and washing wool, making glass and fertilizer. The first US patent to be granted was for making ash lye. A person could make six dollars for 100 bushels of ash (a felled acre). Forty five thousand barrels of ash lye was exported to Europe annually.

ASTOR, JOHN JACOB—
After the War of 1812, Astor monopolized the fur business. To push out the Canadians, he paid a Congressman to pass a law that only an American citizen could obtain a trade license. To destroy competition from independent traders, in 1822, Astor paid Missouri Senator Benton to persuade Congress to abolish government trading houses. In spring, over 3,000 Indians, trappers, woodsman, clerks, voyageurs and adventurers from all over Europe, to camp on Mackinac Island and sell and trade their furs.

BETTY LAMP—
The Betty lamp, named from the German word "besser" or "bête" which means, "to make better," is thought to have originated in Germany, Austria or Hungary. The Betty was most often made of iron and burned fish oil or fat trimmings with a wick of flax, reeds or twisted cloth. It had a lid which helped to confine heat, decrease smoke, and make the oil burn more efficiently. To decrease the risk of fire, caused by tipping over, the lamp was hung on a hook or a chain.

FEVER 'A' AGUE (MALARIA) —
Michigan Malaria mosquitoes bred by the billions in the swamps left behind by the receding glacialiers of the last ice age. Early settlers would sleep with their windows closed in summer as well as winter to protect themselves from the siege of chills and fever,

called “Fever 'N' Ager,” which they thought was caused by miasma rising from the low lands. “The pestilence that walketh in the darkness” struck suddenly, without notice. The chills would shrink the marrow in the bones, followed by burning fever. Not usually fatal to healthy adults, Malaria claimed many children and invalids.

LACROSSE—
A game played by the Native American Iroguois tribe as part of a ceremonial, symbolic, warfare ritual to give thanks to the Great Spirit. The game was played by 100-1,000 players from sun-up to sun-down for up to 3 days on a mile long field.

MASSASAUGAS—
A Michigan rattlesnake that grows to 2-3 feet. The eastern massasauga rattlesnake (Sistrurus catenatus catenatus) is one of only two rattlesnake species in the Great Lakes region. Although it's venomous, the massasauga is a timid snake.

MAST—
Beech mast and acorns fed to pigs to get them fat. This did not harm the pigs, but was poison to cattle, ponies, and sheep.

MORELS—
A mushroom with a sponge looking cap that grows in the northeastern woodlands.

NATIVE AMERICANS OR NATIVE PEOPLE OR INDIANS—
These terms refer to people native to the Americas when the European settlers arrived. Most Natives prefer to be referred to by their particular tribe rather than referred to as Native Americans. "Indian" is the term used in federal law and by major US. Indian agencies and organizations. In modern usage, the term "Indian" usually means an enrolled member of a federally recognized tribe (or one who is eligible to be enrolled in a federally recognized tribe). Native Americans were not made citizens of the United States until 1923.

RED-DOG OR WILDCAT BANKS—

Banks founded by unscrupulous men who would form a bank and issue an unlimited flood of bank notes. If a federal inspector came to insure the bank had enough gold and silver to support the notes, the bankers would send kegs of silver ahead in advance to cover the notes they'd issued. Then, after the investigators left the first bank, the kegs of silver would be sent on ahead of the inspectors to the next bank to cover the notes issued there. These banks started to fail in "37" and people lost their life savings.

SYLLABUBS AND POSSETS—
Two English dairy dishes that probably evolved during the sixteenth century. Syllabubs, made from cream and wine, was served cold in delicate glass pots. The liquid part of the syllabub was sucked through a spout and the froth eaten with a spoon. During the second half of the eighteenth century, the quantity of wine was reduced allowing the syllabub to be whipped up into a thick lather, rather like modern whipped cream. Possets were frothy spiced custards made with cream, wine and eggs, usually served hot in more durable ceramic pots.

OBSIDIAN—
A volcanic glass that naturally occurs when felsic lava extrudes from a volcano and cools rapidly with minimum crystal growth.

OYERS CORNERS—
Present day Springport, Michigan

SECRETARY (also called secretaire, or escritoire) —
a writing desk fitted with drawers, one of which can be pulled out and the front lowered to provide a flat writing surface.

SHRUB—
A 19th century drink made from vinegar, fruit juice (usually cider), and alcohol

SPIDER—
A Cast iron cooking pan that had a handle and three legs used to stand the pan in the coals and ashes of the hearth fire.

SWITCHELL (also called hay-makers punch or ginger water) —
A popular 19th century drink made from water mixed with vinegar and

seasoned with ginger and sweetened with molasses

STOOP or STOUP—
A porch, platform, or staircase leading to the entrance to a house. Term was commonly used before the civil war to describe the veranda of a small house and cabin.

TAVERN—
A tavern is a place of business where people gather to be served food, and in most cases, where travelers receive lodging. After the civil war these placed of business were called a stagecoach stop or hostelry or 'hotel', 'house', or 'inn,' in larger cities.

TOLEDO WAR—
Michigan, still a territory, claimed the Toledo strip, an area along its border with Ohio near the Maumee River (look at the 1805 map below). Ohio, which was already a state, also claimed the land. The "Toledo War" broke out between these two states, over this strip (the "Toledo Strip").

VOYAGEURS—
French fur trappers.

WAR OF 1812—
A military conflict fought from June 18, 1812 to February 18, 1815, between the United States of America and the United Kingdom, its North American colonies, and its North American Indian allies.

WA'MUS—
A warm, knitted, belted work jacket

BIBLIOGRAPHY

The following texts were used as references in the writing of this novel.

Michigan - A History of the Wolverine State
Dunbar, Willis, F
William B. Eerdmans Publishing Co.
1965

The Only Eaton Rapids on Earth
Munn, Scott, W
Edwards Bros Inc.
1951?

Chief Okemos of the Chippewa
Lamp, Thelma, C
Friends of Historic Meridian
1976

Pioneer History of the Settlement of Eaton Co.
Joki, Mike

Indian Reminiscences of Eaton Co.
Caldwell, Helen, Nichols
Joki, Mike

Michigan Pioneer and Historical Society - Collections and Researches
Edited by Burton Agnes, M.
Wykoop Hallenbeck Crawford Co., state printers
1911

Diary of an Early American Boy
Sloane, Eric
Dodd, Mead & Co., Inc
1962

Portrait & Biographical Album of Berry and Eaton Counties, Mich.
Chapman Bros
1891

History of Ingham & Eaton Counties, Michigan
Durant, Samuel, W
D. W. Ensign & Co.
1880

Pioneering Michigan
Freedman, Eric
Altwerger and Mandel Publishing Co
1992

Cadillac and the Dawn of Detroit
Hivert-Carthew, Annick
Wilderness Adventure Books
1994

When Michigan Was Young
Fasquelle, Ethel, Rowen
Avery Color Studios
1981

White Pine Whispers
Massie, Larry, B
The Priscilla Press
1998

Fair Shake in the Wilderness
Harrington, Steve
Maritime Press, Inc
2001

Pioneer History of Eaton County
Strange, Daniel, M. Sc
Eaton County Pioneer and Historical Society Publishing Committee
The Charlotte Republican Print
H. T. McGrath and M. H. Defoe
1923

ABOUT THE AUTHOR

Dennis Swan retired from the Eaton Rapids post office, where he was a rural mail carrier for many years. He also ran the family's 250-acre farm and operated a small antique shop. Dennis and his wife, Kathi still live on the old 'Walworth' homestead in Eaton Rapids, where his parents lived when he was born. He grew up listening to stories from his father, grandfather and great uncles about the days of yesteryear and how things are now so vastly different from early rural Michigan.

His ancestors were the pioneers who came west from the east coast between the 1830s and the 1850s. His third-great-grandparents settled on the next farm south of his. Dennis' second-great-grandfather, W. Wesley, enlisted with G Company, 17th Infantry of the Civil War Regiment of Michigan and was wounded at Fox's Gap in the "Battle of The South Mountain" at Sharpsburg, Maryland. He came home with a bullet still in his shoulder, but left his brother, John, in the Cave Hill National Cemetery in Louisville, Kentucky. Wes married a neighbor girl, Mary Wilkinson, whose grandfather was Joram Chatfield after he returned and built the house where Dennis' second cousin still lives. Dennis' grandfather's oldest brother was born in a log cabin across the road before his great-grandparents built the brick house that still stands there.

Dennis grew up loving history, antiques, old houses, and barns. He loved going around to the cemeteries on Memorial Day with his grandparents, listening to the life stories of those that lived before him. Many of these stories he incorporates into the novels he weaves. He loves living on the family farm with his wife and dogs. His step-daughter and step-daughter-in-law live close by, as do grandchildren and one great-granddaughter, Gracealyn.

Made in the USA
Columbia, SC
17 May 2017